SHADOWS OF FIRE

THE SHADOW REALMS
BOOK 1

BRENDA K DAVIES

BRENDA K. DAVIES

CHAPTER ONE

ELEXIANDRA TRIED NOT to crumple the invitation the crow had delivered as she read it, but her blood pressure rose until it pounded in her ears. The neat, embossed gold lettering was far too cheerful for the words written on the thick parchment.

She'd bet a lot of these invites had gone out through the mortal and Shadow Realms, and that at least a thousand immortals would accept and attend. She didn't reside in the Shadow Realms, but—much to her dismay—King Tove of the dark fae must have decided to include at least some of the immortals who lived in the human realm on his invitation list.

"What is it, Lexi?" Sahira asked as she appeared at Lexi's side.

If Lexi showed her, Sahira would make her go. Her aunt would prattle on about proper etiquette and how exciting it was for them to get the chance to visit the Gloaming, the dark fae realm. But even if Sahira didn't force her to attend, Lexi had no idea how to get out of this.

How did she say no to the king of the dark fae?

She didn't, that was how. But why did he invite *her?*

Sure, her father was a general on the winning side of the war, but he perished in that war, and she was a half vamp, half human who had never entered a Shadow Realm before. The only things separating her from mortals were that she drank blood, as well as ate food, and she was an immortal.

She had no special abilities, no powers, and though she was stronger than a human, she wasn't as strong as a full-blooded vampire. She was a nobody holding an invitation from one of the most powerful immortals in all the realms. And she would prefer to throw it away.

Lifting her head, Lexi pushed back a loose strand of auburn hair as she studied the large manor only fifty feet away from her. At one time, the thirty-room, gray stone building was beautiful and in pristine condition.

Then her father entered the war on the side of the "let's make our existence known to the humans" faction and everything changed.

But then, her father never really had a choice. It was either fight or die, and at least he chose the winning side, even if it wasn't necessarily the right one, but she would *never* voice that opinion out loud.

If he'd chosen the losing side, then the Lord would have most likely taken the manor from them or destroyed it, and she and Sahira would be on the run like all the other rebels.

She was still staring at her home when Sahira snatched the invitation from her hand.

"It's an invitation to a ball!" Sahira gushed.

Lexi winced and braced herself for what was to come. She didn't want to attend some fancy ball, but the sparkle in Sahira's eyes said her aunt was already planning what they would wear.

The invitation specified attending in their finest attire, which meant ball gowns. That was all well and good, but she didn't own anything fancy, and she wasn't in the mood to go shopping.

"It's to celebrate the end of the war," Sahira said, "and the king of the dark fae's sons for helping the Lord win."

Some of Sahira's enthusiasm vanished as she spoke. She may

love the idea of a ball and fancy gowns, but they'd both lost a lot during the war and didn't have anything to celebrate.

She'd lost her dad, and Sahira lost her half brother. They'd lost the luxurious life they once lived and most of the humans who once lived at or worked the manor grounds.

But they weren't the only ones who lost a lot. The human realm lost its innocence about the existence of immortals as well as countless lives. Every day, they continued to lose more.

And the dark fae king planned to celebrate those losses. Lexi found this a little strange considering he'd lost more than half his sons in the war.

She bit her tongue as she lifted her head to gaze into the crow's black eyes. When it tilted its head, the sun created a rainbow hue of colors throughout its feathers. The crow was the dark fae's messenger, and it was waiting for her response.

She didn't know what to say. The idea of going to the Gloaming was tempting, she'd love to see how the dark fae lived, but she still didn't understand why *she* was holding this invite.

She'd never met a member of the royal dark fae before. She knew Colburn—or Cole as he was more commonly known—and Brokk were the only sons the king had left on his side. Out of his nine sons, five died in the war, and the other two survivors fought for the rebels.

Like everyone who chose the losing side, they were stripped of their titles, land, and money. They were being hunted throughout the realms.

Many of the rebels ended up in the mortal realm where there was less magic and they were harder to track. Many others hopped through the Shadow Realms to avoid capture and death.

"We need gowns," Sahira continued, and Lexi closed her eyes. "We'll have to go to the marketplace to purchase them. It will be fun."

The two of them had drastically different ideas of fun, but at four hundred and fifty-three years old, Sahira was four hundred and twenty-nine years older than her. Her aunt had grown up and lived through far different times.

Sahira once attended balls held by kings and czars in the human realm while Lexi grew up in jeans and T-shirts. Sahira would sometimes talk about the old days with wistful sadness while Lexi's old days were bowls of cereal in front of her favorite cartoons.

She often missed those days. They were much simpler, and her father was still alive.

This invitation was making Sahira's year and ruining Lexi's day. She dreaded everything about it, but she knew what she had to do.

Opening her eyes, Lexi used her finger to check the yes box for her and Sahira. Created by fae magic, a gold mark materialized on the invite. She lifted the invite into the air, and the crow swooped down to take it from her.

It clasped the invite in its talons, released a loud caw, and soared back toward the clear blue sky before vanishing.

With a sigh, Lexi looked beyond the manor to the smoke in the distance. She couldn't see the ruined remains of the city a hundred miles away, but every day she saw the smoke rising from it.

A week ago, she dared to travel close enough to investigate the devastation the dragons unleashed on the city, but she was still a few miles away when the roar of a dragon caused her to retreat.

She preferred to stay as far from those beasts as possible.

The humans who survived the massacre continued to filter out of the city every day. She'd heard from some that others were choosing to stay behind to rebuild.

Every day, she watched as broken, ragtag groups of survivors fled the city in search of something more, but there wasn't much left out there. Each morning, she walked out to the road to give those survivors food. Some stopped to talk, but most would simply look at her with haunted eyes before taking their bread and walking away.

The dragons unleashed a fair amount of destruction on the world, but most of their larger fires had been extinguished. Some smaller ones still popped up. Lexi had no idea what started them, and she wasn't going into the city to find out, but their smoke filled the sky, and sometimes they burned for days.

The war ended a month ago. It was too soon to accomplish much rebuilding and far too soon to celebrate the destruction unleashed on so many.

Hell, she didn't think what happened to Earth should *ever* be celebrated, but she was sure many other immortals would disagree... including the king of the dark fae.

Time was moving on, and the war was over. The immortals of the Shadow Realms wanted to continue with their lives. It didn't matter that many in the mortal realm still suffered.

The winning side had gotten their way; immortals didn't have to hide from humans anymore. The mortals were aware of their existence now, and that knowledge had ruined their lives.

Despite all that, a small tingle of excitement sparked in her belly. She would soon enter a Shadow Realm for the first time; vampires usually weren't welcome there, not even half vamps.

And while there was a chance she and Sahira might get killed if they tried to cross into the Gloaming, she was excited to see what lay beyond the human realm.

CHAPTER TWO

TWILIGHT WAS SETTLING across the land as Lexi and Sahira stood before the growing shadows spreading throughout the forest across from them. It had taken them an hour to reach the designated entrance to the Gloaming, and Lexi clutched the invitation that would grant them passage like it was a life preserver in a storm-tossed sea.

Around her, half a dozen other immortals talked excitedly about what was to come, but Lexi couldn't join in their enthusiasm. She was too nervous.

It had been a week since the invitation arrived. In that time, Sahira had managed to barter enough of her potions in the market-place near their home to purchase two gowns for them.

Her aunt then spent the next couple of days getting those dresses to fit properly and adding special touches to them. They were some of the most beautiful creations Lexi had ever seen, but the exquisite gown only made Lexi feel more out of place. She'd never worn anything like it before.

The other immortals and her aunt were all at ease in their fancy clothes while she felt like an imposter. They were also all excited about traveling to the Gloaming, and she couldn't help wondering if she would be allowed to make the journey.

Maybe the invite was sent to them by accident. Her dad did fight for the Lord, but she and Sahira were both half vampire, and vampires weren't exactly welcome in the Shadow Realms. Neither were humans.

When the time came, would they try to enter the Gloaming only to be bounced back or, worse, destroyed?

She tugged at the collar of her dress as the possibility caused a sheen of sweat to dampen her skin.

Trying to distract herself from the risk of impending death, Lexi studied the two dark fae standing at the edge of the woods. They wore only loose-fitting brown pants; their chests and feet were bare. Like all purebred dark fae, they had black hair, black eyes, pointed ears, and lithe builds.

The shadows swallowed them until they flickered in and out of the spreading darkness created by the setting sun. However, the dark fae were known to be a part of the shadows.

From her distance of ten feet, she sensed their power, yet their ciphers didn't go past the middle of their biceps. She'd only encountered a couple of dark fae before, but she knew those black markings indicated the amount of power they possessed.

They said the dark fae king and his sons possessed ciphers that extended to their wrists. The oldest supposedly had ciphers to the tips of his fingers, like the king.

Unable to stop herself, Lexi tugged at the collar of her gown again as the sun vanished. There was a moment when the entire world held its breath as the last of the sun's rays stretched across the sky. Then the shimmering, deep purple entrance to the Gloaming came into view.

Sahira clasped Lexi's arm and practically jumped up and down in excitement. Lexi tried not to gawk as the doorway shifted from deep purple to black and back again. The dark fae standing beside it stepped away from the trees and waved their arms toward the portal.

Lexi gulped and grasped Sahira's hand on her arm. Her aunt was stunning in her maroon gown. Twisted into an elaborate coil, her mahogany hair hung against her nape, and black eyeliner emphasized the striking color of her amber eyes.

Most days, Sahira wore jeans and T-shirts like her. She kept her hair in a bun and eschewed makeup until she looked more like a librarian than the half witch, half vampire she was. Now, she'd embraced the roll of ball attendee.

"It's okay," Sahira whispered.

"What if the portal doesn't let us enter? Vampires were banished to the mortal realm centuries ago."

"It will let us enter, and if it doesn't, then I'll be stuck here with you, but we're invited."

"That might have been a mistake."

"It wasn't."

"Vampires aren't welcome in the Shadow Realms."

"We have an invite, and vampires aren't welcome to *stay*. They can travel through with permission, which we have. Come on, everything is going to be fine."

Lexi wanted to believe her, but her feet remained planted firmly in place.

Sahira tugged at her arm. "Lexi, move!"

Lexi gulped and shuffled forward until she stood at the edge of the portal. Gathering her courage, she closed her eyes and stepped forward. She fully expected to be knocked back on her ass or cut in two, but her feet continued onward.

Her eyes flew open, and she discovered herself surrounded by the dark walls of the portal as she moved toward the Gloaming.

CHAPTER THREE

THE GROWING crowd of immortals made Cole's upper lip curl as he watched them group before the dais in their finest clothing. There was such an array of ball gowns, fine attire, and the tunics of the dark fae that his eye twitched.

The din of voices nearly drown out the music's melodic strains from the minstrels his father hired. Laughter floated on the air, and glasses clinked as the immortals congratulated each other on a well-won war.

A war that most of these self-congratulatory fuckers hadn't fought.

Cole didn't want to think about the amount of carisle his father spent on this affair. He knew his role here, but he hadn't helped in planning it. There were numerous whispers about the dark fae king having bottomless coffers, so the money probably hadn't mattered to his father.

And after the war, those coffers probably tripled as the winners stripped all the losers' lands and money. Thinking about it made his head hurt.

He'd never expected to long for the human world, but as the

noise of the party increased, he would have given anything to be *anywhere* else.

After two years of waging countless bloody battles in a war he hadn't agreed with, being around so many immortals made his skin itch. He kept expecting a witch or warlock to lob a ball of magic into the crowd or a pack of lycan to turn on the others. Instead, they laughed and drank as if all the death and destruction never occurred.

How short their memories are.

But then, they were immortals, so a couple years of bloody war was less than a blink of an eye in their lifespans. And most of those gathered here hadn't stepped foot on any of the battlefields.

They stayed in their realms, in their towers, or by the Lord of the Shadow Realms and plotted the destruction of others. They did not actually fight, so to them, this was all good fun.

To Cole, it was a powder keg waiting to blow.

Before the war, he spent most of his six hundred and seventy-two years in the lap of luxury too. Because of fights and disputes, he'd killed his fair share of immortals during that time, but those deaths were nothing compared to the hundreds he handed out in the war.

Sometimes at night, he would find himself standing on those battlefields again. He was once more using his fae sword to carve his way through countless enemies as blood dripped from his clothes and hair.

The amount of blood coating him added a good ten pounds to his frame, but it didn't hinder him. As he worked to destroy, the screams of the dying reverberated in his head as the injured pleaded for mercy.

Sometimes he would bolt awake, but other times it felt like he was clawing through quicksand as he struggled to pull himself free of the cloying horror of his memories. He often woke in a cold sweat and unsure of where he was, and it sometimes took a few minutes to recall the war was over.

While fighting the war, the death and destruction hadn't bothered him. Since its end, it haunted him.

But the war was over; their side had won. That was all that mattered to the rest of the Shadow Realms. Or at least it was all that mattered to those who hadn't fought in the war.

It's over. Yet a part of him remained on the battlefields, and he suspected it always would.

"We've packed our palace with immortals who would gladly tear out each other's throats," Brokk muttered as he arrived to stand beside him.

"But these are our allies and friends, little brother," Cole replied.

"The dark fae have no friends."

Cole couldn't have said it any better himself.

"Father says it's time to take our place on the dais," Brokk said.

Cole barely managed to keep from sneering at sitting on that dais in front of all these gawkers. However, this ball was to show they were ecstatic about the war's outcome, and he would do his part to keep up the charade.

Brokk adjusted the thin, princely crown on his head. The light reflected off the silver fae metal that had forged the crown. In the center was the black, oplyx stone of the dark fae realm. Located only in the clintick caves, workers only harvested a few of the rare stones from those deep bowels.

Looking at Brokk's crown reminded Cole he had a slightly larger crown perched on his head. He didn't touch it because, if he did, he'd tear it off and throw it away. He was not in the mood for this shit.

Cole slipped from the shadows beside the dais and strode across it. Brokk walked beside him as they put themselves on full display of everyone in the grand ballroom. The candles' flames danced in their golden sconces and cast shadows across the black walls.

The dark fae do have one friend… the shadows.

They thrived in the shadows.

For a few seconds, the room's noise remained at the same level, but as more and more guests spotted them, the noise declined until silence descended. Not even when the hush gave way to a raucous wave of applause that shook the chandeliers overhead did Cole look at them.

He gritted his teeth against the impulse to leap from the dais and punch them all. Beside him, he sensed Brokk's growing irritation.

"How long do you think this will last?" Brokk murmured as they approached two of the three thrones set in the middle of the dais.

"Days," Cole replied.

Brokk's shoulders hunched up as he muttered, "I'd rather be back in the war."

"So would I."

Never had Cole wished to return to those battlefields, but at least he knew what to expect there. He had no idea what to expect from the immortals crammed into this room.

His father rose from the massive throne set in the center of the three. A smile lit his handsome face as he spread his arms. Increased applause followed, but apprehension flashed in his father's eyes as he looked from him to Brokk and back again.

Cole smiled, but he was aware that while he and Brokk were making a good show of seeming perfectly fine to the room, they didn't fool their father. Though they tried to hide it from him, the king of the dark fae knew his sons hadn't returned from the war the same.

But then, the king wasn't the same either. He couldn't be after losing five of his sons.

Cole didn't miss the increased sorrow in his father's black eyes or that he sometimes locked himself away for hours during the day. He hadn't done that since the years immediately following the death of Cole's mother.

With the door to his private solar shut and locked, the king sat in solitude while he grieved his losses. Cole would like to do something to ease his father's sadness, but he had no idea how to help him when some days he felt like he was drowning too.

Their side won the war, but they'd lost so much, and they'd failed to accomplish what they set out to do.

Still, Cole's smile became more genuine as his eyes held his father's. Unlike Brokk and Cole, the king was pure dark fae, and because of that, he possessed the black hair, eyes, and lithe build of all purebred, dark fae.

Cole saw little of himself in his father's narrow face, hawkish nose, onyx eyes, and lean frame. His father also stood a good three inches shorter than Cole's six-seven height.

However, there were similarities in their thick eyebrows, full lips, and steel wills. Like himself, his father's ciphers ran from the tips of his fingers, up his arms, and across his shoulders.

When not wearing a shirt, it was possible to see the ciphers covering his shoulder blades as they traveled down his back before stopping at his waist. He had even more ciphers that he kept completely hidden from view.

The dark fae kept many of their ciphers hidden from others, but these visible ciphers were impossible for them to hide. Some things refused to be caged, and their visible ciphers were some of them.

The ground beneath Cole's feet quaked as the immortal guests stomped their feet and clapped their hands. His father rested a hand on Cole's shoulder before turning to Brokk.

"My sons, the heroes!" his father declared.

Cole hadn't considered it possible, but the cacophony in the great hall increased. Bracing himself, he turned to face the immortal creatures.

They blurred together until he stared out at nothing more than a sea of faceless bodies scattered across a blood-strewn field.

Cole shoved the image aside and turned to sit on the throne to the right of his father. His throne was noticeably smaller than his father's, and it lacked the black skulls perched above his father's shoulders.

Feeling as if his bones might break, Cole gripped the curved, black ends of his throne until his knuckles turned white. Brokk walked stiffly in front of him and settled onto the chair to his father's left.

At six hundred years old, Brokk was the middle of the king's sons. Because of that, he'd never sat so close to his father's side before, but now that they were the only two sons the king had left in the Gloaming, Brokk's chair had been moved to sit next to their father's.

Cole refused to think about what had become of his two remaining brothers. Like the rest of the losing rebels, they were stripped of everything and were now ruthlessly hunted.

No matter how many realms they ran through, it was only a matter of time before they caught Orin and Alvaro. Cole dreaded that day.

At one time, he and his brothers were as thick as thieves, and he'd always known where they were. Now, he knew five were dead and two were on the run.

If they didn't somehow figure out a way to take down the Lord, the next time he saw Varo and Orin, they would most likely be dead or on their way to execution.

Despite having chosen different sides in the war, Cole was glad they'd survived, especially Alvaro. As half-dark and half-light fae, Varo had always been more sensitive than the rest of his brothers. He'd survived the war, but Cole knew Varo wouldn't handle the aftermath of it well.

If *he* was having nightmares, then Varo must be a mess.

CHAPTER FOUR

LEXI ABSENTLY CLAPPED along with all the immortals and tried to keep her mouth shut while she examined the exquisite ballroom and all the beautifully dressed immortals. She wasn't used to seeing immortals dressed like this. In the human realm, they always wore human clothes to blend in.

Even now that the humans knew about their existence, most immortals still wore the clothing of the mortal's. She didn't know if it was from habit or because the immortals preferred to blend in.

She had noticed the dark fae stopped concealing the pointed tips of their ears in shadows, the pixies stopped hiding, the lycan sometimes transformed, and the vampires would transport in public, but for the most part, the immortals continued to blend in with the mortals while on Earth.

And they were about as far from Earth as it got in this place. The end of the line was so far outside of the room that she had to stand on tiptoe to see inside, but what she saw awed her.

The roof and walls of the dome-shaped room were black. Sconces holding torches of wavering flames hung on the walls. The shadows their glow cast swelled and danced as if they were a living entity—and in the Gloaming, they very well could be.

This was the dark fae land—the land of the immortals who were one with shadows. There could be dozens of dark fae standing in those shadows, and she wouldn't see any of them.

She glanced uneasily around but didn't see anyone. Then the stars illuminating the ceiling moved, and she forgot her unease as she went back to trying not to gawk.

Some of the stars were constellations from Earth; there was the Little and the Big Dipper and Orion, but others looked utterly unfamiliar. A rising purple moon was followed by a large, red planet that slid across the top of the dome.

As the familiar constellations shifted out of view, new stars rose to replace them. These were three times bigger and the color of a flamingo as they floated overhead.

She had no idea what realm they were from, but their beauty stole her breath. She could stand here and watch this ever-changing display for the rest of her life and probably still not see everything it offered.

Around her, the applause increased before abruptly ceasing. She kept her attention focused on the dome while she tried to ignore the oppressive heat of the bodies surrounding her. The main hall was gigantic, but the fae king must have invited every immortal who had supported the war as at least a thousand of them filled the room and spilled out the doorways.

She tugged at the collar of her dress as a bead of sweat slid down her neck. It was a beautiful gown, but she'd never worn anything like it before, and she found the copious amounts of material uncomfortable.

When the line started moving, she tore her attention away from the ceiling to follow the others. Beside her, Sahira practically danced as she shifted from foot to foot and twisted her hands before her.

"This is so exciting," she murmured.

This is awful. But Lexi didn't express her feelings; she imagined there were ears everywhere in this realm.

Finally, the crowd moved forward enough for them to enter the main part of the room. Her eyes instantly settled on the golden dais at the far end of the room and the three thrones there.

Strange carvings etched the gold dais; Lexi had no idea what those carvings represented, but she suspected they represented something to the dark fae. Ten steps led to the top of the dais, which meant the king and his sons looked down on the room from their lofty positions.

In the center of the stage, the dark fae king sat higher than his sons and surveyed the room with an air of casual indifference. The crown perched on his head was larger than the ones his sons wore and possessed three of the black stones, while his sons' crowns only had one stone each.

The king's pointed ears poked out from beneath his shoulder-length, black hair. He was handsome with his black eyes and high cheekbones, but the coldness surrounding him made her pull at her dress again as a clammy sensation crept over her skin.

She didn't know how he could appear so indifferent to so many immortals, but it wouldn't surprise her if he yawned. That nonchalance spoke of his power as much as the black ciphers covering the fingers resting on the curved ends of his throne.

Lexi gulped when she saw the two skulls behind his shoulders. The skulls were black, but she had the unsettling feeling eyes once filled the empty sockets.

To the king's left sat a handsome, slender man with disheveled blond hair that almost covered the tips of his pointed ears. The blank expression on his face didn't change as the Shadow Realms' members climbed the dais to greet him and his family.

When she looked to the king's right, she couldn't keep her jaw from dropping.

She'd heard stories about the king's eldest son. She didn't think there was anyone who *hadn't* heard about him, including the humans who now knew immortals existed.

His ruthlessness was legendary. His ability to kill was

becoming mythological. The troubadours already sang about his feats on the battlefield. The few songs she'd heard in the market-place told of his power, his size, and the way women fell at his feet.

Not only did the women swoon for him, but his enemies cowered, and there were rumors some had killed themselves rather than face his wrath.

Lexi was sure there was some truth to the songs and just as sure there were many exaggerations too. Looking at him now, she didn't think any of it was an exaggeration.

Unlike most of the dark fae—who usually stuck to and bred with their kind—the king had spread out to other immortal species and produced nine children. His oldest son's mother was a lycan, and it showed in the man.

His shoulders were broad, and the thick muscles bulging beneath his black tunic differentiated him from the lean builds of the dark fae. He looked like he could tear the head from a bull and bash his enemies to death with it.

Gold edged the sleeves, neckline, and hem of his formfitting black tunic. Beneath it, he wore a pair of black pants. The tunic and pants were the standard garments for the dark fae, but some-how, he made the clothing stand out in a room full of similar attire.

The vibrant, Persian blue color of his eyes was evident across the vast distance separating them. Those striking eyes also differ-entiated him from the purebred, dark fae as they all had black eyes. However, he did possess the dark fae's jet-black hair and pointed ears.

Cut short, his hair emphasized his tanned skin and the angles of his cheekbones. His square jaw had a short, black beard lining it. He was one of the most handsome men she'd ever seen. And it was clear the troubadours weren't lying about women falling at his feet as the ones who climbed the dais to greet him all preened and simpered while openly flirting with him.

She had no idea how they could flirt so brazenly with him

when he stared at them as if he didn't see them, but each new woman who went to greet him smiled as she fawned over him.

One brazen vampire rested her hand on his arm as she leaned forward. Lexi was sure her low-cut dress left nothing to the imagination.

To be fair, they also flirted with the king and younger son, but it wasn't as overt with them. Or maybe she imagined it.

Uncomfortable with the display, she shifted her attention back to the stars but found her eyes irresistibly drawn back to him. As they got closer and the crowd between them eased, she saw that his ciphers ran down his thick forearms to the tips of his fingers.

The black markings resembled flames with their sharp edges but managed to flow like water as they encircled his wrists and hands. She supposed this mix of fire and water made sense as the dark fae could control the elements.

His short-sleeved tunic revealed more ciphers around his biceps before they disappeared beneath the material. They reemerged at the collar of his shirt. Cole's beard hid them, but the way the flames moved up his neck made her suspect the tips of the ciphers licked at his chin.

Having that many ciphers was a clear sign of his power and it oozed from his pores while his steely gaze surveyed those who came before him with an air of disdain. Only the arrogant dark fae would throw this big of a party and seem annoyed by their guests.

As she and Sahira edged closer, Lexi found it increasingly difficult to breathe, and she tugged at the collar of her dress again. She didn't belong here.

What she'd seen of the Gloaming was beautiful, but she was ready to go home, and she did *not* want to climb those steps to introduce herself to these powerful, cold men. She was uncomfortable with this entire show.

What am I doing here? Why did I agree to this?

She yearned to be at home and in bed with a book. She'd give anything to be anywhere other than here. Lexi glanced at the door three hundred feet away and tried to figure out if she could make it out of here before Sahira stopped her.

Escape wouldn't be possible, at least not without drawing a lot of attention to herself. She gulped as she clasped her hands before her and squeezed them.

She'd probably never see any of these immortals again, but she couldn't make a scene. Her father would be mortified if she did.

Still, she gazed longingly at the door as she resigned herself to her fate.

Deciding to get through it as fast as possible and hoping she didn't make a fool of herself, she turned her attention back to the stage and bit back a gasp when she found the lethal prince of the dark fae staring straight at her.

CHAPTER FIVE

COLE COULDN'T TEAR his gaze away from the woman who looked about to bolt from the hall. Her deep auburn hair hung in waves around her shoulders and swayed against the middle of her back as she searched for what he assumed was an exit. The deep red strands of her hair shimmered in the starlight.

She tugged at the collar of the emerald dress hugging her slender body. It emphasized the rounded hips of her hourglass figure. Her full breasts were thrust high by the bodice, but she revealed far less cleavage than most other women in the room.

Despite that, when his gaze fell to her breasts, a bolt of desire hit him. She turned back toward the stage, and when her eyes met his, they widened. They stared at each other before she glanced back toward the doorway.

For a second, she looked about to bolt as she stepped away from the line, but then she closed her eyes and resumed her place. He'd never seen her in the Gloaming before; he would have remembered her.

His hands gripped the ends of his throne as the line snaked forward and the woman moved closer. When she bit her bottom lip, his gaze latched onto her lush mouth.

What does she taste like?

He vowed to discover the answer to that before this night was over.

Cole stalked her every move as she snaked through the throng and shifted from foot to foot while the other immortals crowded around her. She didn't meet his gaze, but her eyes traveled toward him before darting away.

When a male vampire pressed entirely too close against her back and she cringed away from him, Cole almost rose from his seat to kill him. However, he couldn't kill a guest for touching a woman.

Such a thing could set off another war, and he'd had enough blood and death. Although, he suspected more would come soon. The war was over, but another one had been brewing for years; he would find himself at the center of it again.

He didn't know how much time passed, but *finally* the woman stood near the stairs. A male lycan climbed the four steps to the dais in front of her. After he was introduced, Cole nodded to the man, but he didn't hear a word of what the lycan said.

The woman leaned forward and gave her name to their helot, Sindri. Sindri stepped away from her. "Milords, I present to you the ladies Elexiandra and Sahira Harper."

Cole jolted when Sindri announced her last name. *Harper*!

Brokk's head turned toward him, and Cole exchanged a look with his brother. He was sure his startled expression mirrored Brokk's. Between them, their father didn't react, but the king had to know she was here; he'd invited her after all.

Harper.

And now he understood the woman's nervousness. She *had* never been to the Gloaming or any of the Shadow Realms before. Or at least that's what her father told him during one of their countless conversations.

The world shifted and blurred, and for a minute, Cole found himself sitting in a tent across from a man with pale blond hair.

Delano Harper's bright blue eyes twinkled as he smiled and sipped his wine.

"They'll never know what hit them, boys. I can assure you of that," Del said as he finished his drink and gestured for the pretty serving girl to bring him more.

Brokk and Cole gazed at each other before returning their attention to the robust vampire sitting across from them. The wine had reddened Del's cheeks, but his eyes remained clear.

Over the two years they fought together, Cole had learned nothing dulled Del's intelligence. He often used his ability to drink more alcohol than three immortals combined as a way to make others think he was less aware of what was going on around him, while he was keenly aware of everything.

He'd fooled Cole a couple of times before he caught on to the act.

He learned Del was a brilliant master of deception, manipulation, and strategy. He'd also become one of Cole and Brokk's best friends.

Del rarely talked about his daughter over the years, but on the rare occasions when there were no battles to fight, strategies to plan, or enemies closing in on them, he would sometimes speak about her. There was no denying the love in the man's voice, and it was difficult to shut him up once he got started.

Cole had always found this amusing while he listened to the doting father prattle on about his daughter. He'd claimed she was beautiful, but Cole had blown it off. There were many beautiful immortals, and a father was always biased, but Del hadn't exaggerated.

Over the years, he'd spent many hours with Del, they'd saved each other more times than Cole could count, and then, one day, unable to get to him in time, he watched helplessly as his friend died.

And now he was about to come face-to-face with his daughter.

~

LEXI TRIED NOT to bury her hands in the abundant material of her dress as she sought to control the tremble in them. She *could* do this, and she would do it without falling flat on her face.

The king first. Make sure you approach the king first.

She kept reminding herself of this because she was desperate to rush through this and get out of here. If she didn't approach the king first, it would be considered an insult, and the dark fae did *not* like to be insulted.

As the lycan ahead of them left the dais, she threw her shoulders back, lifted her chin, and strode up the steps with a confidence she didn't feel. At her side, Sahira sauntered forward with elegant grace.

When they stopped before the king, Lexi curtsied. Having never done it before in public, she half feared she'd faceplant, but somehow she managed not to fall over.

"Your Highness," she murmured.

"Milady," the king replied with a bow of his head.

Lexi gulped as the power emanating from him rippled across her skin. The number of ciphers he possessed had hinted at his power, but this close, she could tell he was keeping a lot of it hidden and doing a damn good job too.

Lexi forced a smile and somehow managed to keep her hands from shaking as she turned away from him. She approached the younger of the two brothers as Sahira went to the older. Brokk's aqua blue eyes were warm as he studied her.

"Milady," he said and clasped her hand. "It's a pleasure to meet you."

Lexi had no idea what to make of those words and the gesture; she hadn't seen him touch anyone else, so she merely smiled. "You also, Your Highness."

The prince looked about to say more, but a man and his daughter were already being introduced. They were heading up the steps and toward the king as Sahira approached her. If she didn't move now, she wouldn't get the chance to speak with the older brother.

She'd prefer not to talk with the intimidating man, but it would be rude if she left the stage, and one *did not* snub the dark fae. They especially didn't snub the eldest son of the king.

Knowing their time was over, Lexi gave a subtle tug on her hand in the hopes the prince would release her. It took a couple of seconds before he seemed to recall he was holding her hand.

With a small smile, he released her. Lexi's gaze lingered on him, not because she was still confused by his strange behavior but because she had to brace herself before walking over to the older brother.

She had to go now.

Walking away from the brother, she crossed before the king as the father and daughter stepped onto the dais. Acutely aware of all the eyes on her, she tried not to blush, but she couldn't control the riotous beat of her heart.

When she finally lifted her head to take in the prince, she wasn't surprised to find his striking, Persian blue eyes locked on her. She'd felt them burning into her flesh since the second she stepped onto the dais.

She'd never seen a blue so pure or vivid before. They were like looking into a pool of crystalline ocean water on the clearest of days. If she wasn't careful, she could get lost in those eyes.

Her heart lodged in her throat as she stopped before him. Unable to keep the tremor from her hands, she twisted them into the folds of her dress and clutched them until her bones ached.

His leisurely perusal of her body caused her knees to quake. She was used to men examining her, but she'd never experienced it with this kind of intensity before, and she'd never been this unnerved or excited by it.

CHAPTER SIX

COLE COULDN'T TEAR his gaze away from the beautiful woman standing before him. *Elexiandra*, he recalled Sindri saying.

Del had told him his daughter's name, but it was lost to him until Sindri announced it. He would not forget it again.

Up close, she was even more beautiful beneath the radiance of the turning sky. This close, he could tell shards of pure emerald flecked her hunter green eyes.

With her high cheekbones and rosebud lips, she stood out in a room full of immortals. The smattering of freckles dotting the bridge of her slender nose and sun-kissed skin gave her beauty a charming air of innocence.

Looking at her, something inside him shifted, and for the first time in his life, the lycan part of him exerted dominance over the dark fae. And the lycan *wanted* her.

He'd always identified more with his dark fae side and found it more powerful than the wolf, but now the beast was making its presence known as fangs he always kept suppressed throbbed and lengthened.

She'd attracted the attention of more than a few men in the room, and Cole had to keep his mouth shut as he restrained himself from bearing his fangs at them. His claws lengthened until they bit into his throne.

Wood splintered beneath his grip and buried itself deep within his skin. Still, the pain did nothing to ease the turmoil churning through him. His teeth scraped together until he was certain everyone in the room could hear them grinding back and forth.

He didn't know what it was about this woman, but for the first time in his life, he was on the verge of losing control of his wolf. He was still staring at her when the woman she walked onto the dais with strolled over to her.

"Elexiandra," the woman whispered, "we must go."

Elexiandra nodded before speaking. "Milord."

Her voice was as enchanting as her, and when she spoke, he spotted the tips of her fangs. *Vampire,* he recalled.

Half vampire, half human, he recalled Del once saying. Unlike full-blooded vampires, she could go out in the day, but she couldn't teleport, and she wasn't as strong as other immortals.

For some reason, that weakness caused his protective instincts to become more extreme. He tore his attention away from her to glare at the crowd of men openly admiring her. They all looked away from him.

"Milady," he greeted.

Before he could say more, the father and his daughter stepped closer and edged Elexiandra and the other woman away. He opened his mouth to stop them, but the father was speaking, and they were gliding down the stairs.

He watched until they vanished into the crowd.

∼

ALL LEXI WANTED WAS to flee this place. There were far too many immortals here, they were far too comfortable with each other, and she felt like a fish out of water as everyone else celebrated. However, if she left now, they would notice.

Or would they?

She was one of thousands here tonight; surely they wouldn't notice if she and Sahira slipped away before the party ended. Sahira could stay; she was enjoying herself.

Lexi smiled as she watched Sahira being twirled around the dance floor by a handsome dark fae. The flutes' haunting strains and the dark fae's musical instrument, the ocraba, filled the room.

Now that the introductions were over, the night had given way to music and dancing. The black floor, which reflected the stars above, was filled with immortals imbibing in drinks and food. Their laughter filled the air while their bodies warmed the room.

She had a feeling Sahira wouldn't be returning to the room they were sharing with other immortal women until much later tonight, if at all. Which meant, even Sahira might not notice if she slipped away to return home.

She knew how to get back to the portal leading to the human realm. It was probably guarded, but she didn't think they would deny her if she said she was returning home. They probably wouldn't tell the king either. Who cared if someone left before it was all over?

And since her father was gone, she was the one responsible for protecting and watching over their property.

Maybe she could get permission from the king or one of the princes to return early. As soon as the idea popped into her head, she shut it down. The idea of talking to any of those men made her shiver in apprehension. The power radiating from them was more than she'd ever encountered before, and she wasn't eager to experience it again.

Unfortunately, she didn't think she could avoid it. She was in their world, after all, in their home, and at their party.

But did that mean she had to stay here?

Yes, it did. Because it would be rude if she left early, but she could always slip away to her room. At least it was quieter there, and the night would pass faster if she slept. In the morning, she could leave. If she stayed until then, it wouldn't be seen as rude... she hoped.

Lowering her head into her hands, she rubbed at her temples as she tried to figure out what to do. But the more she pondered her options, the more her head pounded.

CHAPTER SEVEN

"LEXI," a voice purred from beside her.

Her eyes closed, and she bit back an inner groan as she tried not to cringe away from the voice. Could this night get any worse?

She had no idea why Malakai Calsov insisted on using her nickname when they barely knew each other, but he'd done so ever since she was a child. Having grown up on neighboring properties, she'd seen Malakai a few times a year.

However, since he was more than two hundred years older than her, they never played together, barely spoke, and the way he looked at her had always scared her a little.

He stared at her like he knew her, no... not knew her. Once she became a teenager, he started staring at her like he wanted to devour her.

The last time she saw him, her father, his father, and Malakai were on a brief visit home from the war. She'd come downstairs to discover them sitting at the dining room table.

She'd ignored Malakai's ravenous stare as she walked over to rest her hand on her father's shoulder. She'd leaned forward to get a look at what they were studying, but her father shoved the papers away before turning to smile at her.

"My beautiful daughter." He took her hand and clasped it in his. "I won't bore you with such trivial things as war."

"It's not trivial," she replied. "I'm interested in what you're doing."

He squeezed her hand. "Maybe some other time. Could you please see if Sahira can bring us some blood?"

She knew he was trying to get rid of her, so she didn't argue with him. Her father preferred to keep the atrocities of war hidden from her. Besides, she disliked being in the same room as Malakai.

She felt his eyes boring into her back as she walked away and decided to avoid him while he was home. Unfortunately, that only lasted an hour.

She was in the stables when he found her and backed her into a corner. With his hands on either side of her head, he lowered his face, so they were eye level with each other.

His disheveled, dark brown hair hung around his handsome face, and his brown eyes burned with an intensity she'd never seen before. It made her skin crawl as she searched for some way to bolt, but she wasn't getting past him.

"Hello, Lexi," he greeted.

"Malakai."

"How have you been?"

She swallowed to wet her suddenly parched throat and forced herself to smile at him. "I've been fine, and you?"

"I've been fighting a war."

Unlike the look of horror, wisdom, and age that shone in her father's eyes when he spoke of the war, the look in Malakai's eyes was one of almost twisted, perverse pleasure. Her stomach churned as she realized he enjoyed the fighting, the death, and the brutality of this unnecessary war.

She could never express how his enjoyment of the war made her feel sick. It was treasonous, and he would use it against her. She was supposed to be *for* the war; she was supposed to want the humans to know about them so immortals could walk the earth freely and stop hiding in the shadows.

But it never bothered her that she had to keep her true nature hidden from the humans. She much preferred hiding to watching the slaughter of countless mortals and immortals every day.

"We are going to win this war," he stated.

"I'm sure you are," she said and glanced over his shoulder again. "If you'll excuse me, I have some things I have to do."

When he didn't move to let her pass, she tried dodging underneath one of his arms. He laughed and lowered his hand to her hip to keep her in place. Lexi buried the anger surging through her at the intimate gesture.

He wanted to rattle her, and she refused to give him the satisfaction of seeing it happen. But she had no idea how to get out of this.

Lifting her chin, she was about to ask him to move his hand when he said something that stole the words from her. "I intend to marry you, Elexiandra."

She couldn't keep her jaw from falling at the statement; she also couldn't stop a nervous chuckle.

"You find that funny?" he asked.

Not funny, more astonishing, but the malice in his eyes caused her chuckle to stop abruptly. "No, I don't find it funny at all."

She'd never spoken truer words in her entire life.

"We come from good families, our properties adjoin each other, and you will give me fine children," he said.

Lexi could only stand and stare at him. She had no intention of marrying him. Of course, she didn't say that to him, but he would soon learn it didn't matter what he wanted. He couldn't make her marry him; her father would never allow it.

Lexi grimaced as she replied, "I'm not marrying you or anyone else."

He smiled as his gaze raked her. Despite keeping her shoulders back, her spine straight, and her chin raised, she had to resist covering herself with her hands. She wore a black sweater and jeans, but she'd never felt more exposed in her life.

"Malakai, where are you?" his father's voice, drifting through the barn doors, didn't make Malakai move away.

"I'm coming back from this war, Elexiandra," he told her. "And when I do, I expect to claim all the rewards the Lord of the Shadow Realms promised us for winning. You will be one of the first things I claim."

"I am *not* a spoil of war."

She was not one to push back or fight against others, and she had no idea where those words came from or how she found the strength to utter them, but she refused to be something he *claimed*.

If she did marry, it wouldn't be to a man who believed he could own her. It would be to someone who treated her as an equal, and that would never be Malakai.

He smiled as he lowered his hand to run a finger down her cheek. Lexi compelled herself not to recoil from his touch; she would not give him the satisfaction.

"But you will be mine," he murmured.

"Malakai!" his father called from outside.

He lowered his finger from her cheek, and before she could stop him, he kissed her forehead. Lexi was too stunned to respond, and by the time she formed a response, he was striding down the shedrow. His swagger caused her teeth to clench.

Now that she could see beyond him, she spotted her father and Malakai's stepping into the barn. His father's irritation was evident on his face, but she couldn't quite make out his clipped words. When they disappeared, her father walked toward her.

The light filtering through the windows and the doorway at the end illuminated his broad shoulders and solid frame. Stubble lined his jaw, and dark circles shadowed his eyes, but they were still sharp as they narrowed on her.

"What did he say to you?" her father demanded.

"He said the Lord of the Shadow Realms has promised to

reward the fighters, and he intends for me to be one of those rewards. He wants to marry me."

Her father snorted as he ran a hand through his pale blond hair. "Well, since he ranks far lower than me, you won't have to worry about that. It's not something I'll ever let happen."

Her shoulders sagged, and she smiled as she linked her arm through his. "So, you don't plan to give me away anytime soon?" she teased.

The smile slid from his face as he patted her hand. "I never want to give you away, and I'm certainly not going to give you to someone you don't choose."

His words had assured her. He was her protector; he was stronger and held more power than Malakai. She never had to fear being forced into marriage.

But that was months ago. Now her father wasn't here to protect her, Malakai's father was dead too, and she was standing beside Malakai, who had that awful, leering grin on his face. It was the grin that said he could see straight through her clothes, the one that said he'd come to claim his reward.

CHAPTER EIGHT

COLE WATCHED Elexiandra as she stood beside Malakai. Her delicate chin jutted out, and fire shown in her eyes as she kept her hands clasped firmly before her. He couldn't hear what Malakai said to her, but he could tell she didn't like it.

Malakai held his hand out to her, and she stared at it before glancing around the dance floor. Cole sensed her panic as she stared at the couples with desperation in her eyes.

He stepped forward to intervene, but Brokk blocked his way. Cole shot his brother a withering look that caused Brokk's eyebrows to rise. "What's gotten into you, killer?"

Cole watched as Elexiandra's shoulders slumped, and she slid her hand into Malakai's. The vamp grinned as he led her onto the floor. When he went to grasp her other hand, she jerked it back, but Malakai grabbed it and placed it against his chest.

Cole's teeth ground together; Malakai fought in Cole's army, but he'd never liked the arrogant vamp who took far too much joy in tormenting and killing others. It was what they all had to do to survive the war, but Malakai was one of those immortals who smiled the entire time they slaughtered others.

Malakai was dark and twisted, and Cole disliked him anywhere near Elexiandra. Resisting the inexplicable urge to go out there and beat Malakai into a bloody pulp, Cole focused on Brokk.

"What is it?" Cole asked.

Brokk continued to stare questionably at him as he took a step back. "How are you enjoying the party?"

"As much as you."

Brokk smiled grimly. "Then you're having the time of your life."

Cole chuckled. "Absolutely."

Brokk clasped his shoulder and squeezed it. Neither of them wanted this, their father knew that, and if it had been up to Cole, this party never would have happened, but it wasn't up to him.

If they were going to keep up the pretense of being on the Lord's side and being thrilled about their victory in the war, then a celebratory ball was a necessity. And they were all going to have to grin and bear it.

"Enjoy, brother," Brokk murmured before slipping into the crowd.

As he walked, some of the women reached out for him, and Brokk stopped to speak with them before moving on. Cole turned his attention back to the dance floor as the musicians continued to weave their magic upon the crowd.

He spotted Elexiandra amid the crush of bodies. Whereas everyone else was smiling while they danced with their partners, she remained rigid, and the look on her face said she'd rather be anywhere but here.

He was shocked to find himself wanting to intervene, but he had no idea why. What did he care if she was uncomfortable? He'd never considered the feelings of anyone outside of his family before. And as a dark fae, he'd only ever had two uses for women… fucking and feeding.

Yet when Elexiandra's gaze darted to the doorway, something inside him stirred at her unease, and he realized it was the lycan making its presence known again. He contemplated this strange development as Malakai grasped the hand Elexiandra had rested on his shoulder and spun her around.

Whereas most women laughed when their partners did such a thing, Elexiandra glanced anxiously around when he pulled her close again. Malakai said something to her, and when she shook her head, he gripped her chin and lifted her head, so she had to look at him.

She tried to jerk her chin free, but Malakai refused to release her. And then she winced.

Before Cole had considered intervening, he found himself striding through the dancers toward them. The action surprised him, but not enough to make him stop shoving his way through the crowd.

Out of the corner of his eye, he saw immortals turning toward him and the smiles on some of the women's faces, but he didn't acknowledge them. He didn't give a shit if they considered him rude; he couldn't stop. He had to get to her.

In the corner, the bow fell away from the cello, and the flute fell silent. Elexiandra said something and tried to turn her face away, but Malakai kept hold of her chin. They were still fifty feet away from him, and he was about to start ruthlessly shoving his guests out of the way when the woman who walked onto the dais with her appeared at her side.

Sahira, he recalled Sindri announcing the woman's name, and then another memory tugged at the edges of his mind. He recalled Del talking about someone named Sahira. It took him a couple of seconds before he remembered the woman was his half sister.

She was half witch and half vampire, which had to be the rarest combination of immortals in all the realms. He wasn't sure how such a thing happened, given how much the witches despised the vampires.

Cole couldn't hear the words they exchanged before Malakai released Elexiandra. She took a few steps back before turning and vanishing into the crowd with Sahira.

~

A GASP CAUGHT in Lexi's throat when she stepped out of the hallway and into a room made of glass on all four sides. For a minute, she couldn't breathe as her head fell back to take in the glass ceiling almost fifty feet over her head.

The gold beams running across the ceiling held the glass in place. In each corner of the room was a gold tree trunk and, carved to look like tree branches, the beams stretched overhead.

Hundreds of brown vines with hand-sized, green leaves covered at least half of the glass walls, but none of the vines touched the ceiling. They left it open to the two moons beyond the glass.

Flowers the size of her head clung to those vines. Their multi-colored blooms lifted their petals to the moonlight spilling through the glass ceiling. They basked in the rays shining down on them.

She'd never seen flowers with colors like the ones in here. There were reds in shades she couldn't begin to describe, pinks that weren't quite pink and might be some color she'd never heard of, and yellows and oranges so vibrant they rivaled the sun. With their large petals and stigma in the middle, they reminded her of hibiscus, except they were larger and more luminous.

She doubted she was supposed to be here, but she couldn't get her feet to turn away. This was the best thing she'd seen all night, and she wasn't ready to leave it.

She had no idea where she was in the castle or what this room was. She'd told Sahira she was returning to the room assigned to them, but she must have gotten turned around somewhere.

Her aunt wanted to come with her, but Lexi insisted she stay and have a good time. It was so rare Sahira ever got to do anything like this, and unlike Lexi, she was enjoying herself.

Lexi glanced behind her; she could still hear the music, but she didn't see anyone. She should go, but she didn't move. Drawn to the flowers and excited to get a closer look at them, she descended the two steps into the room and strolled across the white, marble floor.

This was so wrong and might get her into a ton of trouble, but she felt like Sleeping Beauty being lured to the spindle as she crept further into the room.

It did not go well for Sleeping Beauty, she reminded herself. However, she didn't stop.

She couldn't decide what to look at first, the spectacular flowers or the bright, full moons. Stopping in the middle of the room, she tipped her head back as she stood beneath one of the moons. Her skin prickled from the energy they exuded.

She closed her eyes and breathed in the sweet aroma filling the room.

CHAPTER NINE

COLE STOOD CLOAKED in the shadows of the moon room as he watched Elexiandra descend the stairs. The awe on her face captivated him as her mouth parted. His father would be irate if he found her here; this room was built for his mother and remained a shrine to her.

It was once a place for her to retreat to when she needed to think and rejuvenate. His father spent weeks having it constructed and made sure the room's design made it so a piece of a moon could always be seen from somewhere, no matter what time of day or night it was.

At noon, that piece of moon was found in the far-right corner if he stood with his toes against the glass, but it was there.

This room was his mother's retreat and her small piece of the lycan realm in the land of the dark fae. She'd brought the luna flowers in when they were no more than seeds and grown them until her death.

Cole barely recalled a time when the vines were no more than a foot tall. She died before she ever got to see them grow into something more, but he imagined this was what she'd envisioned for the room.

When he was a child and she was still alive, he'd sit on the bench in the far corner of the room and watch as she cupped each small vine in her hands. While she talked to them, they weaved around her, and some stroked her cheek.

Sometimes, he swore they laughed with her. And on the day she died, they wept with him when he retreated here. He'd come here in the hopes they'd all been wrong and a rogue warlock hadn't killed her.

He'd come here believing he would find her smiling amidst her flowers. He would run to her, and she would envelop him in her arms and dry his tears while she laughed over the silliness of the mistake.

She hadn't been here, it hadn't been a mistake, and he'd lain in this room for days while he grieved her. The servants tried to lure him away, but he remained where his mother's essence still thrived in the plants that hugged him while he cried.

Three days later, his father came for him. Cole recalled watching his father's strong hand slip past the vines that had closed protectively over him while he slept and wept. He recalled being drawn from the vines to discover his father's black, bloodshot eyes staring at him.

Cole hadn't seen the man since he delivered the news of his mother's death. Afterward, he'd retreated to his private solar. Broken and crying, Cole locked himself away too.

He remembered being astonished to see his father. He hadn't expected him to come for him, but as his dad lifted him from the ground, Cole wrapped his arms around his neck and cleaved to him as he started crying again.

His father carried him from the room, put him in a bath, and dressed him. He'd never forget the broken slump of his father's shoulders as he cared for him. Stubble lined his father's normally clean-shaven face, and his tears had swelled his eyes.

Cole was only seven when his mother died, but a part of him

died with her. A larger part of his father followed her into the grave.

Afterward, his father spent years torturing the warlock before Cole's uncle, Maverick, convinced him to kill the monster. When Cole was fifteen, he overheard Maverick telling his father he shouldn't keep the warlock alive and in the same house as Cole.

Maverick was still livid over his sister's murder, but he believed Tove was only extending Cole's suffering by keeping her killer alive. His father must have agreed as the warlock was dead a few days later.

His vengeance did nothing to ease Tove's sorrow. And no matter how many women followed his first and only wife, Cole knew his father never loved any of them like he had his mother.

And now, another beautiful woman stood in his mother's room. And to Cole's amazement, the flowers turned their heads away from the moons and toward her.

He was the only one the flowers reacted to, partly because of his mother and partly because of his lycan blood. Over the years, the peace he received from the flowers and his love for the moon were the most lycan things about him; they were probably the *only* lycan things about him... until he encountered her.

And now, he could feel the beast stirring within him while he watched her.

Was she also part lycan? Was that why the flowers responded to her too?

No, Del had said her mother was a human, and Del was very much a vampire. Or maybe he remembered it wrong? Maybe he only thought Del said his daughter was part human, and he'd said lycan.

Cole believed he would have remembered if she was part lycan, but they'd been fighting a war and there was often a lot of drink involved when Del opened up about his daughter, so Cole could be wrong.

Elexiandra sighed and lowered her head. The serenity on her

face and the moonlight streaming over her caused his breath to catch. The flowers reacted to her because it was impossible not to; she was magnificent.

They didn't respond to her in the same way they did to him, but they weren't indifferent to her like they were to everyone else who entered this room... except him. The flowers' interest in her intrigued him almost as much as she did.

Cole released the shadows cloaking him, and they slid back into their places along the wall. He stepped forward and waited for Elexiandra to realize he was here.

When she opened her eyes, she spotted him and gasped. Her hand flew to her throat, and a panicked look crossed her face. Smiling, he stepped further away from the shadows caressing him and strolled toward her.

He'd been there when she entered the room, but she'd never noticed as the shadows kept him hidden. After she left Malakai behind, Cole lost sight of her and assumed she retreated for the night. Needing some time to himself, he slipped away to what was once his mother's place and was now his.

Her gaze returned to the doorway, but she had to know he'd stop her before she ever made it there.

"Are you part lycan?" he asked as he stopped a few feet away from her.

CHAPTER TEN

A SMALL CREASE formed between her eyes. "No, my father was a vampire."

"I'm aware. I knew your father."

The confusion left her face as a spark bloomed in her exquisite green eyes. "You did?"

"Yes. He was an amazing strategist."

"I didn't know that," she murmured and glanced at the door again. "He didn't talk about the war much."

Of course, he wouldn't talk about the war with her. He recalled Del saying she was young, but even if she was a couple of centuries old, an air of innocence surrounded her, and Del would seek to protect that.

"I spent a lot of time with him," Cole said. "We fought together often, and I considered him a friend."

"Were you...." She paused to swallow as tears briefly glistened in her eyes. "Were you there when he died?"

"Yes."

Her shoulders slumped a little before they went back again and she looked to the doorway. He sensed her urge to bolt as she folded her hands before her and shifted from foot to foot, but she didn't try to leave.

"Was it...? Did he... did he suffer?" she whispered.

Cole recalled watching Del go down beneath the crush of bodies. He didn't know if the man suffered or not, as that was the last time he saw him. By the time they were able to hunt for the bodies of their fallen, the sun was already up and Del was nothing more than ash, but he couldn't tell her that.

"No," he said.

A single tear slid free before she wiped it away. Tears had never moved him before, and he *never* felt sympathy for anyone outside his family, but he found himself wanting to comfort her.

Over the years, he'd probably caused hundreds of tears to fall in his lifetime, and not once had they swayed him to compassion. But he hated the sight of *her* tears.

"Good," she said. "I should go."

At the same time, he asked, "Was your mother a lycan?"

She frowned at him. "No."

"Are you sure?"

"Yes. I never met my mother, but she was human."

"I see," he murmured as he glanced at the flowers still tilted toward her. "The luna flowers are from the lycan realm. I've only ever seen them respond to lycans, such as myself."

He found himself entranced by her as she studied the flowers again.

"I didn't know the lycans had flowers."

"The luna flowers grow in their land. They only bloom when the rays of the moon are shining down on them."

"Amazing," she whispered.

"They're reacting to you like you're a lycan."

When she laughed, the sound made him blink. He'd never heard a sound so clear and sweet before. It reminded him of the joy he experienced as a child when he'd run through the fields with his arms open and the full moon shining down on him.

It was a time before the death of his mother and centuries before the war. A time when he was still innocent too. It was a time so long ago that he'd forgotten about it… until now.

Elexiandra's eyes twinkled when she looked at the flowers again, and her laughter trailed away.

"I hate to disappoint them, but I am a vampire," she said.

As she spoke, he saw the tips of her small fangs again. They would extend when she fed, but no vampire could ever completely hide them like a lycan could.

"I can see that," he murmured.

Her head bowed as a blush crept up her neck and spread across her cheeks. It was so endearing his fingers itched to brush the hair back from her face, but he kept himself restrained.

He didn't know why; he'd always gone for and almost always gotten what he wanted. But though he longed to touch her, he simply stood and watched as she stretched a hand toward one of the flowers before pulling it back.

When Cole clasped one of the flowers, some of the vines slid down to brush his arms as he moved. The flower's petals were as smooth as silk and just as soft as he ran his finger across it before bringing it toward her.

Her fingers inched toward the flower, and when they landed on it, a smile lit her face. In response to her touch, the petals closed around her hand. She jumped and started to pull away but kept it there instead.

"It tickles!" She laughed.

Cole was stunned to realize he was grinning while watching the interaction between her and the flower. Its petals moved over her hand before it released her. Cole carefully returned the plant; it lifted its petals to the moon before twisting toward her again.

"They're amazing!" she breathed.

There was something far more amazing to him inside this room.

"This was my mother's room," he told her. "My father had it

built for her so that no matter where she stood in it, she could see at least a piece of a moon."

A wistful smile played across her full lips as she gazed around the room. "It's beautiful. I'm sorry. I shouldn't be here. I was trying to find the room I was assigned to and got lost."

"That can happen in this place. Sometimes, it changes around you."

"Really?"

When he grinned at her, Cole realized he couldn't recall the last time he genuinely smiled at anyone, but she made it easy to do.

"No, but it's something my father used to tell me when I was a child. I think he was teasing me because I always got lost in this place."

CHAPTER ELEVEN

Lᴇxɪ ᴄᴏᴜʟᴅɴ'ᴛ ꜱᴇᴇ the intimidating king of the dark fae teasing anyone, even his son, but she saw no reason for the prince to lie to her. Then again, she didn't understand why he was talking to her.

Part of her remained tempted to bolt out of here, but he so entranced the other part of her that she found herself eager to learn more.

"Do you still get lost here?" she asked.

"On occasion," he said with a rueful smile.

She didn't know if he was telling her the truth or saying that so she wouldn't feel bad, but either way, it made her laugh. "It is a rather large castle."

"There are over a thousand rooms."

Lexi's mouth dropped; a *thousand* rooms! If that were true, then he wasn't lying about still getting lost in this place.

"What can someone possibly do with a thousand rooms?" she blurted, and then her hand flew to her mouth and her blush deepened as she realized the question was rude.

He didn't seem to find it such as he laughed. "I have no idea, and I certainly haven't seen them all. I could spend the rest of my life exploring this place and never find all of them. Some are hidden. Some are lost rooms only entered by past kings and queens, and those same rulers sealed others away."

His words intrigued her. She would love the chance to explore this place for a week in search of those hidden and lost rooms. It would be fascinating. "I would try to find them all."

"Perhaps one day," he murmured.

As he spoke, more vines moved to brush against him, and a few encompassed his biceps before slipping away again. He was oblivious to them, but Lexi's amazement of the plants grew; not only were they lycan plants, but they craved the touch of a lycan.

Under the silvery glow of the moon, his eyes were impossibly *bluer* as they perused her. Unlike Malakai, whose lascivious gaze seemed to strip her bare, she didn't squirm beneath the prince's inquisitive stare.

He didn't make her feel dirty or exposed before him; instead, she felt as if he was trying to understand her better, and she was becoming increasingly intrigued by him. For some reason, this terrified her more than Malakai's obvious lust.

The dark fae were not known for their kindness or interest in others. They were known for their ruthlessness, power, and ability to turn once perfectly normal beings into mindless sex slaves.

It wasn't something the dark fae did to all of their sexual partners, but they did it enough that cautionary tales about them abounded.

Despite the warnings to stay away, there were still those who got too close and eventually became one of the shadow kissed creatures seeking only sexual gratification.

She would *not* be one of them.

"So, Elexiandra, is this your first time in a Shadow Realm?" he asked.

"Lexi," she replied.

"Excuse me?"

She edged a little further away. "Please call me Lexi. It's what I go by."

He smiled at her as he prowled a little closer. When he was this close, the heat of his body caressed her skin, and her fingers itched to trace his ciphers.

Lexi gulped and shuffled a few steps back. Getting involved with a dark fae was an excellent way to lose her mind.

"Lexi then," he murmured.

"And you're Colburn," she said.

"Call me Cole."

She tried to think of a response, but her mind and common sense had taken a vacation when she required them most.

"Have you ever been to a Shadow Realm?" he asked.

"No, and I admit, I find it fascinating as well as a little frightening."

"I think that is most immortals' reaction to the Gloaming."

Turning, she gazed out the windows and focused on the lush forest outside the glass as she tried to calm her racing heart. "Is there a sun here, or is it always night?"

"There is a sun, and like on Earth, it rises and sets. However, there are always at least two moons visible at one time, and at midnight, all four are clearly seen for at least an hour. There are all kinds of creatures in this land. Some are like the human realm, and others… well, others would give you nightmares for a week."

"Amazing," she murmured.

She'd love to walk outside this castle and into those woods to explore the wonders they hid. She never heard him move, but his chest pressed against her back.

Lexi gulped as her skin tingled like little pulses of electricity were running through it, and her heart raced like a horse pulling a chariot. The hair on her nape rose as bumps broke out on her arms. If she turned, she could touch him and discover what he felt like.

Don't be an idiot!

She tried to remind herself of all the deadly things the dark fae could do and how treacherous they were, but it wasn't doing her any good. She yearned to touch him and ease her curiosity.

She couldn't get any saliva into her suddenly parched mouth as the power he emanated crackled against her until she felt dizzy from it. Clasping her dress, she forced herself not to touch her forehead and swoon like some woman from the past who suddenly got the vapors.

"That"—he leaned over her shoulder and pointed to the moon on the right. When he spoke, his breath brushed her cheek—"is Orius, and that one"—he pointed to the moon on the left— "is Carpton. You can't see them right now, but the other two moons are Dashius and Golen."

Lexi found it increasingly difficult to breathe as his presence overwhelmed all her senses. He smelled of allspice and something else, something musky and powerful, something she couldn't quite put her finger on, but it was alluring.

"They're beautiful," she managed to croak out.

Larger than the moons on Earth, they cast a lot of light upon the realm. And they were beautiful. One was full, while the other was a crescent sliver.

"Yes," he said, and she felt his eyes on her.

Lexi gulped; she shouldn't do it, but her head turned toward him, and their eyes met. They were so close, she could tell that no other colors marred the perfect Persian blue of his eyes.

She didn't mean for it to happen, but her gaze fell to his lips. Sheltered her whole life, she hadn't spent much time around boys or men.

She was aware her father protected her, probably too much, but she'd never argued with him about it. He always said she would have plenty of time for those things when she was older, but she would never be a child again. He was determined she enjoy her childhood for as long as possible.

She'd probably stayed sequestered for too many years, but though the war only lasted a couple of years, the tensions building up to it started years before then. When she might have normally spread her wings, she remained at home to run things while her father became more entrenched in the events unfolding.

And now she was standing with one of the most powerful and deadly creatures ever to walk the realms, and she longed to kiss him. When his gaze fell to her mouth, her breath caught.

Was *he* going to kiss *her*?

She should run as fast as she could from here. Getting entangled with the prince of the dark fae was the worst idea ever, and Lexi didn't want to end up shadow kissed, but she couldn't move away from him.

One kiss couldn't hurt. It took far more than one tiny, curiosity-easing kiss to turn someone into a mindless sex slave. She didn't know how much more, but since she planned to keep her clothes on, she wouldn't have to worry about it.

He was leaning toward her, so close his breath warmed her lips, when a piercing scream shattered their solitude. The prince jerked away as more screams and shouts preceded a loud bang.

"Stay here!" he commanded and ran from the room.

Sahira! Lexi hesitated only a second before running after him.

CHAPTER TWELVE

COLE RACED down the hallways as the shouts and screaming continued. Another bang shook the floor and rebounded off the walls a second before he burst into the ballroom. He scanned the room as he tried to ascertain what was happening.

And then he spotted a group of lycans, vampires, and dark fae fighting on the other side of the room. The musicians had stopped playing, and Brokk, along with some dark fae guards, were carving their way through the fighters and tossing them away.

When one of them punched his brother in the back of the head, Cole snarled as he sped across the room to help him. They hadn't survived the war to be taken down by a bunch of assholes in their *own* home. He'd already lost too many of his brothers; he would *not* lose anymore.

Brokk turned toward his attacker as Cole seized the vamp by the shoulder and threw him away. Guests scattered out of the way as the vamp skidded across the floor before crashing into the wall.

Dark fae guards surrounded the vamp and hauled him to his feet. Brokk nodded his thanks to Cole, but he didn't have a chance to speak before the growing brawl drew his attention.

Power thrummed through Cole as he drew on the air

surrounding him and pulled it toward him. When a couple of vamps and a lycan lurched toward each other, he held his hands out, turned them over, and pushed them apart with his palms facing outward.

The air around him shuddered as he pushed it outward. The impact of the air shoved the fighters back. They hit separate walls with loud thuds. The air rippled as he held out his palms to keep the fighters pinned against the wall.

Brokk punched a warlock in the face before gripping the back of his head and slamming it onto his knee. Brokk kicked the fighter away and lunged over a witch to snatch a candle from the wall.

Lifting the flame to his mouth, Brokk blew on it. Instead of the fire going out, it surged into a rolling inferno that torched those closest to him.

Immortals screamed as they raced away from him or fell to the ground and rolled as they attempted to smother the flames consuming them. The scent of burnt clothes and flesh permeated the air. The fire wouldn't kill them, but they'd hurt.

When a vampire lunged toward him, Cole released his hold on the prisoners and spun to face his attacker. Red eyes met his a second before Cole drove the heel of his palm up and into the vamp's nose.

Blood erupted from the vamp's shattered nose, and it howled as its hands flew to its face and it staggered back. Lifting his foot, Cole planted it in the vamp's belly and shoved it away from him.

"What is going on here?" his father's voice boomed throughout the vast hall. "Who dares to fight in *my* home?"

Footsteps echoed across the floor and rebounded off the ceiling as his father stalked toward them. Immortals scrambled to get out of the way, and more of the innocent guests fell back. Tove's fury vibrated the air around him.

"Guards, seize *every* single one of the fighters," Tove commanded. "They will all reside in my dungeon until I decide it's time for them to go."

"You can't do that!" a vampire protested.

His father stepped so close to the vampire their noses almost touched. "Are you going to stop me? I helped fund the Lord's war. I gave him my best fighters, including my sons, and if you open your mouth one more time, I will give *you* to his dragons."

The vamp blanched but wisely shut his mouth.

"Take them away," Tove commanded.

The guards captured the twenty-five or so fighters. The remaining guests didn't speak as they led the prisoners away. Some of their gazes flicked from the blood on the floor to the king of the dark fae.

Cole didn't have to look at his father to know he was infuriated; it continued to vibrate the air in the room. More of the guests edged away from the king. He was the most powerful being in this room, and everyone knew it.

"This party is over; everyone go home," his father commanded. "Everyone is to be out of here in twenty minutes."

With that, his father turned and stalked away. Cole glanced at Brokk, who stared after their father's retreating back.

"That was a quick celebration," Brokk said.

"There wasn't much to celebrate," Cole muttered.

And then he recalled Lexi. Turning, he pushed his way through the crowd as it funneled toward the exit. Breaking free of them, he jogged down the hall to the moon room, but she wasn't there.

"Shit," he hissed.

He ran back to the main hall, but half the revelers had already left, and more were on their way out. Still, he searched for her amongst those who remained, but she was already gone.

～

"I CANNOT BELIEVE they dared to fight in *my* hall," his father growled as he paced his solar.

The airy room allowed plenty of room for his angry movements as he stalked to one end, turned on his heel, and stormed past the large table in the center of the room. He reached the window on the other side of the room and paused to look down on the courtyard a few hundred feet below.

Silver sconces hung on the walls, and the torches situated inside them cast shadows across the walls and floor. Tapestries decorated the walls. Most of them were landscapes of different areas of the Gloaming, but one was of his mother, and the others were of all the king's sons.

Despite the fact half of his sons fought against their father in the war, he would never remove their tapestries from his solar. They'd stood against him, but he still loved them; he always would.

If push came to shove, the king would lay down his life for those sons. They were now hunted as traitors, but he would do what he could to make sure they survived. Brokk and Cole were under strict orders to save them if they could, but they didn't require any such orders; neither wanted Orin or Varo to die.

Situated in the North Tower, the solar provided a spectacular view of the Gloaming. Cole didn't have to look out the window to picture the fields full of crops rolling into hills. Though the dark fae mostly survived on the energy produced from sex, they also ate enough regular food to make crops necessary in the Gloaming.

During the summer, those crops would fill the fields, but now they were only half grown. Like Earth, the Shadow Realms had seasons, and the seasons in the Gloaming were similar to Earth's.

It was June in the human realm and spring in the Gloaming, but they didn't have winter here. They had a longer spring, summer, and fall. The leaves changed colors and fell in the Gloaming, but new ones sprang forth within weeks of the old ones falling.

Cole's uncle, Maverick, watched Tove as he paced from his seat at the table. A golden goblet full of wine sat before him, but Maverick removed the silver flask from inside his jacket, unscrewed the cap, and took a gulp. His uncle was more of a whiskey than a wine guy.

Taller than Cole by about two inches, Maverick had difficulty getting his six-foot-nine frame to fit under the table and kept his legs sprawled out to the side. His dark brown hair waved around his broad face, and his chestnut eyes shone with amusement as he watched the king.

Maverick was the alpha of his pack, but he couldn't stop some of his members from leaving to fight against the Lord during the war. But then, the lycans always enjoyed a fight.

His pack was not the only pack in the Lunar Realm. Others resided there, and before the war, they often argued with each other. They would battle over land, losing bits and pieces to enemy packs only to reclaim it again the next day or week.

Cole leaned against the wall as he sipped wine from his golden goblet and watched his father. It had been years since he'd seen Tove so enraged. Brokk glanced at Cole and raised an eyebrow. Cole shrugged and drank some more wine.

"What started the fight?" Brokk inquired.

"A vampire grabbed the ass of a lycan's mate. Her mate punched the vamp in the face; someone hit a witch in the ensuing battle. It was a free-for-all after that," Tove replied.

"You can't blame a lycan for defending his mate," Maverick said.

"Maybe not, but they're all going to spend a week in my dungeons."

"You cannot blame a lycan for defending his mate," Maverick repeated.

Tove stopped his pacing and turned to face Maverick. The two men stared at each other.

"They are on our side," Maverick said. "Some of them are part of my pack. They were wrong to fight in your hall. Let them stew in that knowledge for the night, but set them free afterward."

CHAPTER THIRTEEN

A MUSCLE TWITCHED in Tove's jaw as his teeth ground together. Cole didn't say a word, but his uncle was right, and his father knew it.

"It might not be the best idea to make an enemy out of them," Brokk said.

His father grumbled something and paced over to the table. He grasped the chair at the end, his chair, and gazed down the table at his sons and Maverick.

"I'll set them free tomorrow," he relented. "Except for the vampire. He'll stay in there until I say he can leave, and I don't care if that's three centuries from now."

"They can't fault you for that," Cole said.

"No one gives a shit about the vampire," Maverick muttered.

His father released the chair and pulled it back to sit on it. He waved a hand at the two chairs beside him. "Join me," he commanded his sons.

Cole stepped away from the wall and walked down to sit at his father's right side while Brokk took the chair on his left. Maverick sat a couple of chairs down from Brokk.

They had originally planned to have a full coalition meeting with the other immortals seeking to end the Lord's tyranny. However, there was no reason for those members to remain in the palace once Tove commanded everyone to leave.

Maverick was family; it wouldn't look odd if he remained, but it would look strange if the others did.

"I spoke with Talon," his father said.

The warlock was a powerful asset to the coalition, but he was also the most cautious.

"He's determined that we find someone who can sit on the throne before we try to destroy the Lord," Tove continued. "He believes it won't do us any good if we remove the maniac but have no one to replace him."

"The throne and the power are going to rot whoever we replace him with," Brokk said. "Just like it has the current Lord."

Cole still remembered what the current Lord was like before he sat on the throne. He'd been a good man, a warlock who was chosen by the other immortals to take the place of the Lord before him.

Cole clearly remembered Andreas as a smiling warlock with hazel eyes and a boisterous laugh that once rebounded off the walls of the downstairs' hall. He was one of the few immortals everyone liked, and now the throne had corrupted his mind and turned him into a madman who had unleashed hell upon the unsuspecting mortals.

"And each race of immortal wants it to be one of their own," Maverick said.

"I don't know why everyone is so willing to claim the next lunatic as one of theirs," Cole muttered.

The idea behind the coalition was a good one. A few of the strongest leaders from different realms belonged to it, but unfortunately, the idea was better than the execution. They often spent more time bickering with each other than they did undermining the Lord's control.

His brothers had known what they planned and hoped to

accomplish, but five of them grew impatient with the lack of progress and broke off to join the rebels. Only two of them remained.

Cole didn't fear that they would rat out the members of the coalition if they were caught. They may have stood on opposing sides of the war and had differing opinions on handling things, but there had always been a lot of love between them.

None of them had the same mothers, but they all had each other, and their father loved them all equally. They would *never* betray each other.

They were supposed to have stopped him before the humans ever learned about the existence of immortals. Instead, while the war was still waging in the Shadow Realms, the Lord grew impatient with its lack of progress and turned his dragons loose on Earth.

The humans, not expecting the attack and having never seen anything like the creatures scorching their land before, were slow to respond. But it didn't matter; the Lord had gathered enough intel that he sent the beasts to destroy the human's military strongholds first.

No country was safe from the wrath of the dragons. By the time the humans responded, their military was devastated, and what remained of it was ineffective against the dragons.

The war had spilled out of the Shadow Realms by then, and though the coalition spent much of the war working in secret to depose the Lord, Cole realized they'd failed. Now, they were still trying to figure out a way to defeat him, but millions, if not billions, had lost their lives in the process, including countless immortals.

Once the human realm fell, those immortals who fought on the rebel side had nothing left to fight for... other than their lives.

The war continued for almost another year, but it grew smaller and smaller until the rebels turned and fled in the hopes of saving their lives.

"Because they think they might have some sway of the next Lord if it is one of theirs," Maverick said.

"Why? The warlocks have no control over this one," Cole said.

"It makes no sense, but that's the way it is," his father said.

"Hmm...." Cole drummed his fingers on the table and glanced at the empty seat across from Maverick. At one time, Del would have occupied that chair, but his friend was gone.

However, his daughter was still very much alive. Cole pushed aside the image of Lexi's awed face as she gazed at the luna flowers. Now was *not* the time.

"How do we go about finding someone to take the Lord's place?" Brokk asked.

"That's the question no one can answer," Maverick said. "That throne was built for an arach. Those dragons belong to them."

"But they're all dead," Cole said.

"That they are," his father muttered as he poured himself a goblet of wine.

"There has to be someone who can handle its power," Brokk said.

"We haven't found anyone in a thousand years," their father replied.

"There has to be something we can do," Brokk insisted. "We can't sit here and wait for the Lord to decide he wants all our realms, and all of *us*, dead next."

"Someone has to sit on that throne," Maverick said. "The Shadow Realms will be almost as unstable with an empty throne as it is with the Lord on it. The dragons will have free reign of the realms if someone isn't on that throne to control them. And if those things decide to fly free...."

"We're all fucked," Cole finished when his voice trailed off.

"Exactly."

"What if we kill the Lord and instead of replacing him with one immortal, we have a rotating group of them, each chosen by a member of the coalition?" Brokk suggested. "We can pick who we think will be the best choices for the throne."

"And what if one of them sits on it and decides not to give up the throne's power?" his father asked.

"We'll fight that battle if we come to it, but if they're not on it for very long, maybe we can keep the throne from corrupting them."

"I think Brokk's suggestion might be worth discussing with the others. Have you spoken with Circe?" Cole asked.

Circe was the witch on the coalition. No other witches knew one of their most powerful coven leaders was secretly helping other immortals bring down the Lord. They would have been astounded to learn that at one time she was also working with a vampire, but Del's death ended that relationship.

Tove had originally gathered Maverick, Circe, and Talon for this. After years of friendship, he felt he could trust them, and he wanted the powers other immortal creatures could bring to the table.

He later brought in his sons, and Cole was the one who introduced Del. The man was a military genius, but not even Del could figure out a way to get through the dragons to destroy the Lord. He'd been working on something he said might change things. Unfortunately, he died before anyone could learn what it was.

"Brokk's suggestion could work," Maverick said.

"There's a lot of hate between the different species; look at what happened here tonight," his father said.

"There will be a lot more death if they don't get over it," Cole said.

His father sat back in his chair and clasped his hands before him as he stared at the far wall. "I think we might be on to something here. I think the others will approve of each species having equal time on the throne, and we can hold each other accountable."

"It's going to require a lot of trust between the species," Maverick said.

"That's something we've never had before," Cole said.

"The humans never possessed knowledge of us either, and we never believed our families would be torn apart the way they are."

"This may be our only hope," Brokk said.

"I'll talk with Circe and Talon," his father said.

"If they agree, we're still left with the biggest problem of all," Brokk said.

"How do we get past the dragons to kill the Lord?" Cole asked.

They all stared at each other, but no one had an answer.

"Keep an eye out for Varo and Orin," his father said. "Don't put yourselves at risk, but if there's something you can do…."

"We'll save them if we can," Cole vowed, and Brokk nodded.

Cole knew that was easier said than done as the Lord's men were relentlessly hunting his brothers, but he would do what he could to save them.

CHAPTER FOURTEEN

LEXI STROLLED toward the large weeping willow near the lake. She inhaled the sweet scent of spring and the water lilies floating on the water. The gentle breeze caused the small green leaves to dance as she approached the thick canopy they created.

The branches spilling into the water sent small ripples across the serene surface when the wind stirred them. She couldn't see it yet, but beneath the boughs of the tree and against its trunk, she'd erected a small marker for her father.

His body would never reside here, but his memories lingered like ghosts over a graveyard. She heard his laughter as he chased her beneath the drooping branches and through the curtain of tiny leaves.

Her laughter mingled with his when he lifted her from the ground and spun her around. Her feet flew through the air, and for a moment, she was flying and the world was this wondrous place. She never once doubted his love for her.

Over the years, they spent many hours beneath this tree playing, imagining they were in a fantasy world battling pirates or soaring through the air on the Lord's dragons. Sometimes, she would sit on his lap while he read to her for hours, or they would feed the ducks while birds flitted through the branches and the wind whispered through the leaves.

It had been years since they last sat beneath the tree together. The war took him away long before it claimed his life, but she came here often to sit beneath the boughs and talk to him. Only now, he wasn't talking back anymore.

She refused to look at the smoke rising from the burned-out city while she walked; she'd seen enough of it. Arriving at the tree, she pulled back some of the branches and ducked beneath the leaves.

When she released the branches, they swished as they settled into place behind her. Hidden beneath the tree, some of the weight lifted from her shoulders and they sagged.

She'd spent most of the day trying not to think about what the future held after their return from the Gloaming last night. She hoped it wasn't true, but she suspected it wouldn't be long before Malakai turned up here.

She didn't know how much time she had, but she had to prepare. However, she had no idea what to do. No matter what happened, she would *not* join her life to his, but her refusal was not something he would take well.

What would he do to her? To the manor? To Sahira?

She shuddered at the possibilities before shoving them aside. Those were concerns for a later time. Now, it was just her, this secret place, and the small plaque for her father.

The willow's branches encased her, but they provided enough room for her to walk over to the marker without bending. Kneeling before it, she wiped away the leaves that had fallen onto it and sat back on her heels to read it.

Delano Harper.

Beloved father, brother, and friend.

She'd wanted to put so much more onto it, but no stone could ever be big enough to display the depth of her love or the endless magnitude of her grief.

"I miss you, Daddy," she whispered.

A low groan accompanied her words. Lexi froze as the hair on her nape rose and prickles raced across her skin. She held her breath as she waited for something more, but the only sound was the breeze rustling the leaves.

She glanced around the shadowed interior but didn't see anyone else. Rising, she edged to the left of the tree trunk. Her hand went to the hunting knife strapped to the belt on her waist.

Because she was half human, she couldn't transport away from a threat like other vampires. She didn't burn or catch fire in the sun, though, so she supposed it was a good trade-off, even if it didn't feel like one right now.

She hadn't imagined that groan, and if there was a threat on the other side of the tree, she couldn't fend off many immortals if they got their hands on her. Still, she had to know what was there.

She slid her knife from its holster and held it before her as she stepped around the tree trunk. Lexi's hand flew to her mouth when she spotted the man on the other side of the tree.

Red covered him, and it took her a minute to realize it wasn't because his clothes were red. No, torn open and blood-soaked were the best ways to describe what lay before her.

Unsure what to do, she stood and gawked for longer than she should have before reacting. When her feet stopped sticking to the soft earth, she rushed forward to kneel at his side.

She reached for him before jerking her hands back. She had no idea what to do or where to touch him that wouldn't hurt him more. When he groaned again, his head rolled toward her, and a pair of narrowed black eyes met hers.

There was no recognition in those eyes, and she had no idea who he was, but she knew the raven hair, dark eyes, slender build, pointed ears, and ciphers of the dark fae. She had no idea what he was doing here, but whatever propelled him to seek shelter couldn't be good.

"They're coming for me," he croaked.

"Who's coming for you?" she asked.

She inspected the jagged slices filleting his side and chest to the bones beneath. The blood drenching his torn-open black shirt caused it to stick to his flesh.

Carefully peeling away the scraps of cloth, she revealed the jagged tears beneath. A *lycan* had done this.

Lexi suppressed the unease churning in her stomach while she inspected the wound. The Lord of the Shadow Realms had unleashed bounty hunters on the remaining rebel army, and with their superior tracking skills, many of those hunters were lycan.

She should get away from this man and flee to her house. She should pretend she'd never seen him or, better yet, turn him in. He was a danger to her and Sahira, but she didn't move.

She'd never forgive herself if she turned her back on him or, worse, was the reason his hunters finished what they started. Her father had fought against him, but she didn't want to fight, and she was *so* tired of all the violence and death.

"How many of them are coming?" she asked.

When he didn't respond, she shifted her attention from his injury to his pale face. Even his lips had lost all their color, and his eyes were closed. Leaning closer, she listened to his shallow breaths as they rattled in and out.

He was alive, and if she could get him somewhere safe, he would heal, but if she did that, she'd embroil herself in this mess. She could get Sahira; her aunt would know what to do, but she preferred not to involve Sahira in this.

No matter what, she couldn't leave him here to be hunted down and slaughtered. Rising, she made her way to the branches and pulled a couple back to peer out. Birds flitted through the limbs of a nearby maple, and a dog lounged in the sun by the barn, but she didn't see anyone else.

If she could get him into the storm cellar and the tunnels running beneath the property, he could hide there until he healed.

It might be the worst decision she ever made, she already had enough to deal with, but she lowered the branches back into place and returned to the man's side. He didn't move.

He was completely helpless, and if she didn't act soon, he would also be completely dead.

Grasping his arm, she draped it around her shoulder and slid her arm around his back. Planting her feet, she lifted him from the ground. He moaned, and his head fell back, but when she jostled him, it fell forward until his chin rested against his chest.

She may be half human, but at least she had some immortal strength, and she dragged him toward the edge of the tree with relative ease. With a shaking hand, she pushed aside the leaves to peer out again.

Across the field of green grass, the manor stood a couple of hundred yards away. Modeled after her dad's childhood home, the estate looked as if it could have stepped out of eighteenth-century England with its gray stone façade, rounded windows, and five chimneys.

It was far too large for her and Sahira now that most of the workers who once lived there had fled, but she would never give it up. This was her childhood home, her father had loved the place, and she adored its many rooms, sweeping staircases, and fairy-tale appearance.

When she was young, Lexi would imagine she was a queen ruling her subjects or a ghost roaming the halls as she slipped from one room to the next. Now, she didn't pretend anymore, but she hoped that if she ever found someone to love, she would one day raise her children here too.

That was if she didn't get caught and killed for harboring a dark fae who was most likely a fugitive.

"I hope you're not a complete asshole," she muttered before hauling him out from under the leaves and dragging him across the yard.

The storm cellar was only a hundred yards away, but it seemed like a mile as she hurried across the open space while his feet dragged across the ground. To make matters worse, it felt like it got farther away with every step she took. When she finally made it to the cellar, she dug into her pocket and pulled out the key.

Her eyes darted around, but she still didn't see anyone as she shifted his weight before bending to stick the key in the lock. Her fingers were surprisingly steady as she turned the key.

She slid the key back into her pocket and glanced around again. Only the lazy dog remained in view as she pulled open the doors and dragged him into the shadows. His booted feet thudded against the steps as she hauled him into the darkness.

Three feet into the room, she found the string for the single bulb hanging from the ceiling. Holding her breath, she pulled it and breathed a sigh when the bulb illuminated the damp space.

When she left the manor, the electricity was on, but that hadn't meant it still was. Since the war, it often came and went. It had been more reliable lately as the humans started patching pieces of their world back together.

The bulb illuminated the shelves lining the walls. At one time, supplies packed those shelves, but barely anything remained.

This wasn't the best place to leave him, but she had to. If he was a rebel and lycans were hunting him, they would track the scent of his blood here. She slid his arm from her shoulders and let him slump against the wall.

She was halfway up the stairs before she realized that not only was she most likely harboring a rebel, but he could also be a murderer, a criminal, or something far worse.

Why was she doing this? What was she thinking?

Her heart hammered as she spun back toward him. She had to get him out of here!

She couldn't do this. She hated seeing someone else die, but she couldn't put Sahira's life in jeopardy by allowing this man to stay.

If he were a rebel, he'd stood against her *father*. Then, a disturbing possibility occurred to her; he could have been the one who *killed* her father.

Running back to his side, Lexi knelt beside him. She was reaching for him, determined to drag him out of here and into the woods to let him fend for himself, when his eyes cracked open.

"Thank you," he croaked before passing out again.

Her hands froze before falling to her side. Her father may have opposed him, but he would never turn away an injured man, and he would *never* toss a defenseless man to the wolves, literally.

He could be the one who killed your dad.

The possibility hit her hard; it was true, but unlikely. And she still couldn't be responsible for his almost certain death by turning him away.

She pushed herself away from him and fled up the stairs before the hunters showed up while she was still sitting in the dark, debating what to do. She locked the doors and left him behind.

CHAPTER FIFTEEN

UNDERNEATH THE WILLOW TREE AGAIN, Lexi kicked the bloody leaves into the lake to bury the scent of blood on the air. Lifting her knife, she sliced open her palm and let her blood drip onto the earth.

Lycans, or any immortal, could detect the scent of blood on the air, but she hoped with his bloody leaves gone, her aroma would mask the dark fae's. Pushing aside the branches, she slipped out from beneath the limbs and scented the air as she searched for more of his blood.

She discovered more drops of it, and as she walked, she used her foot to smear his blood into the dirt while letting her blood fall onto his. The blood ended at the edge of the lake. Kneeling beside the water, she bent to wash her hands.

Studying the water's pristine surface, she searched for anyone else on the shoreline, but she didn't see anyone in the shadows of the trees. At least half a mile wide and just as long, the dark fae could have entered the water anywhere along the shoreline, but she hoped it was from across the lake.

She had no idea how he could have swum so far in his condition, but entering the water would have thrown off his trackers until he arrived on her shoreline. And she could only hope she'd done enough to cover his scent.

Pulling her hands from the water, she was relieved to see the wound had already healed. Now, she had to take care of her guest.

At one point in time, she would have run into half a dozen people on her way back to the manor; she encountered no one now. But then, there was no one to run into anymore.

When her father was alive, and before the war, a fair number of people worked the manor. Some lived there, but many fled during the war.

They were shocked to discover they worked for someone more than human, and many chose to be with their families. They also hoped to flee the destruction, but there was no escape.

The dragons had leveled most of the major cities throughout the world. What the Lord of the Shadow Realms unleashed on earth was something far worse than any of them ever expected, and now they were all suffering the consequences of it.

The humans knew of their existence, and immortals had gained nothing from it except more death.

Yes, the Lord had the dragons to keep the mortals in line, and immortals possessed abilities and strengths far beyond the humans, but the humans still had weapons that could maim and kill them.

Most immortals could blend in with humans and still choose to do so, but she'd heard tales of immortals who refused to blend in anymore. After years of going incognito, they were embracing their newfound freedom. Unfortunately, that was also causing problems.

After the war, the humans were petrified, broken, and resentful. They never had any warning that something beyond their realm existed before the Lord smashed their reality to pieces. And they hadn't been given much time to adapt before immortals started taking over.

The war between the immortals was over, but she suspected the war with the humans was just beginning. The Lord of the Shadow Realms couldn't destroy them all; vampires and both the light and dark fae fed on humans. They could also feed on immortals, but many immortals did *not* appreciate that, so vampires and the fae mostly relied on mortals for sustenance.

But then, with as crazy as he was, the Lord might decide to destroy *every* human if they became a problem and require immortals to feed only on each other. Things would become desperate then as few immortals allowed others to feed on them in any way.

She didn't know how the light fae were surviving. They'd refused to fight, and because of that, immortals reviled them. At one time, she often saw them in the human realm, but she hadn't seen any in almost a year.

Unlike the dark fae, who fed on the energy produced by sex, the light fae absorbed the joy humans emitted, and even if they weren't scorned and terrorized by other immortals when they were in the human realm, there was little joy left in this world. But that was their problem to handle; she had her own to deal with right now.

Glancing over her shoulder, she made sure no one was around before she entered the manor, strode down the hall, and jogged up the sweeping stairs to the second floor. At the top, the hallway ran straight ahead of her for fifty feet before veering around a corner.

Her steps were muffled by the dark blue carpet running the length of the hall. Unlike the first floor, where most of the rooms had gray stone walls, the upper level was drywalled and painted. The walls were a cream color and lined with family pictures.

The complete silence still felt so odd, and she resisted hugging herself as the lonely feel of the place weighed her down.

Stopping outside a door halfway down the hall, she took a deep breath before gripping the knob and shoving the door open. She didn't look around; she couldn't as tears filled her eyes while the scent of her dad filled her nose. He'd smelled of the outdoors and mint, and those aromas lingered in his room.

She blinked back her tears as she opened his drawers. She removed a black sweater and some socks. Unable to keep up with the flow of tears, she gave up trying as she ran to his closet, pulled out a pair of jeans, and fled the room. Closing the door behind her, she leaned against it as she wiped at the tears streaming down her cheeks.

It had been six months since word of his death arrived, yet the knife of grief digging into her heart made it feel like it was just yesterday. She didn't know if it would ever get better, but she wouldn't be returning to his room any time soon.

Shoving herself away from the door, she buried her misery as she hurried to one of the hall closets and pulled it open. She removed a couple of towels before returning to the first floor and entering the kitchen.

Dinner was already in the oven, but Sahira wasn't around. She had to be somewhere nearby as she would *never* let one of her meals burn, but Lexi was glad her aunt wasn't here; she couldn't deal with questions right now.

She rushed to fill a pot with water before Sahira returned. She ignored the warm liquid splashing over her hand as she glanced around. She could always tell Sahira one of the horses injured themselves, Sahira wouldn't question it or go to the barn to check, but she didn't want to lie to her.

When she finished filling the pot, she left the room and was careful not to spill anything as she rushed down the hall. Her feet didn't make a sound on the red rug covering the gray stone floors. She kept her ears attuned for some hint of Sahira, but the manor remained unnaturally subdued.

No, it wasn't unnatural anymore. This was the way it was now.

She slipped through the library's open double doors and paused to glance back into the hall. From the kitchen, she heard the back door click shut. Sahira must have been out in the garden.

Lexi turned her attention from the hall and crossed the room toward the large, gray stone fireplace. Overhead, the dark wood beams running across the cathedral ceiling didn't block the sun streaming through the skylights. It illuminated the hardwood floors and brought out the gold in the blue and gold Oriental rug in the room's center.

Normally, she loved the way the sun spilled through the skylights and the large, arched windows making up most of the wall on her right, but she barely noticed it now. Just as she barely noticed the thousands of books lining the shelves to her left, behind her, and around the fireplace.

She'd read every book in this room, many of them more than once. She'd always spent a lot of time here, but since her dad died, it had become her favorite sanctuary. Two overstuffed love seats faced the fireplace. The one on the left was hers, while her father favored the one on the right.

Often, as a child, she would lay on her belly on that rug. She'd prop her chin on her hands and kick her feet in the air while gazing at the fire and listening to her father read whatever new tale they were venturing on together. He had a thing for the classics, his favorite being Oedipus. She had a thing for fantasy, her favorite being any Harry Potter book.

She stopped next to the fireplace and glanced back to make sure Sahira wasn't around. Her aunt knew about the tunnels, but she would question why Lexi was entering them.

After every tunnel was built, Sahira would go into it and cast a spell to keep them cloaked from the outside world. No one who didn't know they were there would ever be able to find one of the tunnels.

But she couldn't go back and close the library doors because Sahira would wonder about that too. Lexi had to take the chance she could slip into the tunnels without Sahira knowing.

Standing beside the fireplace, she kept her attention focused on the doors as she pressed one of the rocks. It pushed in, and something clicked. When the inside of the fireplace swung open, cool air drifted out from the shadows beyond. Taking a deep breath, Lexi prepared herself for what she was about to do.

Once she crossed this threshold, there was no turning back from her decision, but then, she'd already come too far to turn around now. She'd already brought the dark fae further onto her property, and now she had to care for him.

CHAPTER SIXTEEN

LEXI PICKED up the bottle of blue potion and lifted it. Inside, the golden liquid sparked a little as it swished back and forth. From behind the counter, the witch with the cool blue eyes and black hair watched her.

"How much?" Lexi asked about the healing potion.

The dark fae in the tunnels had healed some since yesterday, but it wasn't fast enough for her liking. She intended to get him out of her life as soon as possible, and if the witches' concoction helped with that, then she would pay for it. Normally, she would have asked Sahira for this, but she couldn't do that now.

"Two hundred," the witch said.

Lexi suppressed a snort of disbelief and dipped a hand into her pocket. It was highway robbery, and they both knew it, but she couldn't risk drawing attention to herself by haggling today.

She hated being fleeced by the witch, but at least she could rely on the witches' discretion. The sign next to the register announced all sales were final and confidential.

The witches were known to keep the secrets of their clientele. Immortals and humans wouldn't buy from them as often if they were running around discussing their purchases. The witch would never reveal what Lexi purchased here.

She removed her small wallet from her pocket and took out two hundred carisle. She didn't have to look at the Shadow Realms' currency to know that dragons marked the front of it.

The witch smiled as she took the money and slipped it into a leather pouch. She took the potion from Lexi and put it into another leather pouch before giving it back to Lexi.

"Thanks," Lexi muttered and stifled her impulse to add, "for screwing me."

Turning away from the makeshift, wooden counter, she ignored the people gathered inside the small hut as she made her way through the shadowed interior. Everyone else in the store was human; she could tell by the distinct lack of power emanating from them. They all stopped their browsing of the potions and trinkets lining the shelves to watch her go.

The humans didn't have Shadow Realms currency, but the witch behind the counter would take their money. Lexi felt a stab of guilt as she met their curious stares. They all looked tired and more than a little beat down by their new lot in life.

As she passed a woman, the woman shoved a black lump back onto the shelf. A sign above the lump guaranteed it would provide enough food for a week.

Pity tugged at Lexi's heart when the thin woman bowed her head and her lank hair fell forward to shield her features. The humans hadn't asked for this; they'd never known it was coming, and now they were suffering the consequences because a madman wouldn't give up the throne that had corrupted him.

She barely had carisles left, but she found her hand dipping toward her wallet. The price on the stone was fifty dollars or about twenty carisle. The witch had robbed her blind, but apparently, she had a soft spot for the starving masses. Maybe she wasn't such a smug ass after all.

The woman lifted the stone again, and Lexi scented tears

before she put it back and turned away. Lexi stopped and pulled her wallet out. She removed a twenty-dollar carisle and walked over to the woman.

The woman started to turn away, but Lexi grasped her wrist to halt her. When the woman turned back to her, Lexi saw her round belly. She was only weeks away from delivery.

"Here," Lexi said as she shoved the money into the woman's hand.

The woman started to shake her head. "I can't."

"Take it," Lexi insisted.

She could feel the witch's eyes on her, but she didn't look back. The woman's fingers curled briefly around Lexi's as tears rolled down her cheeks.

Lexi pulled her hand away and walked out of the store before she started to cry too. She'd grown up in the mortal realm; she was more comfortable around humans than immortals. She'd grown up with them; they were her people, they were suffering, and she *hated* it.

Stepping onto the crowded dirt road, she ignored the crush of humans and immortals surrounding her as she swung the leather pouch onto her shoulder and slipped into the crowd.

∼

COLE DESPISED the crowded human and immortal markets that had sprung up in the cities and towns since the war ended. He understood their necessity as humans scrambled to survive, and those who still had fortunes sought to get their hands on things they'd only ever dreamed about. He preferred it when the markets only catered to immortals and were hidden from the mortals.

"Watch it," Brokk growled when a passing lycan's shoulder hit his.

The lycan turned to look at Brokk, who lifted his hand in the air. The lycan took in the ciphers on Brokk's hand and kept walking. Not many immortals sought to pick a fight with the dark fae. The lycan was larger and stronger, but they all feared the dark fae's powers.

"Bunch of hairy assholes," Brokk muttered.

Cole didn't take offense to his brother's comment. He couldn't count the number of times he'd called vamps bloodsucking leeches around Brokk.

"I do not have a hairy asshole," Cole said.

"You never know what the future holds."

"It better not hold hairy assholes."

Brokk grinned at him before turning to avoid a herd of humans who scurried past with their heads down. Cole barely acknowledged the humans as he tried not to inhale the stench of dirt and body odor wafting from them. The sweet stench of witches' potions and burnt wood, as well as the ever-present reek of the distant burning city, hung heavily on the air.

The open road that vehicles once traversed was now a thoroughfare crowded with ramshackle huts and hastily assembled buildings. They'd turned the broken and cracked four-lane road into little more than a lane.

Many of the shops belonged to witches, but there were plenty of other immortals looking to sell things they'd crafted and the food they grew on their land. There were also stalls with vamps who sought to pay for blood. The vamp stalls and food booths were the most crowded with humans, but the witches had a fair amount of business too.

He'd prefer not to be here, but if they were going to know what was happening in the world and how things were going, the markets were the best place to go. Plus, there was a chance he might run into Lexi.

It was a small chance, but one he was willing to take. He'd never been to Del's home, but he knew it was somewhere nearby. And if he didn't find her here, he'd....

What?

Hunt her down?

And how would he explain that to Brokk? They were close, they always had been, but he'd never gone out of his way to find a woman. Brokk would find it odd; *he* found it odd.

However, the possibility of seeing her again intrigued and excited him.

As they walked, he listened to the chatter of the humans and immortals who passed. Most conversations focused on securing supplies to keep their families alive, but there were a few murmurs of discontent amongst the crowd.

He ignored those whispers. Of course, these people were unhappy; nothing of the world they knew remained. What he sought were whispers about where some of the rebels were hiding; he wanted to know where his *brothers* were.

He was shifting through the conversations swirling around him when he detected the faint hint of strawberries on the air. He scanned the crowd as he drew the scent deeper into him.

He'd smelled strawberries thousands of times before, but this was different. It was fresh and welcoming, and he knew it was *her*.

Turning, he searched the crowd. He stood almost a head taller than most of those surrounding him, so he could see over them with relative ease.

And then he spotted her exiting a witches' store and shrugging a pouch onto her shoulder. The sun emphasized the different shades of red in her auburn hair and illuminated her delicate features.

She stepped back from a passing lycan before turning and walking in the opposite direction of him.

"I'll be back," he said to Brokk.

Before his brother could reply, Cole started after her.

CHAPTER SEVENTEEN

THE SCENT of baking bread tickled Lexi's nose, and her stomach rumbled in response. She tried to recall the last time she ate, but she couldn't quite remember.

She should eat something, but she had to get back to the manor so she could give the fae the potion and get him out of her life. However, it was a long walk home, and she'd prefer to have something to munch on while she made the trek.

Unable to resist, Lexi stopped at a cart selling all kinds of baked goods. Her stomach rumbled louder, and it took all she had not to lick her lips as she studied the delicious treats laid out on trays before her.

"Can I get you something?" the woman standing behind the cart asked.

Lexi pointed at one of the cinnamon buns. "Yes, I'll take one of those."

The woman beamed at her as she used a piece of paper to pick up the bun. She slid the pastry into a bag while Lexi handed over more of her money. Lexi tried not to drool as she held the bag and waited for change.

In the distance, the faint strains of a guitar floated through the air. The notes were followed by a sweet, lilting voice that barely carried over the din of the crowd.

"I'll take one too," a deep voice said from beside her.

Everything around Lexi went as still as a broken clock. Like the clock pendulum that stopped ticking, she swore her heart ceased beating before giving a mighty thump that rattled her rib cage.

She knew that voice; even if she lived another ten thousand years, she would never forget that voice. She would always recall the deep timbre of his words as he stood behind her in the room full of luna flowers. Always remember the way his warm breath felt against her ear and how it stirred her hair.

She hadn't believed she'd ever see him again, let alone see him again so soon. He was one of the elite immortals, he moved in entirely different circles than her, and she wasn't returning to the Gloaming anytime soon.

However, she didn't have to look up to know Cole stood beside her.

She couldn't stop her head from tilting further and further back until she found his vibrant blue eyes on her even as the woman held a bag out to him. Her breath gave a small hitch. She wanted to touch the tip of one of his ears; would he like it?

The black, mortal shirt he wore clung to his broad chest, and the short sleeves emphasized the thick muscles of his biceps. His jeans were loose-fitting enough to be comfortable but tight enough to make her mouth water.

The corners of his eyes crinkled, and his thick lips curved into the sexiest smile she'd ever seen. He was a good foot taller than her five-seven height and easily weighed a hundred pounds more than her one hundred thirty.

He should intimidate her, and she imagined many were terrified of him, but she didn't feel afraid. Instead, before she could stop herself, she grinned at him like an idiot.

"It's you," she said.

Cole smiled in return. "It's you."

A shout from somewhere to her right drew her attention and dampened her happiness as she recalled where they were. Cole took the bag from the woman who was still holding it out to him and slipped her some money. Clasping her elbow, he led her away from the booth.

"What are you doing here?" Lexi asked and then tried not to blush at the abruptness of her question. "I'm sorry; I didn't mean to sound rude."

A teasing glimmer shone in his eyes. "You didn't expect to find me here?"

"Not at all."

"Why not? There are things here I like to purchase too."

That made sense, but marketplaces such as this always existed in the mortal realm; she'd gone to them often. This one came to life after the war, and unlike the markets of the past, humans also shopped it. There was no reason to keep the immortal markets hidden anymore.

During her many trips to the private *and* open markets, she'd never seen one *royal* fae. She'd heard countless rumors about them while shopping the immortal wares, but they could get everything they needed in the Shadow Realms.

"Plus," he said, "the Lord of the Shadow Realms likes us to keep an ear out for any threats that might arise and to search for the rebels."

His words reminded her of the dark fae locked in her tunnels, and her appetite vanished. She clenched her bag as some of her excitement over seeing him vanished.

She was harboring a rebel, and if he knew about it, not only would he turn in the fae, but he'd hand her over too. It thrilled her to see him, and he seemed happy to see her also, but his loyalty was to the Lord.

She wanted nothing to do with any of the political turmoil the world remained in; however, she'd put herself right in the middle of it when she decided to hide a war criminal.

And she'd pitted herself against this man and the monster who'd ruthlessly unleashed his dragons on countless innocents. She didn't want anything to happen to the fae she hid, but she wanted even less for Cole to become her enemy.

She liked him, and he made her feel alive in a way she hadn't since her father died. It was a bad idea to feel anything other than apprehension for a dark fae, but she couldn't stop the butterflies in her stomach or the increase of her pulse when she was around him.

"Oh," she muttered.

She realized she sounded a little dumb, but she had no idea what to say. *Oh good, you're all looking to kill more immortals,* didn't feel like the appropriate, sarcastic response.

"And what are you doing here?" he asked.

Lexi held up her bag of food. She couldn't bring herself to lie to him, and she doubted she could pull off a convincing lie, so she hoped he would take this as explanation enough.

"They're some of my favorites," he said.

"Mine too."

A commotion from somewhere to her left drew Lexi's attention to the crowd. Startled cries filled the air as humans and immortals pushed back toward them. When Cole stepped before her, his large body blocked the retreating group from shoving her into the food stand.

"What the fuck?" he muttered.

Lexi was thinking the same thing as a higher-pitched scream rent the air and a child started to sob for her mother. Lexi stepped forward; she wasn't a fighter, but she'd be damned if she let someone hurt a child.

Then the crying child, enveloped securely in the arms of her lycan mother, rushed past them. Cole clasped Lexi's arm as he held her firmly behind him. Despite the commotion, she barely stopped herself from gaping at the hand engulfing almost her entire forearm.

Then the crowd parted to reveal a group of lycan shoving through them. With a sinking heart, Lexi spotted Malakai at the front of the pack.

She glanced at the sun beating down on the earth *and* Malakai. Unlike her, he was a full-blooded vampire who never should have been out in the daylight, but as she thought it, the sun caught and reflected off the red amulet hanging from his neck.

She didn't know where it had come from, but she sensed its power and suspected it somehow allowed him to walk about in the day. She didn't understand how anything could be powerful enough to accomplish that. It had to be the amulet as she'd never seen him in the daytime before the war, yet he wasn't catching on fire now.

With his shoulders back, pride and contempt emanated from Malakai as he surveyed the crowd. Then his brown eyes landed on Cole before sliding to her. Surprise widened them for the briefest of seconds, but they hardened when he spotted Cole's hand wrapped protectively around her arm.

A smug smile curved his lips as he stopped in front of them. He was about five inches shorter than Cole, and he didn't emanate power like the fae prince, but his eyes shimmered with malice when they shifted from Cole's grip on her arm to her face.

"Elexiandra," he greeted in a voice that sent chills down her spine.

"Malakai," she replied.

CHAPTER EIGHTEEN

"WHAT IS THE MEANING OF THIS?" Cole demanded.

As he surveyed the lycan gathered around Malakai, he recognized all of them, but they weren't part of his uncle's pack, and he didn't trust any of them. They all fought on the same side during the war, but for completely different reasons.

"We're hunting a traitor," Malakai replied.

Cole resisted smashing the arrogant grin off Malakai's face as he glanced at Lexi again. The intensity of his reaction startled him.

Despite his lycan blood, Cole was colder and more calculating like the dark fae than impulsive and explosive like the lycan. However, the look in Malakai's eyes as he stared at Lexi had him imagining tearing the vamp's heart out and shoving it down his throat.

There was more than anger in the vamp's stare; there was also a lust that made Cole feel more murderous than he had during the entire war. He'd never liked Malakai, but the wolf part of him marked the vamp for death.

"Perhaps *you've* seen the traitor," Malakai said to Cole.

"Who is it?" Cole asked, and the question came out as more of a growl.

"Your brother. Orin. Some of the boys" —he waved a hand at the lycan surrounding him— "almost had him, but he managed to get away."

"We fucked him up real bad," one of the lycans bragged.

Cole managed to keep his face impassive as a knife of dread lodged in his heart and twisted deep. They were hunting *Orin,* and his brother was injured. Was it so bad he wouldn't be able to hide?

"I haven't seen Orin in a couple of years," Cole replied with an indifference he didn't feel.

He couldn't lose another brother.

"Hmm." Malakai rubbed his chin while he studied Cole. "That's too bad. You could always help us look for him."

"You can't handle it yourself, Malakai?"

"Of course I can, but you know him better than any of us. You know how he thinks. Maybe it's you who can't handle watching your traitor of a brother die."

A seething tempest boiled inside Cole until he felt like a volcano about to blow, but he smiled at Malakai. "My brother's been dead to me for years."

It wasn't true. He would always love Orin. Out of all his brothers, the two of them butted heads the most, but Orin would forever be his brother. Orin was the second of his father's children, and only thirty-five years separated them.

They hadn't grown up together, but Cole had watched him grow from a babe to a child to a stubborn adult with a powerful will. And once Orin was old enough, they trained together, laughed and drank together, and developed a bond that came with blood and shared experiences.

And now Orin would be hunted as long as the Lord of the Shadow Realms remained on the throne.

～

LEXI WAS EXTREMELY glad Malakai and Cole were focused on each other as the blood drained from her face and her stomach plummeted into her toes.

Malakai, her *freaking neighbor*, was looking for a traitor. A traitor who was attacked by lycan and *Cole's brother*. A dark fae who was sitting in *her* tunnels.

She had to get away from these two and Orin away from her home. What was she *thinking* by helping him?

It took everything she had not to slump against the stand behind her as the pouch slung over her shoulder suddenly felt as if it weighed a thousand pounds. She'd bought a *healing* potion. If any of them asked what was in the pouch or demanded to see it, she had no idea what she would say.

Sahira easily could have made what the pouch contained; why would she come to the market to purchase it? Her mind spun as she tried to come up with some plausible answer, but the only thing she could come up with was that Sahira was out of the ingredients and they had a sick animal at home.

It was flimsy at best and easy enough to disprove, but it might be enough to get her out of here and back to the manor. She'd have to tell Sahira about it then, but she'd worry about that *if* the time came.

Why had she decided this would be a good idea?

She almost clutched the pouch against her chest, but it would only draw attention, so she restrained herself from doing so.

She glanced around for an escape. There was nowhere for her to go. She couldn't exactly run away without making them a little curious.

So, she had to stand here and try not to look like a cornered rabbit surrounded by powerful men who would turn against her if they learned what she'd done.

And if she managed to get out of this, she had to go home, give Orin the potion, and get him *out* of her tunnels before she put

Sahira in jeopardy. No, she'd already done that with her reckless actions. Now, she had to fix it.

"Then, if you happen across Orin, you'll let us know," Malakai said.

"I'll bring him in myself," Cole replied.

Lexi tried not to wince at the harshness of those words. Cole was talking about his *brother*. They'd opposed each other, but how could he be so callous about his brother?

Because he's a dark fae.

No, it was more than that. He was an *immortal,* and many of them weren't known for their kindness; Malakai and his pack of lycan proved that. She didn't belong here amid these ruthless, cold-blooded men, but she'd inadvertently inserted herself in the middle of this awful mess.

"I'm sure you will," Malakai said before turning to her. "I'll see you soon, Elexiandra."

The look in his eyes made her blood run cold. He would come to her manor soon. Lexi didn't reply as Malakai walked away with the lycan following him.

Gradually, the marketplace came alive around them again. With the Lord's men out of the way, people and immortals resumed their day while she and Cole remained standing by the woman's food stand.

Then Cole turned toward her, and she saw the steely gleam in his eyes. She forced herself not to gulp as she considered what he would do if he learned she was harboring his fugitive brother, a man he would hand over for execution.

"How do you know Malakai?" Cole asked.

How did she answer that question?

He's the bane of my existence. He thinks he's going to marry me, and I'm terrified he'll find a way to succeed.

For some reason, Malakai believed she was his consort, or maybe he didn't. Maybe he saw her as something to own and not as his fated one. The more she considered it, the more she believed that was more likely. He saw her as an accessory and not his consort.

Besides, she'd heard that when any vampire found their consort in another vampire, it was a mutual realization. If she was Malakai's consort, wouldn't she feel it too? And she most certainly *did not.*

But then again, probably not. She couldn't transport like vampires, she walked freely in the sun, and she wasn't as strong as them. She was only half vampire, and that might make it impossible to feel the pull of the consort bond.

She didn't tell Cole any of these things because this man did *not* care about her problems. Instead, she simply said, "He's my neighbor."

"I see," he murmured, but his attention remained on the direction Malakai went.

"I have to go," she said and gave a subtle tug on her arm.

Seeming to recall he was still holding her arm, his thumb stroked her skin. A fiery tendril of heat worked its way out from where he touched her. It spread through her belly and into her legs until her knees almost gave out.

This was a deadly game she played with him. However, she couldn't bring herself to pull her arm away, and when he stepped closer, she didn't move.

He could learn the truth of what she'd done with his brother and destroy her for being a traitor without breaking a sweat, but she didn't care.

No one had ever made her feel this alive, and now that he was awakening her to the wonder of his touch, she craved more of it. She gulped and tipped her head back to meet his piercing blue eyes. He held her gaze while he caressed her skin in slow, tantalizing circles that made her mouth go dry and her heart race.

Her father had sheltered her for her whole life. She'd never understood his fierce need to keep her protected, but she also hadn't rebelled against it. She had hundreds, if not thousands of years, to see the world, and she was in no rush to leave her safe, much-loved home.

But now, her father was gone, and for the first time, she yearned for something more than her home, her friends, and family; she wanted *him.*

And if the way his eyes darkened as they scanned her was any indication, he wanted her too.

CHAPTER NINETEEN

SHE WAS LOSING herself to him when a powerful roar shook the earth. Screams rent the air, and people raced for cover as a blast of wind rattled the boards in the stand behind her. Dust stung her skin as it whipped up from the ground and swirled down the street.

Cole threw his arms up to protect her from the pebbles and dirt blasting against her skin, but it didn't do much to stop it. Another bellow reverberated through the day, and then an enormous shadow passed overhead as a dragon soared over the top of them.

It was so large it blocked the sun and brought an early twilight to the land. Its belly was a paler shade of red than the rest of it. Its wings spread a good hundred feet wide, and its legs were tucked up against its underside.

It extended its long neck as another roar issued from it, but thankfully, it didn't unleash a wave of fire. This creature wasn't here to destroy; it was here to intimidate and remind the world of who ruled it. It was succeeding.

Her mouth parted in awe at the magnificent, beautiful, terrifying creature. As a child, she'd dreamt of riding dragons and pretended she ruled the throne and the beasts who guarded it. As an adult, she didn't find anything fun or fanciful about them.

They were stone-cold killers who were ruled by a madman. The destruction they unleashed on earth wasn't the dragon's fault; they were only doing as commanded. However, she still *loathed* the beast who gave the Lord so much of his brutal power.

She'd never been this close to a dragon before, never felt so small and vulnerable. This thing could kill them without ever knowing they were there, but she was more mesmerized by it than fearful.

Then it was climbing higher into the sky where it met up with two of its brethren, a red dragon with a burst of yellow on its belly and a yellow one with a stripe of black on its back. The three of them rolled through the air as they snapped at each other before separating and soaring toward the smoldering city.

"They're magnificent," she whispered.

"They're something," Cole muttered.

She glanced at him as someone called his name. He turned toward the voice as the people who fled the dragons crept out of their hiding places.

A tall, blond man strode toward them as the marketplace became crowded again. She recognized the man as Cole's younger brother, Brokk.

"They're hunting for Orin," Brokk said as he stopped before them. He didn't notice her as his attention remained riveted on Cole. "Malakai is leading the party."

"I know," Cole said and stepped closer to her.

Brokk finally noticed her, and then his eyes narrowed on Cole's hand on her arm. He frowned at Cole before turning his attention to her. His eyebrows lifted before he focused on Cole again.

"We should help them," Brokk said.

Lexi suppressed a shudder at this sign of brutality from the brothers. She pitied poor Orin, but he had to find a new place to hide.

When Cole looked at her, she saw reluctance in his eyes, but he gave a brisk nod. "We should," he agreed. "It was good to see you again, Lexi."

"You also, Cole," she managed to say in a far more normal tone than she'd expected.

He held onto her for a moment longer before releasing her. She instantly missed the connection between them, but she'd never been so happy to be free. When he walked away, she turned and fled into the crowd.

~

LEXI KNELT before Orin in one of the dozens of tunnels running beneath the manor and spreading throughout the hundred acres of land they owned. Some of the tunnels went beyond their land, but most didn't.

She had no idea why her father had so many tunnels built when she was a baby and young child, but he was adamant she and Sahira learn them all. He'd done all the work of building the tunnels, installing gates, and stacking supplies himself. It took him ten years from start to finish, as he was still constructing them when she was a teen.

When she was younger, he made them run drills to escape the manor if there was ever an attack. Now, she knew the dark, concrete halls beneath the earth as well as she knew the rooms of the manor. She knew where to locate the emergency supplies down here, so they could survive beneath the ground for a few months if it came to it.

The possibility of such a thing made her skin crawl, but after seeing what the dragons did to the earth, she was glad her father had been so prepared. She'd always considered it crazy and overkill, but now the tunnels offered her a sanctuary she'd tarnished by bringing Orin here.

He did all this before the war, but the Lord was talking about letting mortals know of their existence decades before the war. Her father once told her he would do anything to protect his family, including building these tunnels.

"What is that?" Orin inquired in a raspy voice as she removed the potion from the pouch.

"It's a healing potion," Lexi answered as she uncorked the bottle. "I bought it from a witch."

"I'm not taking a witches' brew. I'll heal on my own."

"Not fast enough."

"What does that mean?"

His fathomless black eyes were bloodshot when they met hers, and she saw the pain reflected in them. She moved the potion toward him, but he grabbed her wrist and held it before them. Despite his weakness, his grip was strong.

"What does that mean?" he demanded.

"They're looking for you, and they can't find you here. I have to protect my family. You have to take this and leave here... soon."

"*Who* is looking for me?"

"Malakai and a group of lycans." She paused as she contemplated not telling him about his brothers; he had enough going on without adding that betrayal to the mix, but he needed to know what he faced once he left here. "Your brothers, Cole and Brokk, are with them. They *can't* find you here."

His eyes darkened at the mention of his brothers, and his nostrils flared. "Those bastards."

She didn't blame him for being angry at his brothers; she would be incensed, but something inside her rankled when he called Cole a bastard. Though, she supposed it was an adequate description for the man trying to kill him.

"I can't leave here," he said.

"You *can't* stay here."

A muscle twitched in his cheek as his jaw clenched. He was gorgeous with his narrow face, high cheekbones, pointed chin, and hawkish nose, but he radiated an unsettling brutality. He wasn't as handsome as Cole, but there was no denying the similarities between them, especially when it came to their ruthlessness.

"Are you going to make me leave?" he asked.

She didn't know how to respond because they both knew she wasn't strong enough to *make* him leave. "I'm helping you."

"And you're going to *keep* helping me."

She gawked at him, and then, feeling like an idiot, she closed her mouth, but she couldn't quite keep it closed. "I *saved* you."

She felt like an idiot for saying that. It was obvious he didn't care she'd saved him and was trying to help him. All he cared about was protecting his ass.

Why did you bring him here?

These tunnels were their sanctuary, and she'd risked them by exposing their existence to this ungrateful *asshole*.

She mentally smacked herself half a dozen times, but berating herself wouldn't do any good. It was too late. She'd already done this stupid, *reckless* thing, and she couldn't undo it. It was time to face the consequences.

"You *can't* stay here," she said.

"I can, and I am, unless you plan to turn me in, which means turning yourself in. You knew who I was when you hid me. That's *why* you hid me away. Do you think they'll take it easy on you if you turn me in now?"

"I had no idea who you were when I brought you in here."

"Maybe you didn't know I'm a dark fae prince, but you knew I was a rebel."

She couldn't argue that. "I have others to protect!"

"So do I, which is why I'm *not* going back out there right now."

"You can't stay here."

Her teeth grated together as she resisted hitting him. She'd never hit anyone before, but she'd love to bash in Orin's face.

"I can stay, and I am," he stated. "Get used to it. I'm not leaving here until they finish searching for me."

"You're putting innocent lives at risk."

"I don't care."

Without realizing she was going to do it, she launched a punch at him. Even injured, he was far faster than her, and he caught her hand with ease. She considered trying to hit him with her other hand, but he would catch that one too, and it would only infuriate her more.

She felt like an ill-tempered child as she glowered at him and jerked at her hand. He released her, and she scrambled back before throwing the potion at him. "Drink it or suffer; I don't care what you do."

He fumbled for the potion as it started to seep into the earth. He righted it and set it aside. She tossed the food and water she'd brought for him onto the ground.

"There's enough for a few days," she said before turning on her heel and stalking away.

"Lexi."

She didn't stop to look back at him, but she wished she'd never told him her name. At the time, she'd foolishly believed that because she saved his life, she could trust him with the information. She'd been a naïve idiot.

She wasn't prepared for a world where brothers turned on brothers and where the one she saved turned on her like a rabid dog.

"If you tell them I'm here, I'll tell them you're a scorned lover who decided to turn me in and you've been a rebel spy this entire time," he said.

Her teeth ground together until she swore they'd shatter, but she still didn't look back. If there were any way she could do it and survive, she'd gladly hand him over to Cole and Brokk.

"You keep me safe, and I'll keep you safe," he taunted.

"Screw you."

She stepped through one of the gates her father installed and closed it behind her. She didn't bother to tell him that she would keep him safe. They both knew she wouldn't turn him in, but if he had any doubts about her intentions, she wanted him to fester in them.

"I'll see you soon!" he called after her.

Now she understood why his brothers were hunting him.

CHAPTER TWENTY

LEXI CLOSED her eyes and leaned against the fireplace as she tried to calm the anger coursing through her veins. *That asshole!*

How could he do this to her when she'd put herself on the line to save him?

Because he's a damn dark fae, and I should have known better than to trust him.

It was true, but it didn't matter now. No matter how much she wanted to, she couldn't change what she'd done. She'd put herself in this position, and the best she could hope for was to somehow crawl out of this mess without getting anyone killed.

She stepped away from the fireplace and strode over to sit in one of the chairs. She sank into the inviting cushion and stared at the fireplace as she tried not to think about how long Orin would hold her hostage.

"Lexi?"

She almost squealed and jumped out of the chair when Sahira said her name. She spun in the chair to discover her aunt standing in the doorway. Sahira had been in the garden when she slipped into the tunnels; she often spent a couple of hours there a day, but she'd apparently finished early today.

Thankfully, she hadn't caught Lexi coming out of the tunnel. From now on, she'd have to use a different entrance into the tunnels.

"Yes?" she croaked.

Sahira didn't seem to notice anything off as she smiled at her. "Would you like some tea?"

Lexi glanced at the clock and was amazed to see it was already their normal teatime. Where had the day gone?

"Yes, of course," she said as she rose from the chair and walked toward her aunt.

Should she tell Sahira about Orin? Her aunt might know what to do about him, but then Lexi would have to involve her in this mess.

Right now, Sahira could claim ignorance about Lexi's actions, and it could save her life. Or at least Lexi hoped it could. If she told Sahira, she would be pissed at Orin for his threats, and things could get ugly. Sahira was a strong witch, but she wasn't strong enough to take on a dark fae.

No, she couldn't tell her aunt about what she'd done. She'd already put her in danger by allowing Orin into the tunnels; keeping her in the dark was the best way to keep Sahira safe. Lexi had dug herself into this hole, and she would get herself out without endangering her aunt.

She stepped aside as Sahira entered the room with two cups of tea. Lexi's mouth watered as a sweet scent wafted from the delicate cups. For as long as she could remember, the two of them sat down every day to enjoy a cup of tea together.

When she was little, they would sit around her small table and fill plastic cups with tea. They'd pretend to be queens while they sipped their tea and dreamed of magical worlds far from the human realm.

As part witch, Sahira had traveled to the land of witches a few times and several other Shadow Realms, but as part vampire, she rarely felt welcome in those realms. However, when she was younger, Sahira loved to regale Lexi with those stories as she poured tea and lifted a dainty pinky finger while sipping her drink.

As she grew, they stopped sitting around her little pink table and drinking out of plastic cups, but they always sat together every day. When she got older, she also learned Sahira's stories, though wondrous, were tinged with sadness and adversity.

Sahira traveled to those realms, but they never welcomed her with open arms because she was part vampire and part witch. She learned more about how her aunt never felt welcome in the witches' realm and the intolerance she faced there.

The witches' hatred for vampires hadn't lessened over the eight hundred years that had passed since a vampire killed the witch queen in a fit of jealousy. The two had been lovers, but the queen had decided to take another to her bed, and the vampire was not happy about it.

In retaliation for her death, all the witch covens joined together. Not only did they slaughter the vampire who killed their queen, but they also unleashed their wrath on the vampire realm.

They leveled that realm, making it uninhabitable for vampires and driving them out. When they fled to other realms, the witches' wrath followed them, and they were evicted from those realms by the witches and the immortals who resided there.

No one wanted to incur the witches' wrath by harboring the vampires. Besides, known for their arrogance, vampires weren't well-liked before they killed the witch queen, so not many other immortals wanted them around.

They could have fled to the far outer Shadow Realms, but many of those realms were inhospitable or inhabited by terrifying creatures, so that left them with Earth. When the vampires fled to the mortal realm, the witches, drained from the destruction of their realm, could not continue their attack on them.

The vampires were getting ready to go back after the witches, who wouldn't have been able to put up much of a fight, when the

Lord at that time put an end to it before the two immortals destroyed each other.

Neither the vampires nor witches were happy when the Lord intervened, but they both relented. They either accepted the decision or ended up being hunted by the Lord, and none of them would ever know peace.

However, the witches did succeed in forcing the arrogant vamps out of the Shadow Realms. They contented themselves with this knowledge, though their hatred for the vamps remained, and the vamps' hatred for them was just as intense.

With no place else to go, the vampires remained in the human realm. They'd traveled to Earth before to feed, but it became their home after the witches' attack.

Lexi had no idea how Sahira's father managed to sweet talk a witch into his bed, but somehow, he did it. And Sahira was the one who paid the price.

Her mother left after Sahira was born, and she didn't take her baby with her. Sahira grew up in the human realm with her father and Del, who was only four years older. Del's mother, a vampire, was killed by a warlock shortly after his birth, and Sahira's mother was still alive, but she had nothing to do with her.

Ashamed of her weakness at having not only slept with but conceived a child with a vampire, Sahira's mother left her baby behind so she could return to the witch realm. Sahira rarely mentioned her, but Lexi knew they'd met.

The loss of both their mothers and their close ages bound Sahira and Del together; they grew up as thick as thieves. Their deep loyalty and love for each other continued until the day he died.

Over time, Sahira stopped traveling to the Shadow Realms and remained on Earth. It was easier for her that way. She was as caught in the middle as Lexi, but at least Lexi wasn't torn between two species who despised each other.

Although, that had probably changed now. Before, the humans

had never known she existed. Vampires had always been a thing of legends born from real encounters with vamps, but they were still fantastical and believed to be fake.

Humans knew they were real now, and she doubted that knowledge made them happy. Yes, she was sure the humans probably hated vamps as much as the witches did.

She followed Sahira over to the two overstuffed chairs, but she stopped before taking a seat. She couldn't spend the next hour staring at the fireplace while knowing what lay beyond it.

CHAPTER TWENTY-ONE

"How about we sit outside today?" she suggested. "It's so nice out."

Sahira turned back to her and smiled. "That sounds perfect."

The teacup warmed her hands when she took her cup from Sahira, and the scent of lavender and peppermint wafted to her. Sahira switched the flavor every day, and Lexi was glad she'd chosen these two today as a sense of peace descended over her.

They left the library behind and made their way down the hall before crossing through the sitting room with its delicate antique furniture and a striking grandfather clock in the corner. The pendulum of the clock swayed as it ticked away the seconds.

With its gray stone walls, the room housed furniture mostly done in shades of blue, and sheer blue curtains framed the double doors leading to the patio. They settled into the patio chairs with their thick blue cushions.

Lexi started to rest her cup on the white table when she recalled why they'd stopped coming out here.

"Oh," she murmured as she stared across the vast, once green lawn that had been bordered by a ten-foot-high privet hedge.

Now, only charred pieces of that once perfectly manicured

hedge stood up from the ground. Half the lawn was nothing more than blackened earth.

Beyond the charcoaled remains, humans trudged down what remained of the road. They skirted broken chunks of asphalt as they walked with their shoulders hunched forward and their heads bent against the sun. Dirt streaked their faces and clothes, and many of them looked like they'd crawled out of a coal mine.

These people looked like this because they didn't have much clothing left and because the dragons destroyed most of their homes. Lexi often felt like she'd lost everything, but she realized how lucky she was.

Despite her losses, she still had much more than so many. She did her best to give what they could, but they didn't have much to spare. Normally, she didn't come to this side of the house, but she couldn't hide from her reality anymore.

It was outside her home, and now, it was also beneath it.

"I saw Malakai," she said as she sipped her tea.

"Oh," Sahira said.

Lexi detected the dislike in her voice; Sahira had never been good at hiding it when it came to Malakai.

"He was out in the daytime," she said.

"That's not unusual if it's overcast."

"It was today."

Sahira turned toward the clear blue sky and the sun streaming down on them. Like her, Sahira could tolerate the sun because she was only half vampire.

"Ooooh," Sahira said more slowly.

"He was wearing an amulet."

Sahira set her cup down with a clatter and spun toward her. She looked like Lexi had told her he was dressed as a scarecrow and reciting the Wizard of Oz.

"Really?" Sahira asked.

"Yes. It was…"

"Red," they said at the same time.

"You know what it is?" Lexi asked.

"It's a sun medallion. At one time, there were a lot of them in the vampire realm. They used to mine for them beneath the mountains there. When the witches destroyed their realm and drove the vampires out, most of the medallions were destroyed or lost. The few remaining ones are all held by the Lord of the Shadow Realms."

"So the Lord gave it to him?"

"Yes."

"Which means no one would dare try to take it from him."

"Not unless they want to have the wrath of the Lord unleashed on them."

Lexi shuddered at the idea of that wrath coming down on her. "Why would the Lord give Malakai an amulet?"

"Malakai must have done something to earn it."

"I don't want to know what that was."

"Neither do I."

Feeling unsettled by this development, Lexi lifted her cup and sipped her tea as she watched the people on the road.

CHAPTER TWENTY-TWO

COLE CAUGHT the scent of Orin not far from where he left Lexi. He didn't say a word to the others, but the other lycan tracked it to a forest where even Cole lost Orin's trail. From there, they prowled through the woods until they came across a few houses.

They interviewed the occupants of those homes, but no one had seen Orin. From there, they traveled back into the woods until they came to the edge of a lake. The sun reflected off the water's pristine surface and illuminated the large, gray stone manor across the way.

Malakai stared at the manor while the lycans prowled the water's edge, and Brokk studied the ground like he was bored with the whole thing. However, the set of Brokk's jaw and the way his fingers twiddled behind his back indicated Brokk was paying attention to everything.

Cole studied the amulet at Malakai's throat. The vampire hadn't possessed the powerful sun medallion while they were fighting together, but there was only one place he could have gotten it.

The vampire's possession of the medallion made Cole distrust him more. He was acutely aware Malakai would tell the Lord every detail of their time together today.

He glanced at Brokk, but his brother was wandering idly by as he examined the shoreline as if searching for something. Whatever Malakai did to earn that amulet, it had made the Lord extremely happy.

"I'll be back," Malakai said.

"Where are you going?" the largest of the lycans demanded.

"I have something to do."

Malakai walked away, and Cole watched as he strolled around the lake. As his step's pace increased, Cole realized Malakai was nowhere near as nonchalant as he was trying to act. Something about the manor had Malakai excited.

"I've had enough of that asshole," the smallest lycan grumbled.

"Then let's get out of here. We're not going to find the dark fae," another lycan said.

"He'll report us to the Lord."

"Report what? That we lost the trail. There's not much to report there."

The largest lycan looked at Cole and Brokk, who stared back at them. "I don't care what you do," Cole said.

The lycans didn't say anything before they turned and loped away into the woods.

"Now what?" Brokk asked.

Malakai was almost jogging as he closed in on the manor. "What has him so excited?" he muttered.

"No idea," Brokk said. "We should try to find Orin."

"We will, but let's see what has that asshole in such a rush first."

Brokk frowned as he gazed after Malakai. "Yes, let's."

They started around the lake together.

"What do we do if we find Orin?" Brokk asked as Malakai climbed the steps to the front doors of the manor.

"We'll get his ass somewhere safe if we can."

"Can you smell him?" Brokk asked.

"No, I lost his scent soon after they did, but I might be able to pick it up again if we keep searching."

They were almost around the lake, and the manor doors were still closed when the scent of strawberries hit him. He'd been so focused on trying to find Orin's scent that he'd shut out all others; now, *Lexi's* aroma hit him like a hammer between the eyes.

He suddenly understood why Malakai abruptly left and his obvious rush.

"Shit," he hissed.

"What?" Brokk inquired.

He didn't respond as he moved faster than Malakai had toward the home. His heart beat faster with every step as he recalled Malakai's reaction to Lexi in the Gloaming and the marketplace, and hers to him. It was obvious what Malakai wanted from her and just as obvious the feeling was *not* mutual.

"What are you doing?" Brokk demanded.

"Stopping that prick of a vampire."

～

"How can we make their lives better?" Lexi asked Sahira as she sipped her tea and watched the stragglers.

"The humans?"

"Yes."

"How can we change what has already happened?"

"We can't, but there has to be something we can do for them."

"We're doing the best we can by giving them food. We'd still offer some of them employment, but most don't trust us enough to work for us anymore."

That was true. Only a couple of the people who once worked here were willing to come back, and none of them lived here anymore. Maybe it was because of the war, or maybe it was because they realized they were messed with for years while living in the manor.

For years, Sahira had cast a glamour over the manor and those working in it that made it appear the immortals were aging the same as humans. When the dragons descended on the land, Sahira saw no reason to keep the glamour in place.

Those who saw the truth and realized they'd been tricked were rightfully pissed. Despite the protection the manor offered them, they left. Lexi didn't blame them, but she missed them.

Before Lexi could say anything more, someone pounded on the front door. The blows echoed throughout the house and rebounded down the hallway. The sudden intrusion of the powerful blows caused Lexi to jump. She cursed as tea splashed over the rim of her cup.

"Who could that be?" Sahira asked as she set her cup down.

Lexi's pulse pounded in her temples as she recalled the group at the marketplace. The group who had gone off in search of Orin. Sahira had cast protective spells over the tunnels years ago; they shouldn't be able to detect him down there, but had she missed something else that could have led them here?

Lycans had a really strong sense of smell. Could they have tracked him all the way here? Would they smell him on *her?*

She'd rushed to clean up his trail; she could have missed something. Or maybe someone had seen her with him. She hadn't noticed anyone around, but that didn't mean they weren't there.

Oh shit.

She tried to control the shaking in her hands as she rose from the chair, but she felt like someone was continuously hitting her with a taser as her heart raced.

Get it together! She gritted her teeth together as she willed herself not to blow it completely. Besides, she didn't know who was at the door, but she had a sinking suspicion she did.

Throwing her shoulders back, she strode to the front door with a confidence she didn't feel. Her mouth felt like she'd been chewing on sand as she took one step and then another toward the door... toward her *doom*.

Sahira's footsteps sounded behind her as another loud knock rebounded throughout the manor. Lexi stepped into the hall and almost winced at the harsh sound. It took all she had not to turn and run in the opposite direction.

Instead, she wiped her sweaty palms on her jeans and called, "Coming!"

Walking toward the door, she felt as if she were walking toward the death chamber, but she didn't try to fight her fate. She'd done this to herself. If the consequences of her actions were waiting to drag her away, then so be it.

She told herself this, but inwardly she was screaming that she wasn't ready to die. She'd prefer *not* to be dragon chow.

"Do you want me to get it?" Sahira asked from behind her.

"No," Lexi said.

She stopped in front of the door, took a deep breath, and pulled it open before she chickened out and ran. She plastered a fake smile on, but it faltered when she spotted Malakai on the other side.

CHAPTER TWENTY-THREE

MALAKAI STOOD with his hand resting on the doorframe as he leaned toward her. Her teeth ground together as her heart thumped out a few extra beats.

"Malakai!" she greeted a little too cheerfully.

She was never outwardly rude to him, but she wasn't exactly friendly either. She preferred not to encourage his pursuit of her or make him suspicious.

Gathering herself, she compelled herself to relax as she continued. "What brings you by today?"

"Elexiandra," he drawled in a tone that made her skin crawl. "It's a pleasure to be blessed with your presence twice in one day."

Somehow, Lexi managed to keep her smile in place, but she wanted to slam the door in his arrogant face. She didn't reply as Sahira came to stand beside her.

"Hello, Sahira," Malakai greeted.

"Malakai," Sahira replied in a clipped tone.

Malakai didn't notice the tension in Sahira's voice as his eyes remained riveted on Lexi. When his gaze ran hungrily over her, Lexi managed to stop herself from crossing her arms over her chest.

Making her uncomfortable was exactly what he meant to do. Instead of cowering, she lifted her chin and met his brown eyes when they finally returned to hers.

"What can I do for you, Malakai?" she demanded.

His smile caused her hands to fist. Malakai believed she would be his, and since her father's death, she'd believed it too, but *no* more. She would lose everything before she ever allowed him to claim her as his wife.

Malakai's smile widened as his hand fell away from the door. If she hadn't known better, she might suspect he'd read her mind and found it amusing. However, vampires didn't possess that ability.

"Have you seen a dark fae around here?" he inquired.

"We haven't seen anyone around here," Sahira said.

"This one is injured."

"Which would make him *more* noticeable."

Malakai's eyes narrowed on Sahira, and Lexi almost laughed, but her amusement lodged in her throat when Cole and his brother strode into view.

Can this get any worse?

But even as the thought ran through her mind, excitement hummed across her veins, and a big smile spread across her lips before she could stop it. Seeing her reaction, Malakai stiffened and looked over his shoulder as Cole and Brokk climbed the steps.

They were here, hunting their brother, and she was harboring the fugitive, but she couldn't find it in her to be frightened when Cole's Persian blue eyes landed on her. A small smile curved the corner of Cole's mouth before Malakai stepped in front of him and slammed his palm into the doorframe.

Unprepared for the motion, Lexi couldn't stop herself from jumping at the sound. Exasperated by his intimidation tactics, she scowled at Malakai as he leaned closer. The malicious gleam in his eyes caused her stomach to roll, but she refused to back down from his intimidation tactics.

"Back off," Cole said, and clasping Malakai's shoulder, he pulled him back a step.

For a second, Lexi believed Malakai was going to shove him as they glared at each other. They were two extremely powerful beings, but Malakai had to know he would lose in a fight against Cole.

He didn't seem aware of this as his hand fisted.

~

COLE BRACED himself for Malakai's attack; he would welcome the chance to beat this asshole into a bloody pulp. Malakai believed that because he worked for the Lord, he could do whatever he wanted. He was in for a rude awakening.

"I said," Cole bit out, "back *off.*"

Brokk shifted behind him, but Cole didn't look at his brother. Brokk wouldn't interfere unless he believed Cole might lose. There was no chance of that happening.

Malakai's eyes turned red. "Are you interfering in an investigation that the Lord of the Shadow Realms ordered me to undertake to find *your* treasonous brother?"

Stepping closer, Cole used his superior size to force Malakai back. "I am interfering in nothing. I'm telling you that harassing the daughter of a man who died for our cause will *not* be tolerated."

"I will inform the Lord of your insubordination."

"Go ahead. You are a *lieutenant* in his army, and I am a *general*. You served under *me* in the war, and we know which of us means more to him. We have helped to track Orin, but his trail has grown cold. It's time to move on."

"I'm sure the lycans hunting him with me will disagree with you," Malakai said.

"Perhaps, but you'll have to hunt them down to ask them. They left."

Malakai looked as if Cole had punched him in his too hand-some face. "No, they didn't."

"They're gone," Brokk said. "If I were a betting man, I'd say they're probably already having a drink somewhere."

"They didn't care if you reported them either," Cole said.

Red crept up Malakai's neck as he searched for the lycans and found nothing. Cole didn't know if he was more embarrassed or incensed by this revelation, but he found Malakai's discomfort amusing.

Cole waited for him to launch a punch, but instead, the vamp turned toward Lexi and gave a small bow. "I will see you soon."

The shoulder beneath Cole's hand vanished as Malakai tele-ported away. Cole's hand fell to his side, and he turned to find a pale Lexi staring at the spot where Malakai had stood.

Then, her eyes met his and she smiled.

CHAPTER TWENTY-FOUR

LEXI SHOULD POLITELY THANK him and make some excuse to retreat. She should be on pins and needles and terrified he'd somehow catch a whiff of his brother, but instead, her heart raced with excitement, and she felt almost giddy with happiness.

"It's good to see you again today," he said. "I wish it was under better circumstances."

"Again today?" Sahira asked, and Lexi managed to stop herself from wincing.

"Yes." She turned to her aunt. "I ran into Prince Colburn at the marketplace earlier."

Sahira lifted an elegant brow as she looked between them. "I see." Then her gaze settled on Cole. "And you're helping Malakai hunt down your brother?"

She didn't bother to hide her disapproval over this. No matter what he did, Sahira would have let them draw and quarter her before she ever turned on her brother.

"He is a traitor," Brokk stated.

Somehow Lexi managed to keep herself from wincing at the callous words. Traitor or not, asshole or not, Orin was still their brother. But they seemed not to see it that way.

She didn't know what had caused such indifference from them, or maybe she did; she had met Orin after all. She couldn't imagine what it had been like to live with him for centuries. She wanted to kill him, and she'd only known him for a day.

Despite the fact they'd probably hand her over too if they knew the truth, her smile never wavered. Maybe she was better at this deception stuff than she realized. It was not a discovery she liked about herself.

"Would you like to come in for something to eat or drink?" she asked, and Sahira sniffed disdainfully.

The idea of having them in the manor, above their brother, frightened Lexi, but she wasn't ready to say goodbye. Besides, etiquette required she didn't send two *princes* away without at least offering them something first.

Cole's eyes flicked to her aunt before returning to her. "Thank you, but we should continue our search."

She struggled to hide her disappointment. "Oh, yes, of course."

"I'm sure I'll see you again soon," Cole said and gave her a pointed look that caused her toes to curl and a blush to creep up her neck.

He bowed his head to them. "Good day, ladies."

He turned away, and Brokk duplicated the gesture while murmuring the same words.

Lexi watched them walk away before shutting the door and leaning against it. She closed her eyes as she tried to understand what happened. Malakai was pissed, and he would be back, but she couldn't bring herself to care as she replayed Cole's words in her mind.

"I'm sure I'll see you again soon."

She was a fool for wanting him to return while his brother remained in her tunnels. However, she hoped she saw him again sooner rather than later. She just hoped it wasn't anywhere near here.

"You should stay away from that man," Sahira cautioned.

"Anyone who would turn against their brother is someone who would turn on you."

She opened her eyes to find Sahira studying her with a knowing look. She almost told Sahira she'd turn Orin in too, but there was no way Lexi could explain how *she* knew him.

"I doubt I'll be seeing him again," Lexi said.

"Hmm," Sahira huffed as she folded her arms across her chest. She looked a lot more skeptical about this than Lexi felt. "With the way he was looking at you, I think he'll be back, and you should stay away."

"Sahira—"

"He's no good, Lexi. You're also completely different. He's a seasoned warrior, a prince, and a *dark fae*. You know what they're like with men and women."

She did. She'd heard the stories about the twisted sex fiends the fae could leave in their wake. Heard how they went through sexual partners like most others went through clothes, but she couldn't bring herself to look at Cole like that.

She was probably a fool for thinking he was different. She was sure plenty of other women probably convinced themselves of the same thing, but she couldn't believe he was nothing but a callous immortal seeking only one thing from her... and every other woman he met.

"He's also part lycan," Lexi said. "They're known to be notoriously free with their sexuality until they find their mate, and then they never waver from their partner."

"Lexi—"

"I don't know why we're talking about this. Like you said, we're completely different. He isn't going to return here."

The sadness those words evoked surprised her. She shouldn't want him to return while Orin was here, or even after Orin left, but... but... she *did*.

"I need a shower," she muttered.

"Would you like to finish our tea?" Sahira asked.

She was too annoyed for tea right now. Cole might not return, but Malakai would, and she suspected he would make her pay for the embarrassment he experienced today.

"No," she murmured. "We'll catch up tomorrow."

"Okay."

Lexi started to walk away, but she stopped and turned back to her aunt. "What do you think Malakai is going to do?"

"Nothing, if he knows what's good for him."

"That amulet proves he's close to the Lord. With Father dead, he could make me marry Malakai."

Sahira's shoulders went back, and her nostrils flared. "Over my dead body."

"*That's* what I'm afraid of, and we've had more than enough dead bodies."

Some of the fight went out of Sahira. "Your father also fought for the Lord; he wouldn't throw that away just to please Malakai."

"My father is dead and can't do anything for the Lord anymore; Malakai is alive, especially vicious, and obviously close to him. He might not ask the Lord to marry me. He may ask him to give me to him as his concubine so that way, when Malakai finishes with me, he can toss me aside again."

Sahira opened her mouth to respond, but then she closed it. They stared at each other as her words hung in the air between them. The sad truth was, being used and discarded by him was the better of the two options.

Feeling as if the world rested on her shoulders, Lexi started up the curving stairs toward the second floor.

"Lexi." She stopped and turned back to Sahira. "We won't let it happen."

Lexi didn't say what they were both thinking; there was nothing they could do to stop it if the Lord decided to do it.

CHAPTER TWENTY-FIVE

"YOUR BROTHERS WERE HERE EARLIER," Lexi said to Orin as she set a basket of bread on the ground.

Judging by the color in his face and the fact he didn't wince every time he moved, he'd taken some of the potion. Apparently, his concern over being unable to defend himself outweighed his dislike of having to rely on the witches for anything.

"Cole and Brokk?" he asked.

"Do you have any other brothers?" she retorted.

"Yes, but Varo is well hidden. The others are all dead."

She winced at the reminder his family sustained many losses too, but then, many families lost so much. "I forgot they were dead."

"Your father is dead too, isn't he?" Orin asked.

Lexi stared warily at him as she stepped back. "How do you know who my father is?"

"It took me some time to remember, but I've seen your manor before. I rode by it once, before the war. It belonged to Delano Harper, and I heard that Del did not survive the war."

Lexi wiped her suddenly sweaty palms on her jeans. When she

gave him her nickname earlier, she hadn't believed he would figure out who she was, but she'd been foolish to think that.

He would have discovered that once he left here. It's not like he couldn't find her manor again, but she still didn't like him knowing who she was.

"No, he didn't," she said.

"You're Elexiandra Harper."

"Yes."

"I'm sorry for your loss."

Lexi blinked at him. After his words yesterday, she hadn't expected any sympathy from this callous man.

"Thank you." Then after a few seconds passed, she said, "I'm sorry for your losses too."

His black eyes studied her. "Thank you. What did you tell Cole and Brokk?"

"Well, since neither of us is locked up right now, I'd guess I told them that I hadn't seen you."

A strand of black hair fell into one of his eyes as he examined her. The movement revealed the ciphers on his neck, but her father's clothes hid whatever other marks he bore.

"You don't strike me as a liar, Elexiandra."

"Normally, I'm not, Orin."

He lifted a loaf of bread and broke off a piece. "You are now. And you must be a pretty good liar if my brothers believed you."

When he took a bite of the bread, Lexi contemplated kicking it down his throat. "You don't know what I'm capable of doing."

Orin lowered the bread and leaned toward her. "Neither do you."

Lexi recoiled. "What's *that* mean?"

"Only that I don't think you know what you're capable of doing. I bet you never considered harboring a war criminal or lying to the side your *father* fought on. War changes us and makes us do things we never thought we would. It brings out the worst and best in us."

"The war is over."

"Now you're lying to yourself."

She frowned at him while he ate more of the bread. After a minute, he licked his fingers and looked up at her again.

"The rebels lost the war, but the battle still wages," he said. "And eventually, you're going to have to decide what you will and won't stand for."

"I can tell you that I won't stand for an arrogant fae trying to tell me who or what I am."

His arrogant grin set her teeth on edge. "Obviously, you will, because I'm still here."

"I didn't have much choice," she reminded him through gritted teeth.

"You might be lying to yourself again."

Having had enough of his crap, Lexi opened the bag hanging from her arm and removed a jug of water. She placed it beside him. Then she took out a couple of flashlights and set them down too.

"I won't be back for a few days," she said.

"And why is that?"

"Because I can't keep taking the risk of being discovered emerging from one of the tunnels. You have enough food and water to last you for a bit, if you don't waste it."

"The dark fae must feed in other ways," he reminded her as his gaze perused her.

"Then you'll have to leave here soon because I'm *not* helping you with that."

She didn't wait to hear any more of what he had to say before she turned and walked away. She was glad to be away from him and glad she didn't have to return for a few days, but as she made her way into the darkness, with only a small flashlight to guide her, she couldn't help pondering his words.

He was right; the rebels had lost the war, but the battle still raged, and she had no idea which side she stood on.

No, that wasn't true. Her father was loyal to the Lord because he believed that was right, but there was no way he could have foreseen the devastation the Lord would unleash on the mortal realm.

He never would have fought on the Lord's side if he'd suspected the amount of misery and death the mortals would endure. And she couldn't be loyal to a man who killed without remorse and slaughtered *billions* to get his way.

She couldn't see herself as a rebel either. She wasn't a fighter, but she couldn't stand by and do nothing while others suffered. She had no idea what to do or think anymore, other than wanting him *off* her land.

Lexi tried to figure it all out as she made her way through the tunnels, but by the time she reached the end, she felt as confused as when she started.

She cautiously poked her head out of the opening. Sure she was alone, she slipped out of the tunnel and into the barn. The sounds of the horses munching on their hay and shifting in their stalls greeted her. Inhaling deeply, she allowed the much-loved scent to calm her, but she doubted her calm would last.

~

SITTING AT THE TABLE, Cole studied the club as two women danced around his brother. Brokk ran his hand over a dancer's ass before pulling her onto his lap. The woman squealed as she draped her arms around Brokk's shoulders.

When another woman approached him, Cole shook his head at her and tensed. Normally, he enjoyed coming here, but tonight, he wanted out of this place.

Unfortunately, Brokk wasn't interested in leaving.

The woman took a couple more steps toward him, but when Cole's eyes narrowed on her, she turned to someone else. It had been a few days since he fed, and the dark fae stirred inside him as the scent of sex filled the air, but the idea of touching one of these women repulsed him.

From the corners of the room and the hallways deeper within the building came sounds of ecstasy. This club specialized in making sure men and women got exactly what they desired when they came here.

The workers were trained in the art of sex, and many of them were shadow kissed. Corrupted by the touch of the dark fae, those shadow kissed worked here to satisfy their hunger for more sex. But they would never appease that need.

Over the centuries, he'd left plenty of shadow kissed souls behind him. Some of them probably worked here, but he had no interest in seeing any of them. He stopped having any use for them years ago.

Sitting in the other booths, deep within the shadows of the club, was an assortment of other immortals. The single candle inside the red glass jars on the tables did little to dispel the shadows and helped keep most of the patrons hidden.

And all of those patrons were enjoying the entertainment the men and women working Becca's club provided. Those immortals had come here for entertainment and sex, while most of the dark fae were here to feed.

They were all happy to be here, but his skin crawled when a dark fae woman walked past him and trailed her fingers across his neck. He ducked away from her touch and growled at her. The woman scampered away.

"Now, now, play nice," a woman purred from behind him.

The chair beside him pulled back, and Cole met Becca's gaze as she settled onto it. As she crossed her legs, the slit in her black dress caused it to fall open to her waist. It was obvious she wore no underwear, and just as obvious she wanted him to know it.

The striking beauty of her face was on par with the perfection of her body. The crisscrossing straps making up the top half of her dress only covered the nipples of the lush breasts they pushed up.

"What's the matter, lover?" she inquired.

"We're not lovers," he reminded her. He shifted his attention to Brokk as the woman on his lap laughed. "It's time to go."

The woman whimpered her protest and pressed closer to Brokk. Becca leaned toward Cole as Brokk lifted his drink.

"Back off," Cole warned her, but she didn't move away.

"What's the rush?" Brokk asked.

"We came in search of Orin, and he isn't here," Cole said.

His words didn't matter as his brother was distracted by another woman who came up behind him. She'd tipped his head back and had her breasts in his face as she leaned over to kiss him.

Becca tapped her fingers on the table and smiled smugly. "But he was."

Cole stiffened at her words, and Becca leaned closer to run her fingers over the back of his hand. An involuntary snarl issued from him as he pulled his hand away. He didn't have time to think about where that snarl came from, but it didn't faze Becca.

She sat back and ran her fingers across the top of her breasts before tweaking her nipple until it hardened beneath her dress. Her ciphers encircled the backs of her hands and wrists; he knew from experience they were the only ones she possessed or at least the only ones she revealed.

"When was Orin here?" Cole demanded.

Becca lifted a finger and waved it at him as her almond-shaped, black eyes twinkled in amusement. Her black hair, cut into a sleek bob at her chin, shone in the candlelight.

"Not so fast," she admonished. "You do me, and I'll do you."

CHAPTER TWENTY-SIX

SHE REPULSED HIM, but Cole leaned closer and crooked his index finger. When he beckoned to her with it, she leaned so close he could feel her breath against his lips.

"I had enough of doing you months ago," he told her.

She didn't react for a second, and then she released a bark of laughter and sat back. "Oh my, someone is feisty tonight."

Cole didn't reply as he glanced over at Brokk, who had his tongue shoved down the throat of the fae who stood behind him. The other straddled his lap and ran her fingers down his chest as she undid the buttons on his shirt.

"Brokk!" Cole snapped.

When his younger brother didn't respond, Cole stretched his leg across the way and kicked his chair back. They broke apart when the chair skidded back a couple of feet.

"What the fuck?" Brokk protested.

Cole glowered at him, and Brokk glared back as the women pouted, and Becca laughed.

"In case you missed it, Becca said Orin was here," Cole said.

Brokk blinked at him before shifting his attention to Becca. He slapped the ass of the woman straddling him before pushing her away. "Later."

Both the women moaned a complaint, but they moved away as Brokk focused his attention on Becca. "When was he here?" he demanded.

"Not so fast there, little brother," Becca said as she waved a finger at him before giving Cole a pointed look. "I don't give favors without receiving them."

Brokk glanced at Cole. His brother was aware of Cole's antipathy toward Becca and of Becca's determination to claw her way into the role of a dark fae princess.

During their brief time together, Cole learned she was after far more than a fling, and Cole was *not* looking for a wife. That was something she didn't want to hear, and she had not taken it well.

To Becca, he was the key to her wearing a crown; because, with him, she could become a queen if something happened to his father. It didn't matter that Tove wasn't going anywhere anytime soon; Becca craved the power of the royalty.

She would not get it.

For some reason, she believed he considered her something more than a good fuck. Unfortunately, though he'd walked away, she wasn't ready to give up. When her fingers brushed his arm again, an image of Lexi rose into his mind. He moved away from her touch.

She was the reason he didn't want to be here or anywhere near Becca. He already knew who he wanted, and it was not anyone from this place.

"Don't," he warned her, and Brokk scooted his chair closer to kick him under the table.

Cole shot him a fulminating look, and Brokk waggled his eyebrows as he nodded toward Becca. *"Take one for the team,"* Brokk mouthed.

Cole's hands flexed, and the ciphers on the back of them

shifted. Brokk didn't understand—hell, *he* didn't understand, but there was *no* way he was screwing Becca again.

Last week, despite his abhorrence of Becca, he still would have taken her to bed if it meant discovering what she knew. It had never mattered to him before whether he liked his bed partners or not, and Becca was an expert. She owned this place, she knew what men and women wanted, and she excelled at pleasing her partner.

Her expertise in bed didn't make up for her conniving personality, which she didn't hide well.

"I'm not playing your games, Becca. When was Orin here?" he demanded.

She leaned back in her chair and crossed her legs. She kicked one back and forth as she studied him.

"I don't want you to play a game, Cole. I want you to play with *me*."

"That's not going to happen." Cole pushed his chair back and rose. "We'll find Orin on our own."

He didn't wait for her reply before he turned and strode through the crowd. Immortal creatures scrambled to get out of his way as he stalked toward the stairs and descended to the packed dance floor.

He shoved his way through the dancers, many of whom were having sex on the floor, pushed open the door, and stepped into the cool night air.

Unlike in the Gloaming, where the air was thick with the scent of crops this time of year, the air on earth was heavy with the smell of burnt wood and scorched earth. The aroma of the war and the destruction and death of this planet hung heavily on the air.

The stench had become all too familiar to him recently. So much so that it no longer repulsed him.

"What was that about?" Brokk demanded as he emerged from the club to stand beside Cole. "We have to discover what she knows about Orin."

"I don't care; I'm not fucking her to get the answers."

"It's not like you haven't fucked her for less."

"Things change."

Brokk's aqua eyes studied him. "What is going on with you?"

He wasn't in the mood to discuss this with Brokk, especially since he didn't have the answer. "Let's go."

Brokk glanced back at the *Black Hole Club* before falling into step beside Cole. "*I* was having a good time."

"Then go back."

But Cole wasn't returning. There was somewhere else he'd far prefer to be.

He recalled Lexi, standing in the doorway of her manor, and something inside him twisted. He wanted to return to her, to see her again, and make sure she was safe.

When she'd invited them in earlier, he'd almost accepted, but they'd been so close to Orin, and there was a chance he might still find his trail. He hadn't, and they'd gone to Becca's in the hopes of learning more, but he'd turned his back on their one possible lead.

He loved his brother and wanted to find him, but he didn't regret his decision to leave Becca behind.

"Where are you going?" Brokk demanded as he followed Cole toward the trees.

"I have somewhere to be," he muttered.

"Care to let me in on this secret destination where you *have* to be?"

"Del's manor."

"Delano *Harper's* manor?"

"How many Dels do you know?"

Brokk stopped walking, but Cole didn't hesitate. He shouldn't have left her alone earlier, not after the confrontation with Malakai, and now a desperate urge to get back to her compelled him faster.

"Have you lost your mind?" Brokk demanded as he jogged to catch up with him.

Cole wasn't sure how to respond because he believed he might have lost it a little.

"Is this about his daughter?" Brokk asked.

Cole didn't answer.

"She's gorgeous, but Del was our friend," Brokk said.

Something rippled inside Cole; he didn't like Brokk talking about her like that. "I know."

"Then leave his daughter alone."

"I'm going to make sure she stays safe."

Brokk grasped his arm and pulled him to a stop. Cole's hands fisted as he kept his gaze focused on the woods, but his frustration wasn't for his brother; it was for *him*.

"She's young, Cole."

"I know."

"Then what are you doing?"

Cole's head twisted toward him, and whatever Brokk saw there caused him to release Cole's arm and take a step back.

"Malakai will go back for her," Cole growled.

"And what do you plan to do about that?"

"I don't know."

Cole didn't look back at Brokk as he continued toward the woods and the broken road on the other side of them. That road would lead to the market where he encountered Lexi earlier, and beyond it was her home.

What was he going to do when he got there? Stand guard outside her manor until Malakai returned?

That wasn't possible, but the idea of leaving her vulnerable to that asshole caused the wolf inside him to stir. A wolf that only ever stirred around her. When he flexed his hands, claws scraped his palm.

He jerked his hands up and stared at the claws. They weren't as long as they could be, but he couldn't recall a time when he'd lost control of himself enough that they'd extended without him doing it on purpose.

The crunch of Brokk's step caused him to close his hands to hide those claws, but the look on his brother's face said he wasn't fast enough.

"What's going on?" Brokk inquired.

Before Cole could reply, the crunch of an approaching footstep silenced him. He caught the scent of others and turned as five rebel immortals emerged from a copse of burnt-out trees. Their tattered clothing and bruised bodies gave them away before Cole recognized them as traitors.

The two in the lead were lycans, a dark fae followed them, and two vampires were at the back of the pack. The rebels stopped when they spotted Brokk and Cole standing there.

The dark fae took an abrupt step back. Unlike the others, the fae recognized who he'd run across. The vampires and lycans didn't; large grins spread across their faces, and one of the lycans cracked his knuckles.

Cole's natural inclination was to draw on his fae powers, but the wolf was itching for a fight. He'd disembowel these fuckers for fun if it meant releasing some of the hostility inside him.

"I'd keep walking, boys," Brokk warned.

"Good thing we're not a pussy like you," one of the lycans spat.

"You're going to get one chance to walk away," Brokk said.

"We should go," the dark fae muttered.

"Fuck you," one of the vamps retorted.

The dark fae slipped into the shadows and disappeared.

"At least that one's smart," Brokk said.

Cole didn't speak as he studied the lycans and vamps. Like all male lycans, they stood over six feet tall and were broad through the shoulders and chest. A hint of gold shone in their eyes as the possibility of a fight excited them. Cole felt his excitement rising in response.

And then they attacked.

CHAPTER TWENTY-SEVEN

COLE DUCKED the punch the first lycan threw at him, and when the lumbering beast staggered past him, he clasped his hands together and rammed them into his back. The impact caused something to give way with a crack and knocked the lycan to his knees.

The second lycan charged Brokk, who threw up his hands and hit the lycan with a wave of air. The blast of air lifted the lycan and flung him off his feet. He soared through the air until he hit a tree. The impact shook the tree. The lycan hung there for a few seconds before collapsing onto the ground.

Brokk was starting to go after the lycan when one of the vampires transported and threw himself onto Brokk's back. Staggered by the impact of the weight, Brokk reeled backward. Reaching over his back, Brokk grasped the vamp's hair and pulled the creature over his shoulder.

Cole stalked toward the lycan he'd knocked to the ground, but the other vampire transported, and appearing in front of him, the creature grasped Cole's throat. Throwing his full weight into Cole, the vamp shoved him back. Cole nearly went down but kept himself upright when he planted his back foot and pushed back into the vamp.

When the vamp's hand clamped down and cut off his air supply, Cole grasped the vamp's wrist and twisted to the side. Bone gave way with a crack, and he broke the asshole's hold on him at the same time he swung his head forward.

His forehead smashed off the vamp's. The creature howled as it reeled back. Blood spilled down the vamp's forehead and dripped off his nose. When the vamp lifted his head, his once brown eyes were the color of blood.

The vamp vanished as it launched at him again, but suspecting an attack from behind, Cole spun and swung out with his hand. He couldn't see the vamp, but his claws caught in flesh and tore into muscle.

The vampire materialized a second later. His hands stretched toward Cole, but they froze in midair. Then his hands flew to his sliced-open throat as blood poured forth.

Cole was almost as astonished as the vamp as blood spilled between the vampire's fingers and splashed onto the ground. He hadn't realized he'd unleashed some of the lycan within him until his claws tore into the vamp's throat.

He'd never let the lycan free before, not even during the war. When fighting, he'd always relied more on his dark fae powers, but now he welcomed the rush the release of the lycan gave him.

He smiled as more of the lycan broke free of its cage, and with another slash, he severed the vamp's head. It thudded when it hit the ground and rolled a few feet away.

He turned toward the lycan he'd knocked to the ground. The beast was already recovering and climbing to his feet when Cole launched himself onto its back, seized its hair, and ripped its head back.

He plunged his claws into its throat and hacked through the thick sinew. Twisting the lycan's head to the side, he relished the sound of muscle tearing apart as he succeeded in hacking the creature's head off.

He turned toward Brokk as his brother dispatched the other

vamp. Brokk turned toward the lycan he'd flung into the tree. He took a step toward him as the tip of a sword erupted out the front of Brokk's chest. His brother's eyes widened as they fell to the blade piercing his heart.

"NO!" Cole bellowed as he released the lycan's head and shoved its body out of his way.

He didn't understand what happened until Brokk twisted to the side. The movement revealed the dark fae who slipped away had returned and snuck up behind his brother while Brokk was fighting.

Brokk was reaching for the sword when the fae grinned and ripped the blade free. The rays of the moon shone off the silver blade with its intricate markings. Dismay filled Cole when he realized what the sword was made of...

Fae metal!

The only metal that could kill a fae, and the coward had rammed the blade through Brokk's heart. It was a lethal wound for a fae.

I'll rip off his head and shove it down his throat!

But as the thought ran through his mind, Brokk went to his knees.

No! No! No!

He'd lost too many brothers to this war; he would *not* lose another. He caught Brokk before he fell face-first onto the ground. When the fae lifted the blade to bring it down against Brokk's back, Cole grasped the sword and held it while supporting his brother.

Brokk's hot blood soaked his shirt as the sword bit into his flesh and sliced through his muscle until the blade scoured his bone. The fae tried to rip it away, but Cole refused to relinquish the sword as he yanked it forward.

Not expecting the motion, the fae staggered forward with the sword. Cole grabbed the fae by his throat. His claws dug into the creature's flesh as he tore out his throat and threw it aside.

The fae's hands flew to what little remained of his throat as his blood drenched Cole and Brokk. Cole lifted his hand and delivered a staggering backhand that knocked the fae's head to the side and broke his neck.

Paralyzed by the blow, the fae hit the ground as Cole rose with Brokk in his arms. Cole shifted his hold on his brother to pull the sword free of his palm, and twisting the blade, he grasped the hilt and plunged it through the fae's back and into his heart. Pinned to the ground, the fae's fingers clawed at the dirt for a few seconds before he went limp.

Cole turned his attention to where he'd last seen the remaining lycan, but the beast was gone. He didn't have the time to hunt it as Brokk's body became completely limp against him.

Lifting Brokk into his arms, Cole fled into the night.

~

THE INCESSANT POUNDING on the door rebounded through the hallway until it became a never-ending crescendo that caused Lexi to bolt awake and propelled her out of bed before she realized she was moving. Flustered, she spun as she tried to get her bearings.

What was going on? Had the war started again?

No, that made no sense. Why would the war be banging on her door? It never had before.

Realizing she wasn't making any sense to herself, she struggled to rid herself of her sleep and confusion as the banging continued.

Who was trying to bang down her door and why?

She started to run from her room but skidded to a halt when an image of Malakai entered her mind. The idea of him seeing her in her old T-shirt and nothing else propelled her toward her closet. Their door was about to come off its hinges, but if it was him, then he couldn't see her like this.

She yanked open her closet doors and pulled out her robe. She tugged it on and cinched the belt around her waist before running from her room. From a few doors down and diagonally across the hall, Sahira was exiting her room.

Their eyes met before Lexi ran for the stairs.

"Elexiandra!" Sahira called sharply after her.

When she arrived at the bottom of the stairs, Lexi glanced at her aunt over her shoulder.

"You don't know who's on the other side!" Sahira called as she descended the stairs after Lexi.

No, she didn't, but they were banging so relentlessly that the thick wood door rattled in its frame. There was something desperate in that knock, something that propelled her forward even as dread slid down her spine.

The banging reverberated in her head as her hand fell on the knob and her throat went dry.

"Lexi!" Sahira hissed.

She had no idea who was on the other side, but she had to answer it. Something about the frantic pounding made it impossible to ignore.

After the last time she tried to help someone, she should know better than to do it again. That asshole was still living in her tunnels, but she couldn't stop herself from opening the door.

She gasped, and her hand flew to her throat when she spotted Cole on the other side. His eyes burned the brilliant silver of a lycan on the verge of transforming. Blood slicked his hair, slid down his face, and coated his hands as he lifted Brokk toward her.

Lexi's stomach plunged into her toes as she took in Brokk's bloodstained clothes and the gaping wound in his chest.

CHAPTER TWENTY-EIGHT

"I NEED HELP," Cole said in a gravelly voice distorted by the elongated fangs in his mouth. "I need a witch. *He* needs a witch."

Lexi blinked as his words sank in. She turned toward Sahira as her aunt rushed forward and stopped when she saw Brokk's damaged body.

"Please help him," Cole said.

The pleading and torment in his voice tugged at Lexi's heart-strings. She understood his suffering and panic, and she would do whatever she could to help... even if it bit her in the ass again.

"This way," Lexi said. "Hurry." She pushed past her aunt. "Sahira, get whatever you'll need to help him."

Her aunt closed her mouth, but her eyes remained wide as she glanced from Lexi to Cole and finally to Brokk.

"Lexi—"

"Close the door and gather your supplies," Lexi said more sharply than she intended, but she could feel time running out, and she couldn't deal with her aunt's overprotective nature now.

Sahira took a deep breath before her shoulders went back, and she shut the door. Lexi was aware she might be getting herself into more trouble —she had no idea what happened to them or if their enemies might come knocking on her door—but she couldn't turn them away.

She couldn't turn *Cole* away even if she harbored his other brother beneath her home.

Cole's feet thudded on the steps as he followed her upstairs. At the top of the steps, she threw open the first guest room door she came to and rushed inside. She flipped on the light switch, and a dim glow filled the room. The electricity was powered down again, but at least it was working.

When they lost most of their workers, she and Sahira closed off all the unused rooms.

Now, she yanked the dust cover from the bed and the table beside it. She balled the covers up and shoved them into a corner as Cole carefully set Brokk on the bed.

When his head flopped to the side, Lexi held her breath while she waited for some sign he was alive, but he didn't move. Just as she was beginning to think it was already too late, she caught the subtle rise and fall of his chest.

The air rushed out of her burning lungs, and she lifted her gaze to Cole. Anguish burned in his eyes and etched the lines of his face as he clasped his brother's hand. She wanted to assure him it would be okay, but the words froze in her throat.

She couldn't bring herself to lie to him by promising something that might not be true. Sahira was a talented witch, but she couldn't perform miracles.

The clatter of bottles drew her attention to the doorway a second before Sahira rushed into the room with a tray full of supplies. She set the tray on the table Lexi had cleared.

"What was he stabbed with?" she asked.

"A fae sword," Cole said.

"A *fae* sword?"

"Yes."

"Made of *fae* metal?"

"Yes."

Sahira's eyes flew back to Brokk as Lexi's hand went to her mouth. *How is he still alive?*

"Was it wielded *by* a *fae?*" Sahira asked.

"Yes," Cole said flatly.

"Shit," Sahira whispered.

That word summed it up. Fae *metal* through the heart was the only thing that could kill a fae, besides decapitation, yet as she watched, Brokk's chest rose and fell once more.

The fae forged metal was the strongest in all the realms and a powerful weapon against their enemies, but they didn't use it against each other. Apparently, that was no longer the case.

Lexi gulped at this insight into how far the two sides had devolved into their hatred of each other. If a fae had used a fae weapon against one of their kind, then all bets were off.

"So, the only reason he's still alive is because he's half vampire," Sahira said.

"Yes," Cole agreed.

Lexi's hand fell from her throat. "I'll get some blood."

She turned and ran from the room. She took the stairs two at a time to the entranceway and sprinted past the stairs to the kitchen. Flinging open the doors of the fridge, she shoved aside the meager contents to grab a couple of bags of blood tucked into the back corner.

She closed the doors and ran upstairs. When she returned to the room, she discovered Cole sitting on the side of the bed. His hand rested on Brokk's back as he propped his brother up so Sahira could pour a vial of green liquid into his mouth.

Lexi caught the scent of apples and pixie dust, but she had no idea what else was in the vial. She set the blood on the table before going to retrieve towels and water.

CHAPTER TWENTY-NINE

"You're injured," Lexi said.

When Cole looked up from where he sat at Brokk's side, Lexi gestured to his hand. It had stopped bleeding, but dried blood coated it, and when he turned his hand over, she saw the ragged edges of a raw gash.

Sahira looked up from where she was applying a healing salve onto Brokk's chest. Her hands stilled as she glanced between the two of them while Cole stared at his hand. Lexi marveled at the size of that hand as he flexed his fingers.

"It's healing," he said and lowered it.

"We should still clean it," Lexi said.

His gaze returned to his brother before shifting to Sahira as she rose away from Brokk. "I'll take care of it," she offered.

"It's fine. Though, I should probably clean up." Cole glanced around him and rose from the bed. "We got blood all over your things."

"It's fine," Lexi assured him.

"I'll replace them."

"Don't worry about it. I'll show you to a bathroom and try to find you some clothes."

"I can—" Sahira started at the same time Cole said, "Thank you."

Lexi ignored her aunt's irritated gaze as she moved toward the door. She felt Sahira's eyes burning into her with every step, but she didn't look back as she led Cole from the room and down the hall to one of the guest bathrooms.

She flicked on the light and hurried inside to remove the dust cloths from the vanity and toilet. She shoved them into the closet and pulled out a few towels that she set next to the sink.

"Thank you," he murmured.

His skin remained paler than normal, and his eyes were dull when they met hers. Then his brow furrowed as his gaze latched onto her, and the silver bled out of his eyes. Lexi marveled over the abrupt change as they resumed their vivid blue color.

There was so much in those eyes, but also something raw and primitive, something far more lycan than fae, and something that wanted *her*.

That knowledge should terrify her; instead, she thrilled at it.

∽

COLE STARTED to reach for her when he recalled the blood staining his hands. He dug his nails into his palms as he lowered his hand.

He couldn't touch her with blood on his hands, but the scent of her and the beauty of her hunter green eyes were difficult to resist. A clatter from Brokk's room drew his attention, and he stepped away from her.

"I'll be right out," he said.

He entered the bathroom and closed the door. When he stepped in front of the mirror, his heart sank when he saw the amount of blood coating him. She *never* should have seen him like this.

He also realized washing his hands wouldn't suffice though he scrubbed them before turning on the shower. A knock sounded on the door, and he opened it to discover Lexi standing there with an armful of clothes.

"My dad wasn't as tall as you, but I found some of his biggest clothes. Hopefully, they'll fit," she said.

There was something sad and wistful about her as she held the clothes out to him. *She misses him.*

The thought struck him hard, as did the impulse to cup her cheek to offer comfort. He wasn't one for comforting or for noticing others' feelings, but with her, things were different.

She was different. He had no idea why, but she was.

"Thank you," he said as he took the clothes from her. "Your father was my friend and a good man. I miss him too."

Her luscious mouth parted, and his gaze fell to those ripe lips as Sahira called to her.

"I hope they fit," she whispered before rushing off to see the witch.

Cole closed the door, stripped out of his ruined clothes, and stepped beneath the hot spray of water. He watched the blood swirl down the drain until the water ran clear. He turned off the shower, dried himself, and dressed.

The jeans were too short on him and rose above his ankles. They were also a little too tight around the waist, but they fit well enough. The shirt pulled taut across his shoulders, and he might tear it if he moved his arms too fast.

When he opened the door, he discovered Lexi with her hand raised to knock.

"Oh," she said, and her hand fell back to her side. "I thought you might need this."

She held up a bottle of Sahira's salve, and as he reached for the bottle with his good hand, her strawberry scent engulfed him. It was a scent he would never forget.

"I'll do it for you if you'd like," she offered.

The idea of her touching him was too enticing to resist. "Yes," he said.

When he stepped aside, she pushed past him with far more authority than her slender frame and height would have conveyed. He almost smiled but stopped when he spotted Sahira studying him from Brokk's doorway with blatant disapproval.

"How is he?" Cole inquired.

"He'll survive," Sahira said.

Some of Cole's tension eased. "Thank you."

Sahira's eyes went past him, but before she could say anything more, he stepped into the bathroom and closed the door. He understood Sahira's disapproval; she didn't think he was good for her niece, and she was probably right, but he didn't give a shit.

He'd never denied himself something he wanted before, and he wasn't about to start now.

When he turned, he discovered Lexi standing by the sink with her head bent as she uncapped the bottle of salve. The aroma of herbs and spices filled the air, but they were so varied he couldn't name any of them.

She turned toward him. "Come here," she said.

With pleasure. But he kept that to himself as he walked over to stand across from her.

"Let me see your hand," she said.

He liked this bossy side of her and smiled as he extended his hand. She grasped it tenderly and drew it toward her. When she poured some salve onto his palm and gently massaged it into the wound, all his amusement vanished.

Her touch caused his cock to harden as he imagined those slender fingers working their magic over his shaft. Her long lashes curled upward as she worked with a tenderness he'd never experienced from another before.

"What happened out there?" she asked.

"We ran into a group of rebels who weren't happy to see us," he said gruffly. "The dark fae left but returned to ambush Brokk."

"I'm sorry," she whispered.

The lycan part of him, a part so close to the edge all night, surged to the forefront. Unable to resist touching her anymore, he cupped her cheek and savored the warmth of her silken skin against his palm.

Her fingers stilled, and her breath caught. For a minute, she didn't move, and then her face tilted up, and her eyes met his. The freckles dotting the bridge of her nose were more visible in the light shining down on her.

She was so beautiful it was like a punch to the gut when those hunter green eyes, with their flecks of emerald, met his. Men would kill to possess her, and *he* would kill *them* to make sure she stayed safe.

His need to keep her safe increased as her breath warmed his thumb. His gaze fell to her mouth, and he ran his thumb over her pouty bottom lip.

She was a temptation more alluring than any siren, and he'd encountered a few sirens before. He'd resisted them; he couldn't resist her.

Her warm breath tickled his thumb before he bent his head and replaced his thumb with his mouth. He braced himself for her to push him away, but she remained unmoving with her back against the sink as her fingers clenched his palm.

When she didn't push him away, he ran his tongue across her lips and nearly groaned at the honey and strawberries taste of her. He could spend hours, days, years, kissing her, and he would never grow tired of the taste or the sensation of her lips yielding to his.

The lycan part of him broke free completely, and he completely forgot he was half dark fae as the wolf inside took control. His fangs extended, his claws lengthened, and a tingle raced up his spine as the transformation threatened to take over.

No! Not in front of her. Not like this.

He couldn't recall a time when he'd lost such complete control of himself, because it had never happened. In all of his six hundred and seventy-two years, he'd never been on the verge of transforming without willing it to happen.

Then her mouth parted and her tongue met his. At first, it was hesitant and uncertain, but the longer they kissed, the bolder she became until she met each of his thrusts. He slid his hand into her hair and cupped the back of her head as he deepened the kiss.

He lost himself to the wonder of her as her fingers encircled his wrists. Cole had kissed more women than he could count over his lifetime, and he couldn't recall a single one of them, but he would never forget her.

His hand fell to her waist and slid beneath her robe. The thin material of her shirt pressed against his palm as he gripped her hip. He drew her flush against him, letting her feel his rigid dick.

He released her hip to grip her ass and lifted her so she sat on the counter. Her shirt bunched in his hand, and he growled as he stroked her hip before squeezing it.

CHAPTER THIRTY

LEXI'S HEAD spun as Cole's scent and the feel of his body bombarded all her senses. She stopped feeling the cool counter beneath her ass and stopped hearing the rapid beat of her heart as everything in her became focused on *him.*

Beneath her palms, the corded muscles of his biceps bunched and flexed as the vast amount of power thrumming through him vibrated against her. That power prickled her skin and made her pulse race. The scruff of his beard tickled her face, but she welcomed the delicious sensation.

She'd been around many powerful beings in her lifetime, but she'd never touched one like this before. And she'd *never* been kissed like this before. His kiss demanded more, and she willingly gave it.

Every thrust of his tongue, every touch of his hand, was designed to make her crave more, and it worked. She hadn't known it was possible to feel so destroyed yet so found by a kiss.

It felt as if he was breaking every part of her down to the most basic element and recrafting it into something else, something made entirely for him. Was this what it meant to be shadow kissed?

But no, despite the name, she knew someone had to offer up a lot more than a kiss for that kind of complete possession to occur. Still, he was changing her on a fundamental level that left her shaken and alive in a way she'd never been before.

She couldn't get enough of him.

Her hands slid under his arms and pressed against his back. She tried to draw him closer even as his arms crushed her against him. His hand entwined in her hair and pulled her head back to give him better access to her mouth.

This was going too fast. She'd never been touched in such intimate, knowing ways before, and she had to slow down. He was a dark fae, if she didn't get control of this, she might never regain control, but her body completely disagreed with the rationale of her brain.

She jumped when a booming knock on the door reverberated throughout the bathroom. When she tore her mouth away, his forehead fell to rest against her temple as his hands possessively gripped her ass.

"Lexi!" Sahira called. "Is everything okay in there?"

Lexi's chest heaved as she labored to catch her breath. She tried to wiggle away from Cole, but his arms remained locked around her, and the sound he emitted froze her. When he lifted his head and their gazes met, she blinked at the sight of the pure silver eyes staring back at her.

She'd never seen a lycan on the verge of losing control. However, those silver eyes were a clear indication the beast was close to the surface. It should terrify her, as an out-of-control lycan was one of the deadliest creatures in all the realms, but she couldn't feel any trepidation with his arms locked securely around her.

For the first time, she felt his claws against her ass and saw the faint hint of a cipher at his temple. The outline of his fangs was visible against his closed lips.

If she wasn't mistaken, he was on the verge of transforming.

But as she stared at him, the cipher vanished, and his claws retracted.

She wondered how many ciphers he truly possessed. Immortals whispered that the dark fae hid some of their ciphers from the outside world. The more ciphers a fae had, the stronger they were, but many claimed they only revealed a small percentage of those ciphers to the world so they could conceal the true depth of their power from their enemies.

It made sense to her, but this was the first time she'd seen evidence of it. The emergence of that cipher was as much a sign of his loss of control as his silver eyes.

When his erection pressed between her thighs, she resisted rubbing against him. For a minute, they simply stared at each other. Then her gaze fell to his mouth, and yearning tore through her.

"Lexi!" Sahira called, and a note of panic tinged her voice.

Struggling to breathe, she stammered out a reply. "I'm fi-fine! I'll be right out."

His arms squeezed her, and she sensed his irritation as Sahira sighed. Then her aunt's footsteps sounded against the rug as she strode away

She waited for him to release her, but he remained towering over her with his body locked possessively around hers.

"I should…." Lexi swallowed the lump in her throat. "I should go."

A muscle twitched in his jaw, but finally, and with a reluctance evident in his slow movements, he released her and stepped away. Lexi tugged her robe close around her as she wiggled off the countertop.

She resisted the blush creeping up her neck and into her cheeks, but it was a losing battle. With her cheeks burning, she finished tugging her clothes into place.

"I must admit, you are a bit irresistible in this," he murmured.

When he gripped the lapel of her robe and his fingers played with the material, Lexi frowned. She didn't own anything she would consider irresistible. She glanced down at the pink fabric, and her eyes widened when she spotted the tiny bunnies on it.

With her face burning hotter, she closed her eyes. In her rush to grab clothes from the closet, she hadn't snagged her new, white, fluffy robe. Instead, she'd taken the robe she'd practically worn threadbare as a kid.

Unwilling to part with it, she stashed it in her closet when she outgrew it at twelve. And now she was wearing it in front of *him*.

"I was in a rush," she muttered. "Someone woke me in the middle of the night."

His burst of laughter caused her eyes to blink in surprise. The sound rumbling from him made her toes curl as much as his passionate kiss. It was such a vibrant, warm sound, so much like the man who issued it.

He was still laughing when his head lowered. His eyes were that piercing blue again when they met hers.

Lexi bit her lip as she gazed at him. He was gorgeous, and she longed to run her fingers over the angles of his face before entwining them in his hair and kissing him again. But if she kissed him again, she wouldn't stop, and she was *not* prepared for where it would all lead.

"It's adorable," he said before releasing the robe. "I should return to Brokk."

"Yes, of course."

She started to edge away from him, but his hand on her face stopped her. He wiped something from her cheek. When his hand moved away from her, she realized it was some of the salve she'd put on his palm.

"Your hand—" she started.

"It's fine," he assured her as he held it up between them.

Some of the salve remained on his palm. Beneath it, she saw the healing edges of the deep gash in his hand. "What caused it?"

"I grabbed the blade."

Her eyebrows rose at this statement. She couldn't imagine

doing such a thing, let alone the agony accompanying it, but it didn't seem to affect him.

"Until later," he murmured as he clasped her chin and kissed her once more.

Before she could melt into his kiss again, he broke it off, opened the door, and left the room. She gazed after his back as she pondered his parting words.

What exactly did they mean? Would they continue what they'd started later, or was it just a parting comment?

An uneasy feeling grew in the pit of her stomach as she lifted her trembling fingers to her swollen lips.

Now that the confusion and chaos of the night was settling down, she recalled his brother—a traitor that Brokk and Cole were hunting earlier—was hidden beneath her manor.

The heat Cole's kiss evoked vanished as her blood ran cold.

CHAPTER THIRTY-ONE

LEXI NUDGED the cracked door further open. She poked her head inside the room where she last saw Brokk and Cole to discover Brokk sleeping soundly on the bed and Cole asleep in the chair beside him.

A twinge tugged at her heart as she gazed at Cole's large frame in that chair. He'd stretched his long legs before him, and his head had fallen back. He must have been extremely uncomfortable, but that chair was where she last saw him, and she assumed he stayed in it all night.

She eased the door closed and retreated before rushing down the stairs. She strode down the hall and through the kitchen to the mudroom, where she kept her stable clothes. Removing her sneakers from beneath the row of coats hanging on the wall, she tugged them on.

The sun was beginning to break the horizon as she stepped outside. A low mist covered the open field and danced across the ground as she strode toward the barn. The dew-covered grass dampened her sneakers and the bottom of her jeans as she walked.

Beneath the smoky scent always lingering in the air was the

sweet aroma of spring and flowers as the robins sang. She stopped outside the barn door and slid it open.

At one time, she came to the stables to help because it was something she loved doing. Now, with most of their staff having fled, she came because she had to care for the animals.

She smiled when the nicker of the horses greeted her and they kneed their doors impatiently. As she made her way down the shedrow, she hung their food tubs over the four horses' doors before going to let out the goats and chickens.

Normally, this was her favorite time of day, and she loved this private time as she listened to the sounds of the animals eating. Today, she didn't find any solace in the work as her mind spun over the predicament she found herself in.

She wished she could get Orin out of her tunnels, but she didn't know how to do it without causing a scene that would get her thrown in jail before her beheading. Maybe, if she could talk to him and tell him what happened with his brothers, he would agree to leave, but she couldn't risk going to see him again while Brokk and Cole were here.

Sahira's spell kept the tunnels enshrouded in safety, but she couldn't risk coming back smelling like Orin or getting caught emerging from the tunnels. She had no way to explain either of those things away.

The sun had risen higher in the sky by the time she finished turning out the horses, cleaning their stalls, and setting their feed up for tonight and tomorrow. She left the barn and trudged back across the lawn to the manor.

As the day progressed, the road was filling with humans and immortals starting their day. Most of them walked with their shoulders hunched up and their heads bowed, but some strode purposely forward with the confident swagger of the oppressors savoring their destruction.

Anger and sadness coiled inside her as she watched the downtrodden pass. This was not the way it was supposed to be. This was not what her father had in mind when he fought in the war, or at least that's what she told herself.

No matter what side he chose, she couldn't believe this was the outcome her father sought. He had his faults, she would never deny that, but he was a good man at heart. He'd believed he was doing the right thing when he joined the Lord's side.

There was no way he could have foreseen this outcome, and there was no way he would have approved of it.

Her gaze traveled back to the manor. How did Cole feel about all of this?

He'd fought on the Lord's side and was hunting his brother, yet he didn't relish the battering the human race had taken like Malakai did.

But maybe he did. She had no idea what he did and didn't enjoy. She knew so little about him, after all.

Her fingers involuntarily rose to her lips as she recalled their kiss. Still completely wired from it, she barely slept last night, but there was a good possibility it meant nothing to him.

He was far older than her and part dark fae. They fed on sexual energy as well as food, which meant he'd experienced countless kisses before.

He'd probably forgotten about kissing *her* by the time he returned to Brokk's side, but she couldn't help speculating if it might have meant something more to him.

She dropped her hand and shook her head to clear it of the memories of that kiss. She had enough to contend with without daydreaming about things that could never be.

She trudged back to the manor, entered, and closed the door behind her. She kicked off her sneakers before returning to her room. Some of the tension eased from her as she took in the familiar comfort of her surroundings.

This had been her room since she was a baby. Her nursery's pink walls were replaced by her childhood's purple walls, which became the color-splashed walls of her teens, and were now the dove-gray walls of her twenties.

Photos of her, Sahira, and her father hung around the room. In one, she was sitting on her dad's lap next to the lake. They were both smiling as their heads leaned against each other. Looks of love and serenity lit their faces.

She recalled the night the photo was taken. Only six at the time, she'd walked to the lake while holding her dad's hand. They spent some time looking at the stars while he pointed out the constellations. Later, she learned he made most of them up, but she'd marveled over them as the crickets and tree frogs sang their songs.

When they arrived at the lake, the moon was high in the sky. He pulled out a loaf of bread, and she sat in his lap. He regaled her with stories as the ducks, woken from slumber by the prospect of food, swam over to them.

Sahira snapped the photo after all the bread was gone, and Lexi's head was resting against his chest. She recalled his heartbeat beneath her ear as he held her. She'd drifted off, secure in the knowledge he would always protect her.

He'd seemed indestructible to her, but she'd been wrong. Her hero had fallen on a battlefield, and she had only memories and photos left of him.

With tears clogging her eyes, she turned away from the photo. She tugged off her barn clothes and tossed them into the hamper tucked inside her walk-in closet. One side of the closet contained some of the fancier clothes she wore to the few "special" events she attended in her life, but it was mostly full of jeans, sweaters, and hoodies.

She did have a collection of shoes she loved. Unfortunately, she didn't wear them often as sneakers and boots were her main source of footwear for work around the manor. But occasionally, she would take them out, put them on, and admire them before slipping them away again.

Gathering some new clothes, she left the closet behind and set the clothes on the pale, yellow comforter covering her queen-size bed. She flicked on the bathroom light switch, but nothing came on.

Lexi lifted the flashlight from where she left it on the counter and turned it on. Hopefully, there was still enough hot water in the tank to get her through a shower, but it wouldn't be her first cold shower if there wasn't.

Remodeled when she was fifteen, the bathroom held the claw-foot tub she insisted on having. There was also a stand-in shower with a glass door.

The beige walls were simple and unadorned, but the shelves lining them held various bottles of some of Sahira's concoctions. Lexi pulled down a lavender mix she loved before stepping into the shower.

She'd been looking forward to a hot shower, but the lukewarm water didn't last long enough for that to happen. In the hopes of calming her nerves, she rubbed the lavender over her skin and washed it away before fleeing the cooling water.

Wrapping a towel around herself, she left the bathroom and dressed in a pair of jeans, a loose-fitting T-shirt, and her socks. She stood in front of her bureau's mirror, brushed her hair, and slid an elastic onto her wrist to use later.

When she finished, she left her room and walked down the hall to where Brokk was resting.

CHAPTER THIRTY-TWO

SHE CONTEMPLATED KNOCKING on the door to see if they needed anything, but she didn't want to wake Brokk. He'd been on the verge of death last night and required his rest, so did Cole.

She descended the stairs and strode down the hall toward the kitchen. She stepped into the large, airy room with its gray stone back wall. The rest of the walls had been drywalled over and painted a cranberry color.

To her left was a large window overlooking the barn and paddock. Beneath the window was a basin sink. Sahira stood at the stove at the far end of the large island in the room's center. Thankfully, the gas continued to work when the power was out.

Her aunt was chopping herbs on a cutting block she'd set out on top of the black marble countertops. Whatever she was cooking made Lexi's stomach rumble. However, judging by the vials surrounding Sahira, she wasn't making breakfast. She was replenishing her potions.

Shade, Sahira's black cat and familiar, sat beside the cutting board and watched as Sahira's fingers worked their magic. Shade's tail swung back and forth as he meticulously cleaned his paw. He paused in the middle of his grooming to study Lexi with his golden eyes before resuming his cleaning.

Sahira absently rested her hand on Shade's head, and their eyes met before they resumed their activities. Lexi lifted a piece of bread from the counter before pouring some blood into a mug.

"How's the patient?" Lexi asked.

"When I looked in on him an hour ago, he was doing much better," Sahira replied. "He's still sleeping, but he's healing."

"That's good. Was Cole awake?"

Sahira set her spoon down with a loud clatter. "No."

"Good."

"He's dark fae."

"I know."

She also knew what that meant. Everyone knew the dark fae were lethal and cold. They also only had one use for someone of the opposite sex... to feed on the energy they emitted during sex.

But Cole wasn't entirely dark fae. When she first met him, all she'd seen of him was fae, but last night she glimpsed far more lycan in him. And the lycan were known for their undying loyalty to their mate. They also played the field a *lot* until they found their mate.

And while Lexi didn't think she was his mate—that was *not* what she wanted in her life at all—she didn't think he was like the other dark fae. Not entirely, at least.

Would he break her heart if she wasn't careful? Absolutely.

But she didn't plan on letting him get close enough for that to happen. However, she wouldn't mind if he got as close as he did last night again.

You don't want to become shadow kissed.

She shuddered at the possibility of becoming one of those mindless, sex-starved things the dark fae sometimes left behind. No, she did *not* want to become one of them, but for that to happen, she was pretty sure a lot more than what passed between them last night would have to occur, and she had no plans for that.

She felt Sahira's gaze as she slathered butter on her bread, but Lexi didn't look at her aunt as she tried to act completely nonchalant.

"I'll be in the library reading," she said as she lifted her mug and her plate.

"Hmm," Sahira grunted.

Lexi strolled over to kiss her cheek. "You worry too much."

"I always worry about you."

Lexi squeezed her shoulder before releasing her and strolling toward the door. "I love you too."

CHAPTER THIRTY-THREE

FOLLOWING the scent of whatever was cooking, Cole descended a set of backstairs and entered a large, airy kitchen. With her back to him, Sahira stood at the island in the center. Her fingers flew as she chopped something with easy precision.

Though she remained focused on whatever she diced, the slight stiffening of her shoulders told him she was aware he'd arrived. His feet didn't make a sound as he strode across the kitchen toward her.

She didn't turn to look at him as he approached. "Can I get you something to eat, Colburn?"

He stopped at the countertop and, sniffing the air, caught the faint hint of Lexi. She'd been here recently.

"No," he said. "And call me Cole. You helped save my brother's life."

Sahira didn't look up at him while she worked, but her jaw clenched a little.

"Where is Lexi?" he asked.

Her fingers stopped, and the thud of the knife ceased against the wooden board. Her head remained bowed for a second before she lifted it and met his gaze. Strands of her mahogany hair had slipped loose of her bun to frame her face. Her amber eyes narrowed on him.

"Stay away from her," Sahira said.

Cole almost chuckled in amusement, but there wasn't anything funny about this. Sahira played a large role in Lexi's life, and she didn't like him. Because of that, she would do everything she could to drive him away.

However, after the taste he got of Lexi last night, he wasn't going anywhere. He rested his hand near the stainless steel cooktop with its black, iron burners.

"And why would I do that?" he asked.

"Because she deserves better."

"Better than me?"

"Better than being messed with by a dark fae."

Perhaps that was true, but he didn't care. "You don't like the dark fae."

Sahira tossed a handful of herbs into the large pot on the stove. "*No one* likes the dark fae, *Colburn*."

He lifted an eyebrow at her pointed use of his full name. She was a brazen little witch. *So that's where we stand.*

"I could say the same about witches and vampires, *Sahira*."

She scowled at him while she stirred the pot.

"I could say the same about lycan and humans," he continued.

"She deserves better than to be messed with by a man who is only looking for one thing. She's better than that. She's better than *you*."

Again, maybe that was true, but it wasn't going to stop him. He wanted Lexi, and he would have her. The only one who could prevent it from happening was Lexi. After last night, he didn't see that happening.

He leaned closer to her. "And how do you know what I'm looking for?"

"Because it's what all dark fae are looking for. You have to feed, and you need victims to quell your hunger."

"I can assure you, Sahira, there are no victims in my past. They were *all* willing."

"Did they all know what you are?"

He held her fiery gaze as she stopped stirring the pot. His hand flexed on the countertop as his claws lengthened before retracting again. She wasn't a threat to his safety, but she was a threat if she tried to stand between him and Lexi.

"You know that's not the way immortals work," he said. "Or at least it's not the way we worked before the war. Humans were never supposed to know about our existence, but since you're so curious about my sex life, I can assure you that since they learned of us, they've always known whose bed they've climbed into. For some, their curiosity has only increased their desire for immortals and especially the dark fae."

"Good for you," she muttered sarcastically.

A vein in Cole's temple throbbed. "And has everyone in your past always known what you are?"

"There's a big difference between us; I don't feed on others."

"We all do what is necessary to survive. You are part vampire; you require blood."

"I use blood bags."

"Good for you."

"And is it necessary for you to leave the broken, twisted souls of the shadow kissed in your wake?"

"Anything I've ever done to anyone, they've asked for. No," he said as he leaned closer, "they *begged* me for it."

Waves of dislike emanated from her. He smiled in return.

"Where is Lexi?" he asked.

"She's young, and she just lost her father. She deserves better than to have someone like *you* playing with her."

"You have no idea what I'm like," he said.

"Everyone knows what the dark fae are like."

"And what are the witches like? Or the vampires? You're

condemning the dark fae when all immortals have questionable traits. A witch's temper is legendary."

Sahira pulled the wooden spoon from the pot and slammed it on the counter. The flames beneath the pot rose as her temper flared. Lifting his hand, Cole moved it toward the fire and closed his fingers. The fire went out.

"You're not the only one who can control the elements," he reminded her though the dark fae were stronger and better at controlling the elements than the witches.

The fire surged back to life and wrapped around the corners of the pot. "I am the only one who can cast a hex."

"Are you threatening me?" Cole growled.

He didn't want to upset Lexi by hurting this woman, but he wouldn't tolerate threats from anyone. She had no idea what she was playing with right now. *He* didn't know what she was playing with right now. He barely recognized himself since Lexi entered his life.

"I'm telling you," Sahira hissed. "Leave her alone. She is one of the kindest souls I've ever known, and she deserves the best."

Cole straightened away to study her angry countenance. *She's a mama bear protecting her young.*

Sahira wouldn't be a hindrance to Lexi because she disliked him; she would be a problem because she loved Lexi.

"Now on that, we can agree," he said.

She blinked at him, and some of the anger went out of her, but her stance remained rigid. He turned away before their antagonism toward each other became something worse. He'd find Lexi on his own.

He started for the doorway but stopped when she called his name. He turned back to find her stirring the pot once more.

"I don't care that you're the prince of the dark fae; if you hurt her, I'll find a way to make you pay," she vowed.

He laughed as he walked out of the room. He had no doubt she would do everything she could to keep Lexi safe, but he wasn't afraid of her.

He wasn't going to fight with her either. Sahira could succeed in pushing Lexi away from him, and he wouldn't let that happen.

He strode down the hallway toward the front door. As he walked, the scent of Lexi drew him to a set of open, double doors. Inside the room, he spotted Lexi curled up on the cushion of an oversized, brown chair.

She sat with her legs beneath her and her chin on her palm as she held a book. The sun shining through the floor-to-ceiling windows on one side of the room cascaded over her. Its glow brought out the deeper shades of red in her auburn hair.

Feeling like someone had socked him in the stomach, he stood in the doorway and drank in her beauty. He'd never seen anyone as lovely as her. It was more than the perfection of her face; it was also the soul Sahira mentioned. Its warmth radiated from her.

Stepping out of the doorway, he strolled toward her. He crossed the Oriental rug to settle in the chair a few feet away from her. She was so engrossed in her book she didn't realize he was there until he cleared his throat.

CHAPTER THIRTY-FOUR

LEXI SQUEAKED and almost threw her book when a sound came from only a few feet away from her. Her head shot up, and she spotted Cole sitting in the other chair and grinning at her like the Cheshire cat.

That smile and the carefree way he draped his arm over the back of the chair as he turned toward her caused the rapid beat of her heart to shift from alarm to excitement.

"I didn't hear you enter," she said.

"I know."

It wasn't fair he looked casual and carefree while she felt so thrown off by his sudden presence.

"What are you reading?" he inquired.

Lifting the book, she turned it toward him so he could see the name on the cover. When she entered earlier, she'd sought escape, so she chose one of her favorites.

His smile grew. "Harry Potter and the Sorcerer's Stone."

"Have you read it?" she asked.

"No."

"It's really good. The series is one of my favorites."

His gaze wandered over all the books before settling on her again. "Do you mind if I pick something to read?"

"Not at all."

She couldn't help but marvel over his size as he unfolded himself from the chair and rose with a fluid grace she wouldn't have associated with someone of his size. She knew all lycan were massive, but she hadn't been around many of them.

She tipped her head to the side as she watched him studying the shelves. She was extremely curious to see what he picked. "How is Brokk doing?"

"Much better. He's still sleeping, but his color has improved, and so has his breathing."

"That's great. Will your father be worried about you?"

"I sent him a crow this morning."

Cole stopped his perusal of the shelves and removed a book. Lexi bit her lip as she impatiently waited to see what he chose. He examined the book for a minute before returning to the chair.

"Did you find something you liked?" she asked.

He turned the book toward her, and she laughed when she saw he held the Chamber of Secrets.

"Someone told me it was a good series," he said with a smile that showed off his dazzling white teeth.

"They were correct." She closed her book and held it across the gap between them. "I'll trade you. I've already read it half a dozen times, and it's better if you start at the beginning."

He took the book from her and handed her the one he'd claimed. Leaning back in the chair, she opened the book, but she couldn't concentrate as her gaze repeatedly returned to him. He didn't have the same problem as he flipped through the pages.

The rustle of turning pages was the only sound in the room as an hour slipped past. She was acutely aware of his presence in the room, but it wasn't uncomfortable.

A sense of peace enveloped her as his masculine scent teased her nostrils. She had no reason to feel safe in his presence, but she hadn't felt this secure since her dad died.

When the grandfather clock down the hall chimed the hour, he set his book down and rose. "I should check on Brokk."

Lexi buried her disappointment. He left the room, and she returned to her book, but unable to concentrate, she kept rereading the same page.

She was about to give up when he returned. She hated the leap of excitement her heart made. Becoming more entangled with this man could be the biggest mistake of her life, but she already craved the rush of life he made her experience whenever he was near.

The dark fae were loyal to very few, and she was well aware of what they needed to survive. She would only be one of many to him, but she still itched to feel the corded muscles of his arms around her again.

"Is he okay?" she asked to distract herself from her wayward thoughts.

"He's still sleeping."

"I'm sure he'll wake soon."

"So am I."

He said this, but his brow remained furrowed as he reclaimed his seat. He didn't pick the book back up. Instead, he stared at the empty fireplace. Her gaze swung between him and the fireplace as the unsettling possibility he might somehow see the entrance to the tunnel plagued her.

There's no way he knows it's there. But sweat broke out on her palms and beaded along her nape. *Get it together, or he's going to notice!*

This was true, but she wasn't one for subterfuge, and she could feel herself unraveling as she waited to see what he would do.

"How has it been for you since the war ended?" he asked after a few minutes.

Her shoulders relaxed as she stared at the fireplace and tried not to laugh in relief. The entrance was too well hidden to see. She had to calm down, or she was going to blow it.

When he turned toward her, she recalled his question and pondered the best way to answer it. He probably expected her to tell him things were great, her father's side had won, but she couldn't say that. She lost her dad in the war, and everything had been a struggle since the dragons torched the earth. She couldn't lie about that.

"It's... been... difficult," she admitted.

"How so?"

An unexpected lump formed in her throat. "Not having my dad, for starters. He took care of so much around here, and he was my... everything." Her gaze fell to her hands as she fiddled with the edge of her shirt. "Trying to keep this place running after his death and after so many workers deserted us has been a challenge, but Sahira and I are doing it.

"We have a human handyman who still comes to help Sahira and me with some repairs, but our live-in help is gone. The people who used to work and live here know we're immortals now; there's no point in continuing to hide it from them. Even if we never hurt them and always helped them, they still fear us. And who can blame them?"

"Who indeed?"

"Before, Sahira used to cast a glamour over us to make the humans think we were aging like them, but she gave that up after the war. There was no reason to drain herself by keeping up the pretense."

"It's a big place for the two of you to take care of on your own."

Lexi shrugged. "It's our home, and we're *not* giving it up."

Cole nodded but didn't speak again. When the silence stretched onward, Lexi couldn't stop herself from asking, "How has it been for *you* since the war ended?"

～

COLE STARED at his hands as he contemplated this question. It had been hell for him since the war ended. Pure, unadulterated hell. The memory of those vicious battles lingered in his mind; the blood staining his hands would never come off, and the nightmares....

Well, he was certain the nightmares would haunt him for the rest of his days.

Before the war, he killed others, but he never slaughtered them with the ruthlessness he did during some battles. To him, many of those he slaughtered were innocents. Yes, they'd stood against the Lord, but so did he.

He hadn't fought against the Lord on the battlefield. It had all been behind the scenes, and he'd failed.

However, no one could have foreseen the crazy bastard letting loose his dragons and slaughtering countless humans and immortals with such gleeful, ruthless intent.

Now, all he could do was make sure his brothers and so many others hadn't died in vain by continuing to try to bring the Lord down from within. The ruler of the Shadow Realms, and the dragons, was insane, but he didn't suspect their treason. That was the only hope they had of taking him down.

"It's been... different," he said. "It's certainly been quieter at home with half of my brothers dead and two of the remaining ones banished and hunted as traitors."

CHAPTER THIRTY-FIVE

LEXI'S EYES involuntarily darted to the fireplace before returning to him. When her lungs began to burn, she realized she was holding her breath and released it slowly to not draw attention to herself.

She stared at him as her heart raced, and she wondered if he could tell his words had sent her into a mini panic attack. She didn't want to discuss his brothers, but she couldn't safely steer the conversation away without drawing attention to herself.

She remained outwardly calm as she replied, "That had to be difficult."

"It was," he said. "It *is*. Before the war, we were all close."

This revelation surprised her. He cared for Brokk a great deal, but the dark fae were selfish, aloof creatures. Or maybe that was only the image they portrayed to the outer world. Or maybe it was because his family was a mix of half-breeds and therefore not as cold as the dark fae were said to be.

Orin was pure dark fae and a complete asshole, but maybe the others had bigger hearts. The lycan were known for loyalty to their families; perhaps that was the side of Cole she now saw.

"I'm sorry for your loss," she murmured.

When his head tipped to the side, the sun shining over him emphasized the elegance of his square jaw, chiseled cheekbones, and Persian blue eyes.

"I'm sorry for your loss, too," he said.

Lexi ducked her head as she blinked away her tears. It had been six months, but sometimes it still felt like it had only been an hour, and she would never get over her grief. *This* was one of those times.

"Thank you," she whispered when she trusted herself to speak. And then, because she had to know what her father experienced before he died, she asked. "Was the war horrible?"

When he didn't reply, she lifted her head to look at him again. His hands gripped the ends of his chair until his knuckles turned white and a muscle twitched in his cheek.

Looking at him, she wished she could take back the question. No matter what he said, she would always know the war had sliced many lacerations and scars onto his soul. And now she knew the last of her father's life had been awful.

Of course, it was horrible. It was war. Countless immortals and mortals lost their lives.

He'd fought on the winning side, but that didn't make it any less atrocious. It just meant he didn't have a price on his head and countless enemies hunting him now that it was over.

Even the dark fae with their purported heartlessness would be affected by all the death they waded through to survive. It was only beings like Malakai who came through the war relatively unscathed.

"Yes," he said.

When he didn't elaborate any further, they sat in silence as the seconds turned into minutes.

Then he spoke again. "What happened to your mother?"

"My father didn't tell you?"

Cole's hands relaxed on the chair, and when he looked at her again, some of his tension ebbed. "No, he never spoke of her."

"He didn't tell me much about her either," she admitted. "I know she was human and she died while giving birth to me. He told me he loved her, but I don't think humans are meant to birth immortal creatures."

"No, they're not."

"Her name was Sharon, and he said she was beautiful."

Instinctively, her fingers went to her face, and she touched her cheek. Her father once told her she looked exactly like her mother. There were times when she looked in the mirror and tried to picture the woman who helped create her, but trying to imagine her face on a dead woman was unnerving.

"Like mother, like daughter," Cole murmured.

Lexi's eyes widened as he stared at her. He found her beautiful?

She wasn't an idiot, and she owned a mirror, so she knew she wasn't ugly, but to hear him say this sent a warm thrill of excitement through her.

"What about your mother?" she asked.

"She was killed when I was seven."

Lexi's hand flew to her mouth. "Oh, I'm sorry."

He shrugged, but something in his eyes told her it wasn't such a casual thing. "It was centuries ago."

"It still must have been hard. I miss my mother, and I never knew her. I can't imagine knowing her and losing her at such a young age."

"At least I have memories of her. She was a good woman, kind and gentle. She loved my father and me very much."

"What about your father?" she asked.

"What about him?"

"Did he love her?"

"With all his heart. He still does."

The look on her face must have expressed her shock as he chuckled and draped his arm over the chair back.

"Despite what many think, the dark fae are very capable of

love. In fact, since they so rarely give their love to anyone beyond their family, they often love deeper than most immortal creatures. My father never recovered from her death. He fathered other children, but she is the only one he loved and the only one he claimed as his wife."

Somehow, she managed to keep herself from gawking at him like an idiot. Immortals rarely married, and when they did, it was forever. The bond was severed only by death or extreme circumstances.

"I didn't know he had married," she murmured.

"There's no reason you should. They married hundreds of years ago, and while the dark fae like to think all the realms revolve around them, I realize not everyone feels the same way. I wouldn't expect you to know our history, though many of my kind would."

She chuckled as she rested her chin on her hand. He fascinated her; she could talk to him for hours, if not days.

However, when the clock chimed out the next hour, he rose from the chair. "I have to check on Brokk."

She watched as he strode from the room before picking up her book again. There were so many things she should do today, but she didn't move. She couldn't bring herself to leave as she hoped for his return.

Ten minutes later, he entered the room again. Alert for him this time, she caught his footfall in the hall and lifted her head as he glided toward his chair.

His movements mesmerized her; there was something animalistic about him. Something primal and lethal and utterly seductive in a way that might make her a little insane.

"Any change?" she asked as he settled onto the chair once more.

"No."

"I'm sure he'll wake soon."

"I hope so."

He picked up his book and started reading again. She did the same, though her attention remained mostly on him.

After a few minutes, he set the book down and turned toward her. "What do you like to do for fun, Lexi?"

She lifted her book and waved it at him. "Read."

"What else?"

"Riding, and before the war, I'd often go for hikes with my dad. Sometimes Sahira would join us. I also like to fish."

"Did you go to parties?"

"My father had a few here that I attended as a teen, but I never went to the Shadow Realms until your father's invite arrived. Once the war started, the parties stopped."

"That they did."

"What about you, Cole? What do you like to do for fun?"

There was one thing the dark fae *loved* to do for fun, but she hoped he didn't answer that.

"I also like to read and listen to music, and I attended *many* parties over the years."

"Did you travel to different Shadow Realms?"

"I did."

She set her book in her lap as she leaned forward. "What are they like? Are they all as fantastical as the Gloaming? Which realm is your favorite?"

"My favorite is the Gloaming; there's nothing like home. But the witches' realm is amazing, as is the lycan's, and there are many others inhabited by numerous, immortal species. Many of them, I would never travel to. And then there is the siren realm and the imps."

Lexi propped her chin on her hand as he talked about the different realms and all the many immortal creatures she would never meet. The deep timbre of his voice and the pictures he painted enthralled her.

She could listen to him talk for hours, and though he got up to check on Brokk every hour, that was exactly what they did. The sun was setting when she reluctantly pulled herself away from him.

She went upstairs to clean up another guest room in case he decided to sleep away from Brokk tonight. When she finished, she went out to bring in the horses.

She returned to the manor and discovered him sitting at Brokk's side. She told him about the other room, but she doubted he would sleep in it.

"Thank you," he said.

She bid him good night and closed the door.

CHAPTER THIRTY-SIX

COLE FOUND Lexi in the library again the next day and settled into the chair beside her. He couldn't stop himself from smiling at her as she lowered her book and beamed at him. That smile warmed his heart and could light up all the realms. He basked in its radiance.

"How is Brokk?" she asked as she set her book down. "I poked my head in to check on him, but you were both sleeping."

"He woke in the middle of the night," Cole said as he rubbed his beard. "He was up long enough to drink some blood before passing out again, but he was talking, and he's getting stronger."

"That's great news."

It was certainly a relief to him. He'd never been so happy to hear his brother call him an asshole for leaving Becca's establishment.

"I hope you don't mind if we stay," he said. "I think it will be a few days before he's strong enough to travel."

"Stay for as long as you need."

He picked up the book he'd been reading yesterday, but his gaze continuously shifted to her as she sat with her legs dangling over the side of the chair. Her feet kicked leisurely back and forth as she turned the pages of her book.

He'd dreamt about her last night, and it was the first time since the war ended that he hadn't had a nightmare.

Instead of blood and death, his dreams were filled with her smile and the warmth of her body. In those dreams, he stripped her bare and tasted every inch of her before taking her. Instead of waking with a scream trapped in his throat, he awoke aching for more.

He'd been about to rise and pad down the hall to knock on her door, but as he was contemplating going to her, Brokk woke up.

After that, he couldn't leave his brother's side.

However, his hunger for her was growing, and he didn't know how much longer he could deny himself. He didn't understand *why* he was restraining himself. The only reason he could come up with was that he believed her to be innocent. If he moved too fast, he might scare her away.

He'd never done slow before, but he could if it meant getting her in his bed, where she belonged.

He read for a bit, but he watched her more. Finally, he gave up and lowered his book. "What's your favorite music, Lexi?"

He'd learned a lot about her yesterday, but he was eager to learn more.

She set her book down as she met his gaze. "I love the songs the pixies create and rock music like Five Finger Death Punch and Disturbed. What about you?"

"I enjoy pixie songs and Creedence Clearwater Revival."

"Oh, they are good," she agreed.

He spent the rest of the morning alternating between checking on Brokk and learning more about her. The clock was striking twelve when she rose from her chair and stretched.

"I have some work I have to do in the gardens. Is there anything I can get you before I go?" she asked.

He buried his disappointment; if he had his way, she'd never do menial labor again, but it was not his place to get involved in her life. Unless it resulted in getting her in his bed. An image of Del rose in his mind, but he pushed it away. His friend was dead, and his daughter was an adult who could make her own decisions.

"No, and I know where the kitchen is if I do need something," he said.

She smiled at him before leaving the room. It felt emptier without her, and he didn't like it. Rising from the chair, he took his book upstairs and returned to Brokk.

~

THE NEXT MORNING, Lexi found herself staring at the clock more than her book as she waited for Cole. When the clock struck nine and he still didn't arrive, she began to fear he wouldn't come today.

She squelched her disappointment and kept reading, but she couldn't concentrate on the words. At nine thirty, she almost shouted with joy when he strode into the room and smiled at her.

And then she cursed herself for being an idiot. *He's a dark fae!*

The reminder should have doused some of her excitement; it didn't. It was difficult to keep her distance when she was growing to like him more and more with every passing day.

Freshly showered, his hair was still damp and tousled as he ran his fingers through it. She'd found a few more articles of clothing for him and had given them to him last night, but none fit him properly. The shirt was far too tight through his shoulders and chest, and the pants stopped a couple of inches above his ankles.

On anyone else, the clothes would have looked ridiculous, but he somehow managed to wear them with a sexy confidence that was entirely too tempting. Her mouth went dry as he plopped into the other chair and sprawled out his tall, powerful form.

"Good morning," he greeted.

"Good morning," she replied. "How's Brokk?"

"Better. Sahira came in a little bit ago to put a new salve on him, and he stayed awake throughout it. He's talking, he's fed more, and he's healing. I think he'll be back to normal in a couple of days."

"That's good."

She was glad to hear that, but she dreaded the day he left. She enjoyed talking to him, and he brought a bit of excitement to an otherwise dull and, she was beginning to realize, rather lonely life.

She glanced at the book in his hand, but she already knew he was now on book three when she discovered it missing from the shelf this morning. He must have come down sometime last night to get the book. Deciding to leave him to Harry Potter, she opted for a little bit of horror and chose a book of short stories instead.

"You're enjoying the books," she said and waved at the book in his hand.

Cole glanced at it. "Far more than I thought I would."

"Good."

"That Snape guy is an asshole."

Lexi laughed. "Oh, just wait."

He smiled as he settled into the chair, and when they lapsed into a comfortable silence, she returned to her book. When he got up to check on Brokk an hour later, she finished her book and rose from the chair.

She returned the book to its place on the shelves and clasped her hands behind her back as she circled the room in search of her next read. She scanned the numerous spines until she landed on *Jaws*.

She'd read it a couple of times, but it had been a few years, and she was in the mood to revisit an old favorite. Standing on tiptoe, she stretched for the book. Her fingers had just brushed the spine when she felt Cole against her back.

CHAPTER THIRTY-SEVEN

SHE HADN'T HEARD him return, and it had been days since they last touched, but she would never forget the exquisite sensation of his body against hers or the way he could turn her bones to liquid.

"I'll get that for you," he murmured.

It took everything she had not to lean back into him as she dropped down from her tiptoes. When his hand settled possessively on her hip, it sent a shiver down her spine. He plucked the book from the shelf and handed it to her.

When she took it from him, their fingers brushed and a fiery spark shot through her. Her legs trembled, and she was afraid her knees might give out. Instead of stepping away, the hand on her hip pulled her back and nestled her against his chest.

"*Jaws*," he murmured as he turned the book over in front of her. "One of my favorites."

His breath stirred her hair, and he lowered his head until his lips nearly brushed her ear. Despite knowing she should keep her distance from this man, she'd dreamt about his kiss often and wanted another one.

She shouldn't do it, but she found herself lifting her head and turning toward him. Her eyes held his as his hand slid from her hip to her belly. His muscles bunched around her, and when he growled, his eyes shifted to silver.

The abrupt color change, and what it represented, astounded her, but before she could react, his head bent and his mouth claimed hers. And there was no doubt it was a claiming kiss as it was relentless, possessive, and so demanding the only thing she could do was yield to it.

When her mouth opened and his tongue swept in, the book slid from her fingers. It thudded against the floor. She wanted to turn and wrap her arms around him, but he held her so firmly against him that it was impossible to move.

Then his hand slid beneath her shirt, brushed against her skin, and caused her knees to shake. His touch left her desperate for more.

Each caress of his fingers and stroke of his tongue awakened something inside her that she'd never known existed. She knew what it was like to wake aching from dreams, and she'd satisfied that with her fingers, but she could never douse this hunger with anything less than *him*.

Was this what it was like to be shadow kissed? The possibility should terrify her, but she couldn't bring herself to care as his fingers skimmed up her belly and across the bottom of her bra before his thumb circled her nipple.

When her knees gave out, his other arm cinched around her waist, and he held her up as he touched her more intimately than anyone ever had before.

She wanted—no, she *needed* more.

This time, when she tried to turn, he let her. She moaned when his hand fell away from her breast, but then he gripped her hips and lifted her off the ground without breaking the kiss. Her legs instinctively encircled his waist, and the rigid evidence of his erection rubbed between her thighs.

She clung to him as he braced one hand against the shelves while his other hand cupped her ass. Her pulse raced as every part of her became centered on him. It felt as if the very fabric of her being was shifting and becoming something different, something more alive and *free*.

She'd never expected to feel this way, but she relished the freedom, abandon, and carefreeness she'd never experienced before.

Over the years, she'd read countless romance novels and seen more than a few love scenes in movies and on TV, but she'd never expected this all-encompassing yearning for another.

Her fingers sliding down the front of his chest pushed aside buttons until her hands met his flesh. Beneath her palms, his skin was hot, and she felt the solid, thundering beat of his heart. When her nails scraped his flesh, he nipped her bottom lip with fangs he didn't have only seconds ago.

Only when he first arrived and was out of control with his terror for Brokk had she seen his fangs and silver eyes. Those two things were signs a lycan was losing control, and a lycan on the verge of losing control was extremely dangerous, but his slipping composure only excited her more.

She didn't know what that said about her, and right now, she didn't care.

When he bit her lip again, she mewled and wiggled against him. She stopped caring that he was part dark fae or that he would probably feed on her and break her heart if she wasn't careful; she just wanted more of him.

CHAPTER THIRTY-EIGHT

BEFORE SHE COULD EXPERIENCE that more, a heavy round of knocking reverberated throughout the manor. A tingle of annoyance shot through her, but she ignored it, just as she ignored the knocking.

Her fingers entangled in his hair, and the kiss deepened. When her fingers brushed over the tips of his ears, he groaned. She loved the feel of the point beneath her fingers, and if his response was any indication, he enjoyed it too.

When another round of knocking sounded, she couldn't ignore it anymore.

She reluctantly tore her mouth away from his, and Cole's hands tightened on her. Lowering his head, he kissed her neck before sliding lower to her collarbone.

The heat of his mouth caused Lexi to shiver, but another round of knocking dampened her lust. Like a bucket of ice water was dumped on her head, reality returned.

She'd been about to give herself to a *dark fae* in *her* library. With the doors open, Sahira could have walked in at any time, and Lexi could end up one of the many mindless, shadow kissed souls if she wasn't careful.

The hairs on her nape rose at the possibility. She liked him, but not enough to become one of *them*.

The knocking grew louder and more incessant. The last time someone sounding more than a little annoyed was pounding on her front door, Cole arrived with a half-dead Brokk in his arms.

Now, she had no idea who stood on the other side of her door, but it didn't sound good.

Releasing his hair, she rested her hands on his shoulders and unlocked her legs from around his waist. She slid down the front of him.

The friction between them created a new firestorm in her body. Her legs wobbled when her toes touched the ground, and she almost jumped back into his arms.

"Ignore them," he whispered in her ear before he nipped her lobe.

She wanted to do exactly that, but Sahira had to walk past the library doors to answer the door, and her aunt couldn't find them like this. At the possibility of such a thing happening, her cheeks started to burn.

"I can't," she said.

His arms locked around her, and for a second, she didn't think he was going to release her. Then he let her go and stepped back.

Lexi's eyes widened as she took him in. His silver eyes burned like hot coals, his fangs were clearly visible behind the lips flattened into a thin, white line, and his shoulders hunched forward in a way that said he was straining to retain control.

She recalled some of the horror stories she'd heard about lycans who lost control. They became beasts that shredded everything in their path and tore through their victims like they were no more than pieces of paper instead of flesh and bone.

She didn't think he would hurt her, but she didn't dare move. And then, she spotted that cipher near his temple again.

Something about her rattled not only his control over the lycan part of him but also the dark fae. She didn't know if she should relish that knowledge or be terrified of it.

Either way, she became aware that the power Cole revealed to the world was only the tip of the iceberg. Far more of it thrummed beneath his surface.

Enthralled by him, Lexi almost jumped when another series of loud knocks bounced off the walls.

"I have to get that," she said and was happy when her voice didn't tremble.

Cole stepped further away from her, but when his gaze swung toward the library doors and his lips skimmed back, she worried he might attack whoever had arrived.

Lexi gulped, but she couldn't let the knock go unanswered, and she couldn't let Sahira find them like this. They weren't touching anymore, but her aunt would know something had happened.

Lexi straightened her shirt and threw back her shoulders. He started to reach for her, but his hand stopped and hovered in midair before falling to his side. They stared at each other before Lexi edged away from him and started for the doors.

She almost glanced at the fireplace but stopped herself before she did. It couldn't be Orin at her door. He was probably growing increasingly angry at her for not returning to him, but he was still safely tucked beneath the manor.

Or she assumed he was. When she hadn't returned, he might have gotten pissed off enough to leave, but she doubted he would risk capture by coming to her front door afterward. At least she hoped he wasn't that stupid.

~

COLE INHALED a shuddery breath as he strained to regain control of himself. He was no longer just battling the lycan part of himself but also the hungry dark fae. It had been over a week since he last satisfied his dark fae urges.

He hadn't gone this long since childhood, and he hadn't realized how ravenous he was until now. As he stared at the wall of books and willed his erection away, he tried to recall when he last fed.

He didn't remember the woman, but that was nothing new; he didn't remember most of them. The rare few made return appearances in his bed, and it was never because he wanted more of them, but because they ran in the same circles, like Becca.

But as Cole recalled the last time he fed, he realized it was before meeting *her*. His head swiveled to watch Lexi as she glided toward the doors, and his softening erection stirred again.

Shit, he sucked a breath in through his teeth and fisted his hands. His nails dug into his palms as he willed himself to let her go.

Not only was he hungry, but every part of him craved her, and it was only a matter of time before he had her. He would *not* be denied much longer.

He rested his hand against the shelf as she vanished into the hall, but another round of knocking, and not being able to see her anymore, spurred him into motion.

She was at the door when he stepped into the hallway. From the corner of his eye, he saw Sahira emerging from the hall leading to the kitchen. She was wiping her hands on a dishtowel as she walked. When her eyes met his, he saw the concern in them as she stopped a few feet away.

Lexi cracked the door open, but she didn't open it enough for him to see who stood on the other side. However, a familiar scent caused his hackles to rise.

"Elexiandra," Malakai purred from the other side of the door.

Sahira stiffened, and when he glanced at her again, he saw a hardness that had never been there before. Not even when she was warning him away from Lexi had she looked so tense. Her chin jutted out as her eyes met his again.

She gave a subtle nod of her head toward the door. Cole didn't need her to tell him to intervene in this, he already planned to do so, but it astounded him that she found him less of a threat to Lexi than Malakai.

He hurried to intervene.

CHAPTER THIRTY-NINE

LEXI'S HAND tightened on the door as Malakai rested his hand on the frame and leaned toward her. His brown eyes burned with an intensity that made her stomach churn. A cruel maliciousness burned in those eyes as he smiled at her.

It took everything she had not to step away from him, but she managed to hold her ground. The unraveling control of the dark fae prince made her a little uneasy, but Cole never made her skin crawl like Malakai did.

Malakai was smiling at her, in complete control of himself, and couldn't make her one of the shadow kissed, but he was far more of a menace to her than Cole.

For one thing, Malakai wanted to marry her and rule over her life and lands. She'd rather be tied behind a horse and dragged naked over a field of glass before being dumped in a vat of rubbing alcohol than have such a thing happen, but staying free of him could become the biggest battle of her life.

She had a feeling he would make that life miserable until he got his way.

"Malakai," she greeted flatly.

His eyes fell to her lips and narrowed. She almost touched

them but stopped herself. Now that he'd drawn her attention to them, she realized how swollen Cole's kisses had left her mouth.

"Is there something I can help you with?" she asked.

"I came by to speak with you about something. I thought we could take a walk."

Lexi glanced at the sun and then the amulet at his throat. *What did he do to earn it?*

Knowing Malakai, it was something awful. She inwardly recoiled from him even as she remained standing where she was. He unnerved her more than a child speaking in tongues, but if she revealed that to him, he would use it to his advantage.

She suspected he knew he unnerved her, and he *liked* it.

"I'm too busy for a walk," she said. "I'm sorry you wasted your time coming here."

She started to shut the door, but he threw out his hand to keep it open. Leaning closer, his grin revealed all his perfect white teeth, but it didn't reach his eyes.

If the eyes were the window to the soul, then Malakai's soul was more rotten than meat left out in the summer sun for weeks on end.

"I'm sure you can spare a few minutes of your time, Elexiandra. I have some very important things to speak with you about," he said.

She suspected some of those important things were marriage, and she was *not* in the mood to deal with that. Even before Cole entered her life, she was determined not to bind herself to this man. But now that she knew what it was like to desire another so completely and *like* them, she would never agree to marry Malakai.

Unfortunately, she might not have a choice.

"I can't, Malakai," she said. "You've come at a bad time."

A flash of red ran through Malakai's eyes before he managed to suppress it. Whereas the signs of Cole losing control excited her, this loss of restraint from Malakai caused her blood to run cold. Cole wouldn't destroy her life; Malakai would.

"I have to go," she said and tried to close the door again, but he refused to remove his hand.

He leaned closer as he hissed. "I'm not playing, Elexiandra."

"Neither am I," she grated out as she glared at him.

Yes, he terrified her, and he might force her into a loveless and most likely brutal marriage, but she would *not* let him push her around. She would not give in to him without a fight.

"Please leave," she said.

This time when his eyes flashed red, Lexi braced herself for him to lash out at her, but before he could hit her, an arm enveloped her waist. Cole tugged at the door, and she released it to him.

As he opened the door further, he pulled her possessively against his chest. His posture was casual, but hostility coursed through his coiled muscles.

Malakai rose away from her and his mouth parted before he closed it. Then he gave her a scathing look as his lip curled in disgust.

Lexi's shoulders went back, and her chin lifted defiantly. Getting involved with a dark fae was a *stupid* decision, but she decided to make it, and she wasn't going to be judged for it by this asshole.

"What's going on here?" Cole inquired.

"I've come to speak with Elexiandra," Malakai said in a clipped tone.

"As she said, she's busy right now."

Lexi glanced between the two men. Out of the two of them, there was no doubt who was more powerful, but Malakai was not the type to fight fair.

When Malakai's attention shifted back to her, there was no denying the loathing in his eyes. "I'll be back soon."

Cole's fingers tightened on her hip, and before she could reply, Malakai vanished. She stood staring at the spot where he'd been before Cole guided her back and closed the door.

"That should keep him away for a while," Cole said.

"He'll be back," Lexi muttered. "He always comes back, except he'll be pissed off next time, and you won't be here."

Needing to be alone, Lexi shrugged out of his hold and backed away from him. Cole reached for her, but she dodged his hand and hurried down the hall as she resisted running.

There was nowhere for her to go, and she didn't know who she was running from, Malakai, Cole, or herself and her shitty decisions.

As she strode down the hall, she spotted Sahira standing in the shadows next to the stairs. Sahira opened her mouth to say something, but whatever she saw on Lexi's face silenced her.

She didn't say a word to her aunt as she went up the stairs to her room.

CHAPTER FORTY

COLE FOLLOWED Lexi for a few feet before stopping to watch as she disappeared into the hallway above. She'd purposely avoided him, and she needed some time alone. In truth, so did he as the echo of her words continued in his head.

When the click of her door closing sounded a few seconds later, his attention shifted to Sahira. She stood with her shoulders slumped forward and her eyes closed.

"How bad is it with him?" he asked her.

Sahira opened her eyes and met his gaze. "He won't stop until he gets what he wants."

"And that's Lexi."

"Lexi, the manor, and the land. He intends to marry her."

Cole felt like she'd kicked him in the nuts. Not only could he not stand the idea of Lexi as Malakai's wife, but he couldn't imagine her married to that asshole. Malakai would destroy her.

However, Malakai must want her and everything she offered badly if he was willing to marry her for it. Marriage was sacred to immortals, and it was rare when something other than death severed the bond.

"He's been asking for her hand in marriage since she was fourteen," Sahira continued. "Her father always refused him."

"Fourteen? She was only a child."

"She was beautiful, even then."

"I'm sure she was, but immortals don't marry for beauty or lust."

"Malakai's different. His property abuts ours, and not only does he want her, but he's also after both lands."

"And when Del refused to let them marry, she became an obsession to him."

"When Del refused to let her be his *concubine*, she became an obsession," Sahira corrected.

"He wanted to take her as a concubine at fourteen?"

"Yes. He later offered marriage, but my brother was *not* going to let that happen."

Cole's claws lengthened and retracted as he glanced over his shoulder at the closed door. He'd never liked Malakai, but now he despised the man even more.

"And now that Del is gone, he thinks it's open season on her," Sahira said. "And nothing is going to stop him."

"I will."

Sahira laughed mirthlessly and rolled her eyes. "And *why* would you do that?"

Why *would* he do that? He wanted and liked Lexi, but why involve himself in her life? He'd never given a single fuck about any of the other women he'd desired before.

Lexi wasn't like those other women. For one thing, her father had been his friend and co-conspirator against the Lord. He was a man Cole respected, and he could not forget Del's love for his daughter or the fact they were friends.

Cole kept his gaze focused on the front door as he recalled the red in Malakai's eyes and the hatred on his face. Malakai coveted Lexi, but he also despised her.

Her father had turned him down—*she'd* turned him down and

became the one thing he couldn't have. If he ever got his hands on her, he would destroy her for that.

"Del was my friend, and I can't forget that. We saved each other's lives many times during the war, and I won't leave his daughter unprotected," Cole told Sahira.

There was more to it than that, but he wasn't in the mood to figure it out. Cole stalked away from the door and started up the stairs. He'd only traversed a couple of them before Sahira spoke again.

"And who is going to protect her from *you*?"

He stopped walking, and his head turned toward her. When he met her steely gaze, Cole glowered at her, but the witch didn't back down.

Turning away, he stalked up the stairs. When he arrived at the top, he spotted Brokk leaning against the doorway of his room. Cole's step faltered at the sight of his brother's sweat-streaked face.

"Who indeed, brother?" Brokk inquired.

Cole's shock faded as he scowled at his brother. "What are you doing out of bed?"

"Who could sleep with all that pounding?"

Cole strode toward him, and clasping his arm, he swung it around his shoulders and supported Brokk's weight as he steered him into the room. "You shouldn't be up."

"I had to make sure someone wasn't coming to kill us," Brokk muttered as he let Cole lead him back to the bed.

Cole lowered his arm from his shoulders and sat him on the edge of the mattress. Brokk fell back with a groan. Grasping his legs, Cole swung them into the bed.

"I'm not an invalid," Brokk protested, but as he pushed himself up to rest his back against the bed, he winced and lifted his arm to wipe the sweat from his brow.

"You're barely any better," Cole muttered as he jerked the blankets over his brother.

"I'm doing a lot better."

"Yes, you managed to stand today. You're doing fucking fantastic."

Cole ignored the finger Brokk gave him.

"What game are you playing with the girl?" Brokk asked when Cole finished getting him settled.

Cole sat in the chair he'd become far too familiar with over the past few days. "I'm not playing any game with her."

Brokk winced as he pushed himself further into a seated position. "I heard your conversation with Sahira. We're not exactly known to do things out of the kindness of our hearts, but I've never known you to play with an innocent's head."

"I'm not playing with her head."

"She's young, and we both know she's inexperienced. She's led a sheltered life here."

"How can you say that when you barely know her?"

"I know she's an innocent, and so do you. I remember how Del talked about her and how he kept her protected from the worst of the realms. He was our friend, and she doesn't know how to handle creatures like Malakai or us. You've never been one to take advantage of that, so what game are you playing, Cole?"

Cole gripped the ends of the chair. "I told you, I'm not playing any game. I owe it to Del and her to keep her safe, and I plan to do exactly that. They took us in here, and they kept you alive; I will repay that debt."

Brokk's head fell back and hit the headboard with a small thud. "It's a debt I'll repay too, and she is beautiful. They both are."

"Stay away from Lexi," Cole warned.

Brokk lifted his head and met his gaze, but his brother was smart enough to keep his mouth shut.

CHAPTER FORTY-ONE

LEXI POKED her head into Brokk's room and was pleased to discover him sitting up with his back against the headboard and a book on his lap. When he looked up at her, he smiled as she stepped into the room.

"How are you feeling?" she asked.

He laid the book down as she approached the bed. Though he remained paler than normal, his eyes were bright, and the color had returned to his handsome face. His blond hair was disheveled, and he could probably use a shower, but he was on the road to recovery, which meant he and Cole would leave soon.

Lexi pushed aside the pang of disappointment accompanying the realization as she stopped next to his bed. She would miss Cole, which meant she was an idiot who allowed herself to get too attached to a dark fae.

"I'm much better," Brokk said. "Thank you for taking me in."

She waved away his gratitude. "Anyone would have done the same."

"No, they wouldn't, and we both know that."

His aqua eyes perused her from head to toe, but she didn't

sense any sexual interest from him. However, the intensity of his gaze made her shift uncomfortably.

"Can I get you anything?" she asked.

"No, I'm good," he said.

"We have a TV downstairs, and the electricity is working right now; I can bring it up so you can watch it. There aren't many channels left, but sometimes they air something decent."

"I'm good. Cole gave me this book to read." He held up the first Harry Potter book for her to see. "Have you read this?"

Lexi bit back a laugh as she stared at the cover. "A few times."

"It's really good."

This time, she couldn't stop herself from chuckling. "I told your brother the same thing."

And he'd liked it enough to recommend it to his brother, which meant she'd turned him into a Potter groupie. Now she had someone to discuss the books with as Sahira refused to read books about wizards. She claimed she had enough witches and warlocks to deal with without reading about them.

"I can't tell you the number of times Cole has been wrong over the years, but he wasn't wrong about this," Brokk said.

"He may have been wrong a lot over the years, but *I'm* always right," she said.

Brokk laughed. "Over the years, I've learned most women are always right."

Lexi glanced around the room, but there was nowhere for Cole to hide in here. She couldn't stop herself from asking. "Where is Cole?"

"He decided against spending another night sleeping on the chair, so he's settling into the guestroom you gave him."

Lexi clasped her hands before her. "Are you sure you don't need anything?"

"Some company," he said and waved at the chair. "My brother's not exactly a barrel full of laughs."

She strode around the bed and settled into the chair Cole often occupied. "I'm not sure I'll be much better."

"You have to be better than a pissy lycan with the arrogance of a dark fae."

A burst of laughter escaped her. "You're right; I'm a lot better than that."

"I thought so," Brokk said. "So, Elexiandra—"

"Call me Lexi."

"So, Lexi, has my brother been driving you crazy?"

She leaned back in the chair. One of his brothers had infuriated her, but she couldn't tell him that. The other one had been.... Well, she wasn't entirely sure what Cole had been doing to her, but yes, he was making her a little crazy.

"It's been nice to have some company," she admitted. With his dazzling smile and twinkling eyes, Brokk was incredibly easy to talk to. "Though I wish you'd come here under better circum-stances."

"So do I."

His eyes ran over her, and he studied her with that strange intensity again, but she still sensed only curiosity from him. Unlike Cole and Orin, he was easy-going, which was odd considering he'd nearly died.

"It looks like you'll be good to go soon," she said.

"I should, but I don't think Cole's in any rush."

Her forehead furrowed, but before she could respond, Cole stepped into the room. His massive frame took up most of the doorframe as he gazed at them with an expression she couldn't quite figure out. He looked annoyed but also amused and a little shocked.

Then his gaze settled on her and a sexy smile curved his lips. Butterflies erupted in her stomach as that smile warmed her to her soul. Yes, she was an idiot who had allowed herself to get too close to a dark fae, and she was going to miss him when he left.

"Cole!" Brokk greeted loudly. "We were just talking about you."

Lexi tried to suppress the blush creeping up her neck and into her cheeks, but she failed. She'd been hoping Cole hadn't heard their conversation, but Brokk was happy to inform him that he was their topic.

A steel edge settled into Cole's eyes when they flicked to his brother. "I heard."

Lexi rose from the chair. "I should go. Are you sure you don't need anything?" she asked Brokk.

"No, thank you."

She strode around the bed and toward the doorway, but Cole didn't move out of her way. Her step slowed as she approached him. Memories of what passed between them in the library flooded her, and her mouth went dry.

If he didn't move, she'd either be stuck in this room with them or forced to squeeze past him. And if Lexi touched him again, she might kiss him, and if she did, she didn't know if she would stop.

"You don't have to rush off on my account," Cole said as his gaze raked over her.

Her step faltered. "I'm not."

Though she was.

After the library events, and then with Malakai, she wasn't entirely sure what to do about him. She couldn't deny she was coming to like and even care for him, but if she allowed herself to get closer to him, it would only lead to heartache, and her heart had been battered enough this year.

And since they were leaving soon, she had to put some distance between them.

～

COLE RELUCTANTLY STEPPED out of her way so she could pass. She glanced at him, but her gaze fell to the floor as she slipped by him. The blush warming her cheeks was endearing and adorable.

It took all he had not to clasp her wrist and halt her, but he didn't move as she left the room. Stepping back, he watched the sway of her hips as she strolled down the hall and descended the steps.

When she was gone, he turned his attention back to his brother, who grinned at him. When Cole scowled at him, the smile slid from Brokk's face.

"I'm warning you, Brokk, don't fuck with her."

Brokk pushed himself up higher on the bed. "Unlike you, brother, I have no intention of doing so."

"I'm not fucking with her," Cole said.

"Maybe not, but it's obvious you desire her. And not only is she an innocent, but she's a good person, and I like her. Del was also our friend, and I don't want to see his daughter hurt."

"That's not going to happen."

"You're part dark fae, Cole. It's what the fae do."

"You're as much dark fae as I am."

"I didn't say I wasn't, but I'm also not trying to screw our host. So, in that sense, I'm less dark fae than you while we're here."

"I'm not trying to *screw* her," Cole said.

"Yes, you are. You can deny it, but we both know the truth. It's what the dark fae do. But this time, before you act, take a look at what you're leaving in your wake."

"You nearly died, but I'll still beat the shit out of you."

Brokk laughed as he lifted his book. "You could try, but we both know you love me too much to mar the perfection that is me."

Normally, Brokk's arrogance made Cole smile, but as his gaze returned to where he last saw Lexi, he didn't feel much like smiling. What did he want from her?

No doubt, he planned to have her in his bed, but what would the aftermath be for her? She was an innocent; he couldn't deny that. After hundreds of years, he knew how to spot one, but so what?

She wouldn't be the first woman whose innocence he took, and she wouldn't be the last. Something inside him recoiled at the idea of taking another woman to his bed, but he was dark fae, and that was what they did.

It's what he'd done his entire life, but even after he moved on, he would make sure she stayed safe from Malakai.

"I'm enjoying this book," Brokk said.

"I told you it was good," Cole muttered as his attention shifted back to his brother.

"These witches and wizards are much more likable than our witches and warlocks, though."

This time, Cole did laugh. "That they are."

CHAPTER FORTY-TWO

THE HOWLING wind rattling her windows woke Lexi. She blinked into the darkness before rolling over to stare at the night pressing against the glass.

Rain plastered the window as the wind blew it against the panes and whipped it across the land. Normally, she loved the sounds of a storm, but there was something about this storm that made her feel lonely. It was as if the world beyond that window had ceased to exist and only she remained.

Pushing aside her blankets, she rose and walked over to the glass. She rested her fingers against the cool surface as a rolling wave of thunder built to a crescendo that shook the manor. In the distance, lightning pierced the earth.

Electricity crackled the air as more bolts illuminated the scorched earth beyond the glass. The broken and barren landscape didn't help her feel less alone in the world. She turned away from the window.

She eyed her bed, but sleep would elude her for as long as the storm raged. She grabbed her robe—her adult one—pulled it on, and tied it. Leaving her room behind, she padded down the hall to find something to munch on while watching the storm.

She was almost to the end of the hall when a muffled shout halted her. Straining to hear over the rain beating against the roof and the howling wind, she listened for another sound but didn't hear anything.

Had she imagined it? Did the storm create the noise?

Turning, her eyes fell on Brokk's door, and she crept toward it. Had he experienced a setback?

Her hand fell on the knob, and she hesitated before starting to turn it. She didn't want to knock and risk waking him if he was sleeping, but she couldn't just walk in there.

When the thunder faded away again, another muffled shout sounded, and she realized it wasn't coming from Brokk's room. She retreated from his door and retraced her steps down the hall until she stood outside the room she'd given to Cole.

She rested her hand on the knob but didn't turn it. When another muffled shout started seconds before another clap of thunder boomed through the night, she knew she couldn't walk away without checking on him first. For all she knew, someone had broken into the manor and was attacking him.

That possibility speared her into motion, and before she could think about it anymore, she turned the knob and inched the door open. If someone was attacking him, then she couldn't alert them to her presence.

The element of surprise was her biggest advantage here. And if no one was in the room with him, then she didn't want to wake him.

When the door opened enough for her to see into the room, she realized he was alone. Flashes of lightning revealed the small dresser, fireplace, and bathroom door across from the king-sized bed. Dark blue curtains framed the windows.

On the bed, Cole lay entangled in the dark blue comforter. His face was turned away from her, and his hands were twisted into the sheets. The corded muscles of his arms and neck stood starkly out.

Black ciphers ran from the tips of his fingers, up his arms, across his shoulders, and a few of the flames licked at his chin. She couldn't tell if they went down his back, but there weren't any on his chest.

When his head turned toward her, Lexi prepared to bolt. She was about to be caught entering his room. However, when his eyes remained closed, she realized he was having a nightmare.

Some of her tension eased, and she started to retreat, but a muffled sound of anguish stopped her. She'd heard sounds like that coming from wounded animals before, and it tore at her heart.

She couldn't walk away from any creature in distress, let alone *Cole*.

Knowing she was playing with fire, she stepped away from the door and closed it behind her. She stared at it for a second before taking a deep breath, gathering her courage, and cautiously approaching the bed.

Uncertain of what to do, she stood beside him as thunder boomed and lightning illuminated the room. This close to him, she couldn't help but marvel over the power he emanated.

He was nearly twice her size, and though he was also a half-breed, he was a combination of two of the most powerful immortal creatures in existence. His half-breed status made him *more* powerful, unlike her.

Her human half made her weaker; she was immortal, and she was faster and stronger than any human, but she didn't possess the same strength as a full-blooded vampire. She couldn't even transport.

When he thrashed on the bed and his head twisted away, Lexi buried her trepidation and stretched a hand toward him. A bolt struck right outside the manor; its electricity caused the hair on her nape to rise at the same time her fingers met his flesh.

She wasn't sure if it was the electricity pulsing through the room or the contact with him, but her entire body tingled and her heart raced. She didn't have time to figure it out before his eyes flew open, his hand seized her wrist, and he jerked her forward.

Before she had a chance to react, he pinned her beneath him, and his hand was enclosing on her throat. Then her air cut off.

CHAPTER FORTY-THREE

THE THUNDEROUS BOOM of the dragons ravaging the earth reverberated around Cole. He was swept up in a sea of death, surrounded by enemies, and hacking his way through their bodies as he sought to destroy the adversaries closing in on him.

Why couldn't they all die? And where were they all coming from?

Blood coated his hair, slid down his face, and plastered his clothes to him. Those clothes weighed him down, but he continued to hack and carve and slaughter his way through the immortals surrounding him.

The stench of blood clogged his nose as it caked his nostrils. Breathing through his mouth was the only option, and when he did, he inhaled blood until it coated his tongue.

He spit the blood out, but it filled his mouth faster than he could rid himself of it. The dragons released another wave of fire upon the world. Their flames leapt so high that shadows of fire danced across the land until it looked like a black inferno was spreading toward them.

One of his enemies grasped his sword hand, and spinning

toward the faceless beast, Cole seized its throat and smashed it into the ground.

The roar of dragons and the pulse of blood filled his ears as his hand tightened on his enemy's throat. Their fists battered him, but he barely felt the blows as blood dripped from his hair and splashed onto his victim.

The punches hit him harder; his victim squirmed beneath him, but he kept them pinned as he sought to destroy them. *I will not let them win.*

He bared down as his faceless victim shifted and blurred. He glimpsed red hair as the smell of strawberries pierced through the stench of blood. Cole blinked to clear his mind of the image, but the woman... no, *Lexi* didn't go away.

A fist hit him square in the jaw. It snapped his head back at the same time it knocked away the remaining dregs of his nightmare and threw him back into reality.

He wasn't strangling some nameless opponent; he was strangling... *Lexi!*

With a shout, he threw himself away from her and rolled across the bed. Her wheezing, choking sounds followed him. Even more than the blood and death of the war, he knew those sounds would haunt him for the rest of his days.

"Fuck, fuck, *FUCK!*" he snarled as he launched to his feet.

Turning back toward her, he watched as she rolled across the bed and slid off the other side with a hand on her throat. He didn't recall moving, but suddenly he was around the bed and going toward her as she huddled against the wall. Her fingers touched her temple before pulling away.

He spotted a red lump on her forehead along with what looked like a bit of silver. He glanced at the bed frame; she must have hit her head on it when she fell off the bed. She rubbed at the mark, and the silver vanished, but the lump remained.

When she saw him coming, she held out her palm to stop him.

The wild beat of her heart and the pungent stench of her terror froze him.

"Shit, Lexi. *Shit!* I didn't.... I wasn't.... I didn't mean to hurt you. I would never...."

His next words froze in his mouth. Cole couldn't say he would never harm her when he just had, but he hadn't meant to.

Kneeling in front of her, he ached to draw her into his arms as her striking green eyes studied him warily. He didn't reach for her and instead rested his fingers on the ground.

"I would never hurt you on purpose," he said.

He'd cut off his hand before he ever hurt her on purpose, but that hand had also left red welts along the delicate column of her throat. When he leaned closer to her, she shied away from him, and he recoiled.

"And who is going to protect her from you?"

"Who indeed, brother?"

Sahira and Brokk's words ran through his mind as he gazed at her. He'd promised to keep her safe from Malakai, but *he* was the one who did this to her.

He slammed his hand onto the floor. "Fuck!"

Her eyes widened, but she didn't recoil from him again; even still, more waves of self-hatred swamped him. He should be trying to calm her; he was making things worse.

"Lexi," he whispered. "I'm sorry. I didn't mean to.... I would never do this to you on purpose. I swear, I would *never* do this on purpose. I...." He glanced at the windows as a crashing wave of thunder shook the house.

His nightmare rushed back to him; only it wasn't a nightmare. At one time, it was as real as the storm raging outside. He'd stood, covered in blood, on that field. The thick liquid had clogged his nose and filled his mouth as he hacked his way through so many.

When the falling bodies littered the field, he climbed over the growing mound they created. He lost himself to the bloodlust as he sought to survive, but he didn't let the lycan part of himself take control.

He relied on his fae magic, superior strength, and fighting skills to carry him through the battle. However, knowing she was in danger—even if *he* was the threat—caused the beast to prowl beneath the surface. His claws scraped the wooden floor as they lengthened and retracted.

"It won't happen again," he said as he edged away from her. He'd make sure Malakai stayed away from her, but so would he. "You should go."

But he didn't want her to leave. He'd give anything to shelter her from the world as he lost himself to her kiss again.

She would chase away the nightmares, he was sure of it, but in the process, he might become *her* biggest nightmare. He refused to let that happen.

"What... what were you dreaming about?" she whispered in a hoarse voice.

The rawness of her voice made him wince, and he crept further away. His fangs extended as his teeth ground together.

If anyone else had dared to do this to her, he would have torn them to shreds, but he couldn't destroy himself... no matter how badly he wanted to.

"It doesn't matter," he said.

"It does matter," she whispered.

"No, it doesn't."

He rose, and when her eyes became saucers that latched onto his waist, he recalled his nudity.

CHAPTER FORTY-FOUR

LEXI FORGOT about her sore throat as she took him in. The thick wall of carved muscle was so deep across his stomach she could dip a fingertip into the hollows they created. A trail of black hair ran down from his belly button, and when she looked....

Her jaw almost became unhinged as she took in all *of* him. She should look away, but her attention remained riveted on the limp cock resting against his thigh.

She'd never seen a naked man before, and it was as fascinating as it was startling. Her hand fell away from her throat as she tried to process everything she was seeing.

It was rude to stare, but she remained riveted on him. And then her gaze traveled lower to his thighs and legs as he stood with his feet braced apart. Despite her every intention not to look again, her gaze returned to his dick before he turned away.

She found herself staring at his taut ass and wondering what it would feel like to grip it in her hands before he moved out of view. Once he was gone, the fire burned up her neck and face.

She'd been openly ogling him, and he'd seen her do it. What was the matter with her? He'd just been choking her, and she was pondering what it would be like to grab his ass.

The lack of oxygen to her brain had caused some damage.

Resting her hand against the wall, she took a deep breath and steadied the tremble in her legs before rising. As much as she'd love to remain huddled on the floor, she couldn't do it.

However, she had to walk around the bed and in front of him to leave the room. She wasn't sure her shaky legs would carry her that far.

As she waited to make sure she wouldn't make an ass out of herself by falling on her face, she turned to discover him sitting on the other side of the bed with his hands on his knees.

More ciphers ran across his shoulder blades and down his back, where they stopped at the edge of his waist. He had far more of the markings than she'd realized.

How powerful is he?

Her attention was drawn away from the markings as his shoulders hunched forward and his head bowed. Misery radiated from him. If it wasn't for her throbbing throat and the panic still thrumming through her, she would have climbed onto the bed, hugged him, and offered him some solace.

When she considered doing that, she flashed to him on top of her as his hand clamped around her throat. His mouth had twisted into a snarl that revealed his four fangs as she beat against him.

When his eyes flew open, she'd seen savagery, the likes of which she'd never witnessed before, in their silver depths. She'd also seen an emptiness that turned her blood to ice.

Before, when he looked at her, she always felt seen. But when he was choking her, he looked straight through her to something else. She'd realized he could kill her without knowing it was her.

Her struggles had increased, and she'd beat against him, but it hadn't lessened his hold. It wasn't until she landed a blow that shot his head back that he emerged from the grip of whatever controlled him.

She saw the clearing in his eyes and the devastation on his face when he realized what he was doing before he released her.

And now, she saw the dejected despair enshrouding him. Whatever he'd been dreaming about, it still haunted him, and so did his actions.

Still, she couldn't stay here. He'd nearly killed her.

Her gaze traveled to the doorway as she edged around the bed. She couldn't bring herself to look at him as she compelled herself not to run for the door.

He'd leave tomorrow. She did not doubt it. Even if Brokk weren't ready for travel, he would go after the events of this night.

She ignored the sadness accompanying this realization. It would be better if he left. They should stop this treacherous game they played, but she didn't want him to go.

She told herself she wouldn't look back, but when her hand fell on the knob, she couldn't stop her gaze from returning to him. His shoulders tensed as another round of thunder boomed throughout the room.

Darkness descended before lightning illuminated the room in a series of flashes. She recalled listening to the dragons as they ravaged the land. They sounded like this, and their fire had flashed over the walls the same way the lightning did.

Then she recalled his reaction when she asked him if the war was horrible. She remembered his hesitation before speaking and the anguish on his face.

It had been the look of a man who had committed and experienced atrocities she could never imagine. It had been the look of a man who hadn't been broken by those atrocities, but they had forever altered him.

She hadn't known Cole before the war, but she had no doubt he wasn't the same man now as he was then.

How could he be?

He'd lost most of his family during the war and more than a few friends.

Her hand fell away from the knob as he remained sitting with his shoulders hunched forward, his head bowed, and his hands gripping his knees. He'd terrified her tonight, but she couldn't bring herself to walk away from him while he was like this.

After Orin, she should have learned her lesson about trying to help others, especially the dark fae, but she found herself creeping toward him. Her mind screamed at her to run; this was a bad idea, but her heart and her feet propelled her onward.

He wasn't Orin. He wasn't an asshole who would turn on her like a rabid dog.

This was Cole. This was the man she'd spent the past few days getting to know better as they shared books and discussed their lives. This was the man who made her feel alive every time he touched her.

She briefly contemplated those who became shadow kissed before pushing them aside. It was a fear for a different time. This moment was only for them.

She would have asked him again what he was dreaming about when he attacked her, but she already knew the answer. He was lost to the nightmare of war, and she so badly wanted to find him.

When she stopped before him, his shoulders tensed as if he expected a blow and his hands tightened on his knees.

Unsure of what to do, she remained where she was. She'd been so certain while crossing the room, but now doubt wiggled its way in to fester at her mind.

He was a powerful, immortal being who was well versed in all the realms, and she was... well, she was *her*. She lived and worked on her small manor, her life revolved around her family, and she'd only ever left the mortal realm once in her life.

What could she possibly offer him?

Lightning flashed around the room again, and when he lifted his head, his silver eyes met hers. In his gaze, she saw such a mixture of distress and hope that melted her doubts.

He was the most powerful being she'd ever encountered, yet there was something broken about him, something she longed to heal. She wasn't entirely sure how to do that, but some instinctive part of her told her she could.

She was a simple, not-so-powerful immortal, but she could offer him exactly what he needed.... She could help him heal.

When she cupped his cheek in her palm, his beard rubbed against her skin.

"Go, Lexi," he said gruffly.

Instead of going, she lifted his face and bent to kiss him. For a second, she worried he would turn away, but he didn't. Instead, his mouth was a grim, flat line against hers as he remained unmoving on the bed.

She'd made a mistake; she was making a fool of herself. She'd overestimated their connection, and he was about to pull away, laugh at her, and tell her to get out. He would remember her as the stupid fool who had been a game while he waited for his brother to heal.

If he remembered her at all.

The possibility he was toying with her had never occurred to her before. He was dark fae, but he'd come across as extremely honest.

She'd believed the passion behind his kisses and touch was real and not part of some game he was playing to pass the time. However, as he remained unmoving against her, she couldn't help thinking she'd made a gigantic mistake.

She was starting to pull away when his arms encircled her waist. She had no time to react before he pulled her between his thighs. His hand slid up her back, his lips melted against hers, and he took possession of her mouth.

All possibility of making a huge mistake vanished when his tongue stroked her lips. It slipped inside her mouth, where it created a firestorm inside her.

Her fingers bit into his thick shoulders as he kissed her with a desperation she'd never experienced from him. His need for her was evident in every thrust of his tongue and the way his arms cinched around her.

He wasn't going to let her go, and he wouldn't be satisfied with a kiss this time. She'd known that as she crossed the room to him, but it hadn't sunk into her conscious thoughts until now.

When she released the doorknob and returned to him, she'd known she was making a decision she could never take back. That she was walking a path she'd never walked before, and it could lead her straight off a cliff.

He would most likely break her heart, but at least she would get to experience that part of life. She would at least know what it was like to have him hold her and feel his body moving against hers.

His hand slid up her back to her nape before rising to entangle in her hair. Apprehension coiled inside her. He was so different from her, so much more experienced, and so sure of everything, while she was fumbling her way blindly forward.

When she returned to him, she'd hoped to keep him from drowning in a sea of memories and despair while trying to experience more of life. She was completely out of her depth here, but when his other hand slid down to cup her ass, some of her trepidation vanished as desire bloomed.

CHAPTER FORTY-FIVE

HE SHOULD PUSH her away and order her to run. He'd nearly killed her tonight, but now that she was in his arms, he wasn't going to let her go.

Refusing to let her go made him a selfish prick, but he wouldn't part from her. He'd always been a selfish prick, and he wasn't about to change when he was holding the biggest temptation he'd ever encountered in his arms.

He pushed aside her robe and his hand bunched in her T-shirt as he pulled it up. When he slid his hand down to cup her ass again, his cock became rock-hard as his fingers traced the lacy edge of her underwear.

He slid his fingers over those edges before tugging her underwear down to cup her firm ass. She was so right and beautiful, and he couldn't believe he was holding her. After what he'd done to her tonight, she should hate him, but instead, she'd come to him.

Growing frustrated with her underwear, he carefully sliced them from her silken skin, and the ruined material fell to the floor. Sensing her uncertainty, he cupped her ass again before sliding his hand down and between her legs.

He would keep her so aroused she wouldn't have a chance to

change her mind. She gasped as she swayed toward him. His fingers slipped between her thighs and touched upon the wetness spreading between her legs.

He'd considered himself hard before, but now his dick throbbed with its need for release. Plucking her from the ground, he lifted her and settled her on his lap.

He could be inside her in seconds, something he wanted more than his next breath, but he didn't take her. Instead, he planned to cherish every bit of her and this moment before entering her.

By the time he finished teasing her, she would be mindless and panting with need. When he finally did enter her, he would ensure the pain of her first time was minimal.

He teased her clit until she trembled against him. He teased her until her legs were trembling around him.

Rising from the bed, he broke the kiss while he lifted her. She locked her legs around his waist and clung to him as their eyes met.

The hunter and emerald green mixture of hers had darkened, and her pupils were dilated. Her lips, swollen from his kisses, were as lush as her. She licked them as her gaze fell to his mouth.

"You should run, Lexi," he said.

He didn't know where the words came from; he certainly hadn't expected to utter them, but he had to give her one last chance to leave. She had to realize that once he possessed her, he would never let her go.

It had been a while since he fed, and the fae was hungry, though he wouldn't take from her tonight. Tonight, it would be about her.

For the first time in his life, he planned to deny himself. The realization would have been shocking, but he was far too lost in her to absorb it fully.

When her beautiful green eyes continued to hold his, he didn't see any sign of her changing her mind. There was apprehension in her gaze, but it wasn't of him. How she didn't fear him, he didn't know, but it only made him care for her more.

And he did care for her, he realized with a start. He didn't want to protect her because she was Del's daughter; he wanted to protect her because she was *his*.

Excitement pulsed through him at the realization. She was his, and he was *not* going to let her go.

He squeezed her ass before turning to lay her on the bed. When he set her down and stepped back to gaze at her, her eyes fell to his erection.

He thought she might change her mind and bolt then, but she bit her lip and looked to him again. Her fangs had extended until the sharp points showed over her bottom lip.

With tender care, he traced the tip of one of those fangs, and when it pricked his thumb, he ran the blood across her lips. When her tongue darted out to taste his blood, a spark of hunger flared in her eyes.

He smiled as he pulled the robe from her before gripping the bottom of her T-shirt and sliding it up to reveal her belly. Tugging it higher, he exposed her pert breasts before pulling the shirt from her.

He tossed the clothing aside and gazed down at her. She was long and lean, and her time working on the manor had toned her body. However, she still possessed shapely thighs and luscious curves that begged to be explored. And he was more than eager to do exactly that.

His mouth watered as he climbed onto the bed beside her and cupped one of her breasts. It filled his palm and spilled over a little as he ran his thumb around her nipple before bending to suck it into his mouth.

Her fingers entwined in his hair, and she pulled him closer. He ran his other hand down her stomach. It slipped between her legs where he rubbed her clit before dipping a finger into her. She arched beneath him as he turned his mouth to her other breast.

Her hips rocked as she fucked his hand until her breath came faster. Releasing her breast, he lifted his head to gaze at her as her head fell back.

While she was so focused on the pleasure he gave her, he slipped another finger into her. He stretched her further in preparation for his invasion when it came.

As she rode his hand, he drank in the beautiful sight of her while he pushed her closer and closer to orgasm. When she came apart, he muffled her cry with his kiss as the walls of her sheath contracted around his fingers.

He broke the kiss and leaned back to savor her beauty as her eyes fluttered open. A sexy smile curved her swollen lips while the lightning bolts illuminated her sun-kissed, silken skin and exquisite beauty.

She was the most stunning woman he'd ever seen, and she was *his*. The wolf within him bellowed this knowledge over and over again.

Always the more subtle part of himself, he wasn't used to having the primal lycan part of himself seeking to take control, but it had been asserting its dominance since she walked into his life.

He had no idea what would happen if the beast broke free, but he was willing to find out if it meant making her his.

∽

LEXI FLOATED on a haze of passion as Cole remained kneeling beside her with a look of wonder and something more on his face. She couldn't quite place what that something more was —confusion, disbelief, a dawning understanding that seemed out of place —but when his silver eyes met hers, the wildness in them made her breath catch.

He was magnificent, powerful, and on the verge of losing control. After what transpired earlier, and her still sore throat, that should frighten her. However, when his fingers skimmed her belly and the tips of his claws grazed her skin, she felt no fear of him.

He'd been lost to a nightmare earlier—no, not a nightmare, he was trapped in a memory when she tried to wake him. He was with her completely now. And he would never physically harm her while awake.

He might end up breaking her heart, but that would be her fault as much as his. She'd walked into this knowing what he was, yet she was still here.

"You should have run, Lexi," he said in a gravelly voice distorted by his fangs.

She probably should have run, but she hadn't, and she was glad. There was nowhere else she'd rather be.

Gripping her legs, he shifted until he knelt between them. When he leaned over her, the thick wall of his muscle and the heat of his body encompassed her. He propped his hands beside her head as he held himself over her.

His silver eyes flickered, and for a second, she was staring into their Persian blue depths again. There was something so open and honest about that gaze, something so vulnerable it dug its way into her heart, and though her heart might end up shattered, she would never run from him.

And then the blue was gone and the silver was back. She ran her fingers over his high cheekbones as he lifted one hand and grasped his shaft to guide it into her. The head of it parted her and pushed inside.

Biting her lip, she kept her attention focused on him as sweat dampened his skin and the powerful muscles surrounding her vibrated with his barely leashed restraint. As he moved deeper into her, she tried to ignore the discomfort their joining created.

And just when she believed he was going to bury himself inside her, he stopped moving and put his hand beside her head again. They stared at each other before he bent and reclaimed her lips.

The tender caress of his tongue was so different than his demanding kisses earlier that she didn't know how to respond at first, but when his tongue entwined with hers, Lexi relaxed beneath him.

Her arms slid up to wrap around his shoulders, and she pulled him closer. She marveled at the differences between them. He was so unyielding and massive.

He made her feel small and fragile but also cherished and safe as his thumb rubbed her cheek and the tenderness of his kiss dug its way deeper into her heart.

Her fingers bit into his back, and as she adjusted to having him partially inside her, she lifted her hips invitingly toward him. She wouldn't accept anything less than all of him.

CHAPTER FORTY-SIX

WHEN SHE RELAXED BENEATH HIM, Cole pushed past the barrier of her virginity and buried himself deep inside her. She stiffened as her fingers bit into his back.

He continued to kiss her and tried to get her to relax again by stroking her flesh while her tight sheath gripped his shaft. The lycan part of him demanded to take possession of her, claim her, and own her.

It craved her with a savagery he could never unleash. If it broke free, he would hurt her, and he could never do that again.

However, the demand of the lycan was so strong that the ravenous, dark fae part of him ceded control to the lycan, something it had never done before.

And that cessation of control caused the lycan's need to grow. It wanted to mark every part of her as it claimed her completely.

He labored to control his more savage urges as he remained unmoving within her. If he did to her what his instincts screamed at him to do, not only might he possibly destroy her, but he would also terrify her.

He couldn't let himself go, but he could relish every second of their time together, and he planned to do exactly that as he slid a hand under her ass and lifted it to give him better access. Her fingers entwined in his hair as he started moving within her.

Her body yielded to his as she relaxed further and gave herself completely over to him. She was so supple, so beautiful, and so amazingly *right* in his arms.

Yes, she was his, and no matter what happened, he was never going to let her go.

His cock swelled as he resisted sinking his fangs into his mate.

Mate!

The realization didn't hit him over the head like a hammer. In fact, it wasn't as astounding as it should have been. Because the dark fae part of him had always been the more dominant one, he'd never expected to encounter his mate.

Yet, here she was in his arms, and the lycan had taken control for the first time in his life. And it felt as natural as the rain beating against the windows. She belonged in his arms, and he would do everything in his power to keep her there.

Growling, he thrust into her. He kept the worst of his impulses leashed as the wolf savored the exquisite pleasure of its mate.

∼

ONCE THE PAIN FADED, all Lexi felt was the joy of their joining and the awe of being with him. She'd never known life could offer such an amazing experience as this, and she couldn't get enough of it.

He enveloped her in his arms, and lifting her off the bed, he braced his knees apart as he kept her embedded on him. Wrapping her legs around his waist, she cleaved to him while he guided her up and down his shaft.

Something started to build within her. She recognized the pressure, the excitement, and *need* of a building orgasm, but this was so much more intense than anything she'd experienced before.

She clung to him as the scent of allspice and something musky enveloped her. She buried her face in his neck as the pressure building within her released. Her back bowed as waves of ecstasy crashed through her.

She stifled her cries against his neck as the very fabric of her splintered apart until she was only pieces of the woman she once was. And as those pieces started to reform themselves, she realized she would never be the same again.

～

WHEN HER SHEATH clenched around his shaft and she cried out against his flesh, Cole wrapped his hand around her neck. A tingle ran down his spine, and he came with a shout that the storm drowned out.

He held her as she went limp in his arms while more lightning illuminated the room. He watched the flashes as he cradled her and suppressed the pacing, irate lycan denied its full claim and the famished fae stirring to life.

He'd never come so hard in his life, but he wasn't completely fulfilled. He hadn't claimed his mate, and he wouldn't until he discussed it with her. She was not a lycan; she wouldn't feel the call of the mate bond like he did.

She was part vampire, and they had fated consorts. She might feel the call of that, but he couldn't consider that while he was grappling to control his darker nature.

Keeping himself restrained was easier to do when her naked body was flush against his. It didn't matter that he wanted more; she was with him, which was enough for now.

Laying her back on the bed, he gazed down at her exquisite body as he kissed her again and slowly withdrew from her. He'd already started to harden again when he pulled out; she wasn't ready for that.

There would be plenty of other nights where he would take her over and over again; he would make sure of it. This would not be one of those nights as she needed time to heal.

She groaned in disappointment when he pulled out of her, and he kissed her again.

CHAPTER FORTY-SEVEN

COLE HELD her closer as Lexi nestled against his chest. Thunder continued to roll, but he no longer heard the sounds of battle.

Instead, all he felt was a sense of peace as the rain plastered the windows and the wind howled across the land. This peace was something he'd never experienced before in his life. For the first time, he felt content and settled, and so happy he couldn't stop grinning.

His entire life, the dark fae had dominated the lycan part of him, but now that Lexi was in his arms, he realized the lycan was making itself known more than he realized.

The dark fae had dominated power-wise, but he hadn't realized the incessant, churning emptiness within him could be silenced. He'd always assumed that was what drove the dark fae from one partner to the next, but now, it was gone, and he now knew it had been coming from the lycan part of him.

She'd calmed that loneliness.

It was not completely silenced; the lycan still clamored to claim her to be completely pacified, but it was quieter and more content, and it would stop completely once he officially made her his.

But that could wait. She was just learning the ways of a man and woman; he would not tell her about his intentions to claim her for all eternity yet. He would do it soon, but for now, he intended for her to enjoy what was developing between them without any added pressure.

As he held her, he recalled watching as she wandered into the moon room. The luna flowers had reacted to her as if she were part lycan; they must have sensed she was his mate before he did. They'd been seeking to welcome her because they'd known she would become an integral part of his life.

He held her closer as he kissed the top of her head. The sweet scent of strawberries filled his nose and further calmed the lycan. The dark fae was still hungry, but it could also wait.

He wouldn't feed on her without her permission, and even if she didn't give it, there wouldn't be any other women for him.

~

LEXI FLOATED on a haze of euphoria as she remained cradled safely in his arms. She'd never felt so protected or cherished before. She wasn't sure how long this feeling would last as he would eventually move on, but she was completely content to enjoy it for now.

The solid beat of his heart beneath her ear caused her to smile. She caressed the wall of muscle as she ran her fingers across his chest. She'd never dreamed of experiencing such a rush of pleasure or such wondrous contentment afterward.

She never wanted to leave this bed or his arms.

But reality was returning, and so was the realization she was wading into dangerous territory. She'd told herself not to develop feelings for him, but it was already too late. Even if it resulted in a shattered heart, she would ride this adventure to the end.

Was this what it was like to be shadow kissed? The possibility made her mouth go dry. She *couldn't* become like one of them.

"Cole?" she whispered.

"Yes?" he asked as he twirled a strand of her hair around his finger.

"Will I become one of the shadow kissed?"

His hand stilled on her hair. "No."

"Are you sure?" She lifted her head so she could look up at him. "I don't want to be one of them. I know…." She gulped. "I know it's what the dark fae sometimes do, and I… I… can't be one of them."

"Then you won't be. The shadow kissed are like that because it's what *they* crave. Yes, the dark fae help guide them there, but the choice is theirs to make. Some let the dark fae feed on them and go on with their lives, and others seek more. Instead of shutting those cravings down, they search out more and more until it consumes them."

She pondered this as she tapped her fingers on his chest. "So, it's like some humans with their drugs?"

"Yes."

After what she'd experienced with him, she could see how easy it would be to become consumed by the need for more. She'd hate to walk away from him, but she would choose that over being shadow kissed.

"So, I won't become one of them?"

"Not unless you allow it," he murmured as he nuzzled her temple with his lips. "The shadow kissed have to let us corrupt them. As long as you don't allow it, you'll be fine."

He could be lying to her and playing one of the dark fae games, but she didn't think so. She wouldn't fool herself into believing he was a kind, compassionate man, but he wasn't a liar.

"Okay," she said.

She stifled a yawn and her eyes closed. She was starting to doze when she recalled what happened earlier. They flew open again. She felt safe in his arms, but he was awake now.

What would happen if he fell asleep again?

That dose of cold reality smothered some of her happiness, but she refused to let it ruin the joy she'd discovered in him. The rain ticked against the glass as it pelted the windows.

He shifted to pull the blankets more securely around her. "You should sleep."

"I'm okay," she murmured as she stifled a yawn.

He clasped her hand and stilled it against his chest before kissing her head and her cheek. She warmed to the tender gesture and lifted her mouth to his.

When Brokk was better, he would leave, and she might never see him again. Until then, she planned to enjoy every second of what little time they had together.

She started to melt into him again when he pulled away and kissed the tip of her nose.

"Rest," he commanded and tipped his head back to rest it against the headboard.

She tilted her head up to take in the vast expanse of his chest and dark ciphers. She traced his markings before her hand fell onto his stomach and her eyes closed again. Another clap of thunder caused them to fly open once more.

If he fell asleep and the thunder caused him to dream of the war again, what would happen?

CHAPTER FORTY-EIGHT

WHEN HER LASHES fluttered open to tickle his chest again, Cole realized what was keeping her awake... fear. He ground his teeth together as self-hatred swelled within him. The last thing he wanted was for her to be nervous around him, but he couldn't blame her for being wary.

"Go to sleep, Lexi. I'll stay awake," he promised.

"I'm not that tired," she murmured.

"Yes, you are. Get some rest, and I'll keep watch."

"That's not fair," she protested.

"You're safe with me, and I'm going to make sure you stay that way. Rest."

He ran his fingers through her thick, silken hair and let it cascade across his chest as he marveled at the different shades of red within the striking color. When he glided his fingers down her back, he delighted in the small shiver it elicited from her.

"You have to rest too," she said.

"I'm fine," he said.

He let her hair fall, settled a hand on her ass, and gave it a small squeeze. His cock stirred again, but his concern for her shoved aside his growing lust. She was *not* ready for what he desired to do to her again.

$$\backsim$$

Lexi rested her hands on his chest and started to rise. She hated leaving the security of his arms, but she couldn't stay here if it meant he spent the rest of the night sitting up, awake, in the dark.

His bright blue eyes met hers as his hand returned to her hair. He brushed it away from her temple before cupping her nape.

"You're beautiful," he whispered.

Lexi thrilled at his words as he kissed her again and pulled away. She almost moaned in disappointment but managed to stifle it.

"And you're extremely handsome." The words were out of her mouth before she realized she was about to say them. She hated the blush burning across her cheeks.

He grinned at her. "I'm glad you think so. Now, are you going to sleep or not?"

"I should return to my room. You need to sleep."

His arms locked around her, and he pulled her firmly against his chest. "No. I want you to stay with me far more than I want to sleep."

"But—"

"I want you to stay here... unless you'd prefer to go."

"No, I wouldn't."

"Then relax and stay here with me. I promise you'll be safe."

"I know I will."

And she *did* know that. Despite what happened earlier, she trusted him not to hurt her again.

$$\backsim$$

COLE HELD her firmly against his chest as she rested her head on him once more. Her thick lashes tickled his skin as her eyes closed. This time, they didn't open again.

He held her close as he listened to the rain. A dull throbbing in his jaw drew his attention to it. He rubbed it absently as he recalled the blow that propelled him out of his nightmare. He smiled; his mate packed one hell of a punch.

Her body relaxed against him, and her breathing slowed as sleep claimed her. Even after what happened earlier, she trusted him, and he would do whatever it took to make sure he earned her trust.

He might never sleep again, but it would be worth it if it meant he got to hold her every night. Because, if he had his way, she would be in his bed every night for the rest of eternity.

CHAPTER FORTY-NINE

LEXI SPENT most of the next morning walking around in a haze of euphoria. She finally understood what someone meant when they said they were walking on cloud nine as she turned the horses loose and cleaned the stalls.

She fully expected that cloud to burst sometime soon, but for now, she was content to ride it.

When she returned to the house, she showered and changed before going to the kitchen to make her breakfast. Thankfully, Sahira was nowhere around.

She couldn't handle her aunt's questions right now, and she knew they would come as she couldn't get rid of the stupid grin on her face.

After eating her breakfast, she went to the library and settled on her chair to read. Her gaze kept traveling to the fireplace. She'd done a good job at shoving Orin out of her mind, but after last night, she couldn't deny the guilt nagging at her.

Orin was a complete asshole, but she didn't want to see anything bad happen to him. However, after last night, she couldn't help but feel guilty over harboring him beneath her home. Cole and Brokk were hunting him, and she knew where he was.

Not for much longer. The first chance she got, she was going to get him out of her tunnels, and she didn't care if he wanted to go or not. He didn't have a choice anymore.

Or maybe she'd get lucky and he'd find his way out. He was probably pretty pissed she hadn't returned yet. Until she got the chance to kick him out, she would have to deal with her guilt over keeping this from Cole.

She did so by ignoring it.

Almost an hour passed before Cole entered the room, closed the doors behind him, and strode toward her. It was the first time he'd shut them, and it would draw attention to them, but she didn't care as he prowled toward her in his too-small clothes and bare feet.

There was something almost feral about him as he approached. Her heart picked up, and her skin prickled as her body responded to the hunger he emanated.

He stopped before her and, with tender care, slid his arms under her and lifted her from the chair. He settled her on his lap as he sat on the chair. The intimate, possessive gesture surprised her.

She didn't know what she'd expected from him today, but now that he'd settled her across his legs, with his arms around her, she realized a part of her had worried he'd pretend the whole thing never happened or ignore her.

She wasn't sure which one of those things would be more painful.

He'd been dressed and about to leave the room when she woke this morning. He bent to kiss her and told her he was going to check on Brokk before leaving. Things had been normal, even sweet, but she still hadn't known what to expect from him.

"How are you feeling?" he asked as he lifted a strand of her damp hair and twirled it around his finger.

"Happy," she admitted.

Maybe it was wrong to be so honest with him—dark fae

weren't known to care about other's feelings—but he'd asked, and that was more than she would have expected from a dark fae.

When he smiled at her, the twinkle in his eyes made her heart do a strange little stutter before melting. It wasn't fair that he was so damn irresistible.

"How are *you* feeling?" she asked.

"Happy," he replied.

Lexi's mouth parted at this admission. Was he happy because of *her*?

She didn't dare ask him.

Then his smile faded as his eyes fell to her neck and the faint bruises marring her skin. They were fading as she healed, but his fingers trembled when he rested them against the marks. At least the welt on her head was gone.

"This will never happen again," he vowed.

"You were dreaming about the war, weren't you?" she asked.

She held her breath as she waited for his reply. Would he admit the truth or deny it, or maybe she was wrong completely and something else had pushed him to such a point last night.

"Yes," he said.

"Do you dream about it often?"

His eyes met and held hers as he replied. "Not since coming here."

"Why not?"

"Who knows."

She suspected he knew, but she didn't push him on it. He'd been far more open with her than she'd ever expected, and she wasn't going to take the chance of him shutting down.

"The thunder and lightning must have set the nightmares off last night," he said as he stroked the bruises on her neck.

"I'm fine," she assured him when self-loathing filled his gaze.

His fingers stilled on her. "Are you sore?"

"No, I told you already; the bruises are almost gone."

"I didn't mean here." He tapped her neck before running his

fingers down her breasts. He skimmed her belly and slid his hand between her legs. She gasped when he cupped her. "I meant *here*."

It took her a minute to sputter a response as fire burned her cheeks. "I was earlier, but not anymore."

"Good," he said as he caressed her through her jeans.

Lexi lost herself to his touch until she was panting and her body begged for release. Undoing her jeans, she helped slide them down her thighs, and she kicked them off with her feet.

Leaning back, his eyes turned to silver when they latched on to her lacy, purple underwear. She'd selected the sheer pair in the hopes he would like them. It was obvious he did as he tugged them off.

She shouldn't let this happen here, but she couldn't bring herself to stop it. When he tugged her shirt up, she lifted her arms as he pulled it over her head. He smiled when he saw her bra matched her underwear.

"The doors," she managed to pant out when he removed her from his lap and settled her on the chair before kissing her belly.

"I locked them," he said as he left a trail of kisses across her skin.

A shiver ran through her when she realized this was what he anticipated when he entered the room. Making his way steadily lower, he slid off the chair and knelt on the rug. He grasped her legs and spun her toward him.

She didn't know what he intended until he slid her legs over his shoulders. She started to pull away, but he gripped her ass and held her in place. His eyes burned as they met hers.

"I've imagined tasting you since the moment I saw you," he said.

Her eyes widened at this revelation, and before she could protest, he lowered his mouth to her core. At first, she was so stunned, she couldn't react.

And then his tongue delved deep inside her. She remained rigid for a few seconds, but his tongue melted any of her uncertainty about such an act.

Forgetting all about her shyness, her fingers entwined in his hair as she pulled him closer. His short beard rubbed the inside of her thighs in the most delicious of ways. He kept one hand on her ass while the other roamed up her body to cup one of her breasts.

Lexi arched into him as his mouth and hand worked their magic over her body. Her heels dug into his back, and her fingers gripped his ears as he brought her to climax. She bit her bottom lip to stifle her cries.

She was still floating on a cloud of bliss when he lowered her legs from his shoulders and rose. With deft movements, he quickly shed his clothes.

Though she'd seen all of him last night, she still couldn't get over how powerful and large he was. Gripping her hips, he shifted her on the chair and turned her, so her hands rested on the chair arm.

Lexi wasn't entirely sure what he intended until he stepped behind her and lifted her hips. His dick slid inside, and he buried himself deep within her. Unlike last night, her body swiftly adjusted to having him inside her.

Her fingers bit into the thick cushion of the overstuffed armchair as he introduced her to this new position. There was something so thrilling about having him behind her, controlling her, and demanding more that it aroused her even more.

As he pulled slowly out of her before thrusting deep again, she closed her eyes and gave herself over to him. He guided her hips as her breasts swayed, and his movements became more demanding.

"Fuck," he groaned. "You're so fucking hot and tight, and you're *mine*."

That last word caused her eyes to fly open, but as her mind scrambled to understand what he meant, he reached around to cup her breast with one hand while the other slid between her legs. She forgot all about her shock at his words as he caressed her clit.

Her back bowed, and her head fell back as she came again. Cole plunged into her once more before shuddering. She felt the pulse of his cock as he released his seed.

He sagged against her and pressed his cheek to her back before kissing the hollow between her shoulder blades. His mouth and tongue left a trail of heat down her body as he moved steadily lower.

With tender care, he pulled out of her and shifted his hold so he could slide onto the chair. He pulled her onto his lap once more. She curled up against his chest and rested her head on his shoulder. Beneath her hand, his heart raced.

"That was… nice," she murmured.

His laughter startled her. She lifted her head to take him in as his chest rumbled and his blue eyes twinkled in amusement.

"You might be the death of me, and the best you can say is 'that was nice.'"

"The death of you?" she asked.

"Yes, but what a fantastic way to go."

"Very true," she agreed, and he laughed again. She nestled against him again as his arms enveloped her. "I'm not on…."

Damn it, she was starting to blush again. She tried to suppress the heat scorching her cheeks and failed miserably.

If she was going to have sex, then she was going to discuss these things without blushing. She told herself this, but it didn't change anything as her face burned.

"I'm not on any kind of birth control," she muttered.

"I am."

She lifted her head again. "You are?"

"Yes. I get a potion from a warlock that I take once a month." There was no amusement on his face or in his eyes as he gazed solemnly at her. "I won't leave a trail of children behind me."

She gulped. *A trail of children.* She was concerned about the possibility of *one* child, and he was concerned with having many of them… with numerous women.

This realization doused some of her contentment. *He's a dark fae!*

She would be only one of many to him, and she had to keep reminding herself of this. While she was lost in a sea of happiness, he would move on and probably never recall his time here.

Sorrow bloomed in her chest, but she pushed it aside. She could mourn the loss of what she'd discovered here when he was gone, but she wouldn't turn into a melancholy mess while he was still here.

"Have you fed from me?" she asked as she decided to change to subject.

"You would know if I had, and I wouldn't do it without your permission."

She frowned at him. "Aren't you hungry?"

"Yes, but you're just starting to learn the pleasure a man and woman can give each other. I'm not going to add my need to feed into the mix. That will come in time."

"In time?"

"Yes, we have plenty of it."

"You think Brokk will have to stay here for a lot longer?"

"No, I think he'll be ready to leave tomorrow, and I'll escort him back to the Gloaming, but I will return." And then his eyes narrowed on her. "Unless you would prefer it if I didn't come back."

"Of course not!" she blurted before she could stop herself. "But...."

Her words trailed off as she tried to think of what to say.

"But?" he prodded.

"But you're dark fae."

"I'm also lycan and man."

"What does that mean?"

"It means that I'm *coming back*."

He stated this with such authority that she didn't know how to respond. She'd never allowed herself to entertain the possibility he might decide to stay, but she couldn't help feeling doubtful.

"For how long?" she asked.

CHAPTER FIFTY

COLE BURIED his irritation over her disbelief. He knew the reputation of the dark fae—it was well-deserved and earned, but that wasn't who *he* was.

But wasn't it? It's who he'd always been, who he'd always planned to be... until she walked into his life.

It wasn't who he was anymore, and he hated her doubt in him.

When he saw the uncertainty in her gaze, his annoyance faded. She wasn't asking him these things because she wanted him to leave. She was asking because she was afraid.

"What are you afraid of, Lexi?" he asked.

Her mouth parted, and her eyes darted away from him. "I'm not... I'm not sure what you want from me."

"I want *you*. I thought I'd made that pretty clear."

"But for how long?"

Her words were like a punch to his gut. He wasn't going to leave her, and he needed to make that clear. But before he could respond, a knock rattled the doors.

"Lexi!" Sahira called in a voice tinged with panic. "Lexi, are you in there?"

"Yes," she said.

An oof of air escaped him when she planted her hand on his stomach and pushed herself up.

"Sorry," she muttered as she scrambled out of his lap.

He almost pulled her back as he missed holding her, but she'd already scurried away from him. Cole rose as Lexi hastily tugged on her clothes.

He hated this interruption, but he started to dress too. Something about Sahira's tone didn't sit well with him. He was pulling on his jeans when a thunderous boom shook the earth.

Lexi released a startled cry and staggered to the side when the boom quaked the house. He caught her hand and steadied her before she toppled over the chair. Her eyes flew to his as a growl swelled within him.

He didn't know what was going on, but he would destroy it if it threatened her.

He tugged his jeans on but ignored his shirt as he stalked toward the doors. He glanced back to make sure Lexi was dressed before he unlocked and opened the doors. Sahira took a startled step back as her gaze roamed over his chest.

There was no doubt about what transpired between them inside that room, and he was glad of that. Sahira didn't want him to be a part of Lexi's life, but she didn't have a choice, and she would learn that.

He turned back to Lexi as she hurried toward them, straightening her shirt. She kept her eyes averted from Sahira's as her cheeks burned. He stretched a hand back to her as another boom quaked the house.

When a sound like the earth being torn apart reverberated through the air, he grabbed Lexi's arm and pulled her against his side. The blush vanished from her face, and her skin paled when she looked at him.

"What is going on?" he demanded of Sahira as he embraced Lexi protectively against him.

Sahira's shocked expression vanished as she gave him a steely look. Beneath her fury, he saw a flash of unease before she covered it up.

"Dragons," she said.

An uneasy feeling coiled in his stomach as another boom rattled the windows, and from somewhere in the manor, glass shattered. Sahira turned and strode toward the front door as the shrieking bellow of a dragon rent the air.

"Shit," he snarled.

He wanted to push Lexi back into the library and shelter her from whatever was happening, but he wouldn't part from her. Instead, he kept her tucked against him as they followed Sahira outside.

The sun beat down on them, the sky was a crystalline blue, and the serenity of the day was broken only by the birds filling the sky. Another bellow drown out the cries of those birds.

He didn't see any of the monstrous creatures until they turned the corner of the manor and one of the beasts soared into view. It swept low over the land with its fifty-foot wings spread wide, its head extended, and its tail out behind it.

The sun glinted off its red scales as a plume of fire erupted from its mouth and it rained destruction on the land. Chunks of earth flew up as it plowed a ditch into the fire-scorched ground. Pieces of wood shot into the air as trees and the marketplace's ramshackle buildings toppled beneath its onslaught.

When its fire went out, the dragon soared high into the sky. The sun created a glow around its wings as it hovered in the air.

Then it roared and dove toward the earth. Another wave of fire erupted from it. The marketplace was half a mile away, but Cole's position allowed him to see that nothing remained of it.

"No!" Lexi gasped.

She jerked free of his arms and lunged forward. She ran toward the road as Sahira started after her. Cole caught her before she made it ten feet. He pressed her against his chest as she struggled in his grasp.

"There's nothing you can do," he told her.

"But... but... they didn't do anything!" she protested as tears shone in her eyes. "It's killing them, and they didn't do anything!"

He despised her tears and the heaving breaths shaking her slender frame, but he couldn't do anything to stop this. Not yet, anyway. But one day, he would end this.

He cradled her while the smoke rising from the burning remains choked out the sun. He didn't care about the mortals and immortals at the market, he was tired of senseless violence, but their lives weren't important.

What he cared about was what would happen if the Lord continued to unleash such destruction on Earth. Eventually, he would run out of things to destroy and turn his insanity on the Shadow Realms, including the Gloaming.

And Cole did care about immortals there. He'd already lost most of his family; he would *not* lose any more of them.

He also had Lexi to protect now. And no matter what he had to do, he would keep her safe.

"It doesn't matter if they did something or not," he said.

And that was completely true. It didn't matter if the humans and immortals at the marketplace were innocent; if the Lord deemed them a threat, he would destroy them.

"Holy shit," Brokk breathed as he arrived beside him. "What is going on?"

No one answered him; there was no reason to reply. He could see what was happening with his own two eyes.

The dragon released another roar before turning and swooping toward them. Cole held Lexi against his chest, but there wasn't enough time to turn and flee with her. If the dragon decided to unleash its wrath on them, they couldn't stop it.

∿

LEXI DUCKED a little as the gigantic beast soared toward them. The beat of its wings kicked dirt up from the ground and fanned the flames of the marketplace fire as the screams of the wounded and dying filled the air.

So *many* wounded and dying. So *many* faces she knew. And they were burning.

She tried not to vomit as the scent of burning flesh mingled with the burning wood and earth stench. Her heart thumped a little faster, her mouth went dry, and she gripped Cole's arms as she tried not to cower.

If it unleashed a wave of fire on them, they'd be crisp fried as soon as it hit them. And then the dragon soared over the top of them.

Despite its formidable power and the death it just unleashed, something was captivating about the ruthless beast. When it twisted to the side, the sun's angle turned its scales the color of blood.

She tried not to be awed by the thing, but she couldn't stop her mouth from parting as she gazed at its underbelly. It was *huge*! It blocked the sky until it was all she could see.

When it flapped its wings, the wind it created blew her hair back from her face and plastered her clothes to her. Dirt swirled around them until the cascade of particles briefly blocked out the underbelly of the beast.

By the time the dust settled, the dragon was past them. She turned to track its movements as from one second to the next it vanished.

"Where did it go?" she breathed.

"It returned to Dragonia," Sahira said.

Lexi stared at where it had vanished before shifting her attention back to the ravaged marketplace. People and immortals crowded the road as they fled the destruction, but there were a lot less of them than there should have been.

"We have to help them," she said.

CHAPTER FIFTY-ONE

COLE STUDIED the smoldering remains of the marketplace as he leaned his hand against the windowsill. The full moon was the only illumination over the ruined land.

In the dark of night, the glowing coals of the torched buildings looked like the eyes of some beast lying in wait to spring its trap. But then, that trap had already sprung.

He'd mistakenly believed that once the Lord won the war, he would stop unleashing his dragons. Cole hadn't expected the insane man's ruthless determination to wipe out anyone he perceived as an enemy.

The breeze drifting across the land carried with it the stench of fire and the faint aroma of burnt flesh. He started to close the window against the stench when a crow flitted down to perch on the sill.

He wasn't surprised to see the bird; he'd sent a message to his father after they returned to the manor.

After the attack, Lexi insisted on going to the marketplace to see if they could help the survivors. By the time they reached the fires, any survivors had fled, and those who weren't fortunate enough to be able to run were dead.

The unexpected attack hadn't left much of a chance for survivors. Though he felt the distress emanating from her, Lexi kept her chin high and her shoulders back as they returned to the manor.

Once there, he led her to her room, and while she showered, he sent a letter to his father.

Now, that response had arrived.

He glanced back to where Lexi lay ensconced in her blanket. It had taken her a while to fall asleep, and she hadn't spoken while she lay nestled in his arms.

He didn't talk either. After what he witnessed today, the memories of the war were closer to the surface and raw. The only thing that helped ease the screams and the cloying scent of blood haunting his memories was holding her in his arms.

And so he'd kissed and held her, but he didn't try to do anything more. Finally, she fell asleep in his arms, and when she did, he rose from the bed and walked over to stare out the window. After the events of today, he didn't dare fall asleep with her in the room.

The crow dropped the letter on the windowsill. Cole lifted it and slid the window closed. He walked over to the chair in the corner of Lexi's room and sat. He sank onto the cushion of the plush, baby blue chair and opened the note.

He recognized his father's elegant scroll immediately. *The Lord received word traitors were in the marketplace. He took the necessary quick and effective action.*

Cole knew his father had a lot more to say about what happened today, but he couldn't put them in a letter that might be intercepted. Cole crumpled the letter and threw it in the trash can only a few feet away from him.

He leaned back in the chair and clasped the arms of it as he contemplated his father's response. *Who* told the Lord there were traitors in the marketplace?

Cole hadn't seen any sign of such activity taking place there.

Most mortals and immortals were too scared to do anything more than sell their wares and go home. But someone had put it in the Lord's head that something more was going on there.

And there was also the chance the Lord never received any such word. It was just as likely he'd made it up so he could use it as an excuse for slaughtering a bunch of innocents. Though, he didn't need any reasons; no one could stop him while he controlled the dragons, and there were far too many of those beasts to slaughter.

Even knowing all this, he kept picturing Malakai walking through the marketplace with that smug look on his face. Cole wouldn't put it past the vampire to report traitors in the market just to watch it burn.

Cole had no way of knowing who was whispering about treachery in the Lord's ears, but he suspected that the vampire had a hand in what happened today.

Malakai had done something to earn that amulet.

Cole drummed his fingers on the ends of the chair as he gazed around the room. Much like the woman who slept in the bed, there was something delicate and feminine about it. The curtains surrounding the windows were a pale blue that matched the covers pulled around her.

Pictures of her father and Sahira decorated the walls, and he found himself staring into Del's grinning face. A small pang tugged at his heart; he missed that smile and the man who bore it.

He didn't know how Del would react to his relationship with Lexi, but he doubted his friend would be thrilled. Del had gone out of his way to protect Lexi; he would not want her entwined with a man who was front and center in the war.

As much as he missed his friend, he also didn't give a fuck what Del wanted for her. Cole was *not* giving her up.

When Lexi whimpered in her sleep, he padded across the cool, hardwood floor until he stood beside the bed. He pulled back the comforters and slid into bed beside her.

Tonight, she was the one having nightmares, and he despised it. What happened today never should have occurred. If there were traitors in the marketplace, then there were other ways to handle the situation, but the Lord was too far gone in his madness to see that.

Drawing Lexi into his arms, he kissed her temple. She murmured something before settling down and relaxing against him.

He was exhausted, but he wouldn't sleep tonight. As long as he held her, he didn't trust himself to sleep, but he wasn't going to let her go.

∼

A TAPPING at the window drew Cole's attention the next morning. Shifting his hold on Lexi, he slipped out of bed and walked over to the crow perched on the other side of the glass. The crow's black eyes watched him as he opened the window, and then it set a note in front of him.

Cole ran his fingers over the bird's soft feathers before it flew away. He closed the window against the stench of the fire and lifted the note. He opened it to read his father's words.

If Brokk is capable of the journey, it is time to come home.

Cole crumpled the note and tossed it in the trash before lifting his gaze to the glass. A heavy fog had settled over the land; its silvery tendrils hugged the window and obscured the destruction of the marketplace.

"What did it say?" Lexi asked.

He turned to find her sitting up on the bed; her auburn hair tumbled around her shoulders in tousled waves. Her green eyes were troubled, but she looked achingly lovely as she gazed at him.

"My father wants us to return," he said.

The slight clench of her jaw was the only indication she didn't like this news before she gave a small nod.

"Come with me," he said.

Her eyebrows rose as her mouth parted. "I can't."

"It will only be for a couple of days."

"I can't leave Sahira here to deal with everything on her own. She hates the stables; she claims they smell. And now that the market is gone, it will be harder to find food, and our gardens aren't ready to be harvested yet. I have too many responsibilities here to go, even if it's only for a couple of days."

And no matter how much he didn't want to leave her, especially after yesterday's events, he had too many responsibilities to stay. There were far too many lives depending on him to return.

But staring at her, he didn't care about those lives, the war, or how insane the Lord was; he preferred to stay with his mate. But he did care about his brothers and father, and if they didn't stop the Lord, her life was in jeopardy too.

Nowhere was safe from the Lord and his horde of dragons.

Cole stepped away from the window and crossed the room to her. She'd fallen asleep in a baggy T-shirt that somehow managed to hide her lush curves but still made her look sexy as hell.

He could drag her into the Gloaming; she'd fight him every step of the way and probably end up hating him, but it was better than leaving her here where he couldn't protect her.

"What about Malakai?" he asked.

"What about him?"

"What if he comes back while I'm gone."

She gave him a sad smile as he stopped beside the bed. "It won't be the first time I've had to deal with him, and it won't be the last."

That may be true, but he hated the idea of leaving her here. "Come with me."

"I can't."

Cole wasn't used to anyone telling him no, but he especially wasn't used to the women he was sleeping with saying it. She had no reason to fear becoming shadow kissed.

"What if I *insist* that you come with me?" he asked.

"Don't," she said simply.

"Don't?"

"Yes, don't. Because I won't go, and you won't become a tyrant like the Lord or Malakai."

He almost recoiled at her words but managed to stop himself. No, he wouldn't be like either of them, but the idea of leaving her here....

He looked to the trash can and the note again. He couldn't stay, and she wouldn't leave. He could make her go, but that would destroy the trust between them. A large part of him did not care, but the smaller part wanted to keep his mate happy.

And if he forced her into the Gloaming, she would not be happy. *But what does her happiness matter if she isn't safe?*

Cole rubbed at his temple. He hadn't expected to find his mate, but once he did, he'd assumed it would be easy. He hadn't expected her to be stubborn and set in her ways.

But he wouldn't have Lexi any other way. Lowering his hands, he met her quizzical look. "I'll return as soon as I can," he said.

He could return to the Gloaming and be back in a day. She would be okay for a day, and after what happened last time, he doubted Malakai would return any time soon.

Bending, he rested his hands on her hips and plucked her from the bed. She gasped but didn't protest when he slid onto the bed beneath her and settled her so she straddled his lap. She draped her arms over his shoulders.

CHAPTER FIFTY-TWO

LEXI DIDN'T KNOW how to respond to the fact he was leaving or that he wanted *her* to go *with* him.

She'd known this day would come, but she still wasn't ready for it. And as much as she yearned to, she couldn't go with him. She had far too many responsibilities here and a certain dark fae to remove from beneath her manor.

Maybe if Orin wasn't lounging in her tunnels, she would have asked the handyman to help in the stables like he did when they traveled to the Gloaming. But she couldn't do that now.

But he was asking her to go *with* him! What did that mean? Why would he want such a thing? Didn't dark fae usually forget all about their past partners when someone new popped up?

That's what she'd always heard, and while there was no one new yet, there would be once he left the manor. There would be countless new then.

If she was with him, would he stay away from those women?

She shut the possibility down. It didn't matter; she couldn't go, so traversing down that path wouldn't do her any good. Pondering it for too long would only make her crazy, and she planned to enjoy what little time they had left together.

If he returned, great. If he didn't, well then, she would move on. It would hurt, but she would get over it.

When he lifted her and slid naked into bed, the image of the flames from yesterday tried to push their way back into her mind, but she shoved them aside. He was leaving, and no matter what he said, she might never see him again.

Gripping her hips, he guided her along his erection. She shuddered at the sensation of him slipping between her legs. The head of his shaft teased her clit as the brilliant blue of his eyes shifted to silver.

His hungry gaze excited her almost as much as the hands pushing her shirt up. He lifted it and pulled it off before tossing it aside. His eyes latched ravenously on her breasts as a small smile curved his lips.

"You're gorgeous," he murmured as he gazed at her.

He stroked her breast before teasing her nipple with his thumb. Then he lifted his hand to cup her cheek. He ran his thumb across her bottom lip before slipping it into her mouth to prod at one of her canines. Her fangs lengthened in response, and he smiled.

"You haven't fed from me," he said.

"I've never fed from anyone," she said.

A spark of something lit his eyes. "We are going to have to remedy that."

Her gaze fell to his neck as excitement twisted in her belly. Lexi wasn't sure if she could do it without hurting him, but she was impatient to find out as she watched his blood pulse through the vein in his neck.

"Have you fed from me?" she asked as she played with the hair at his nape.

"No, but I'm going to," he murmured as he ran his thumb across her lip again before pulling it down a little.

"Will I know when you do?"

"Yes."

"Will it hurt?"

"No. Many say it enhances the pleasure."

"Impossible."

He chuckled as he cupped her nape and pulled her close for a kiss.

"Will I hurt you if I feed on you?" she asked when the kiss ended.

"No. And even if you did, I want it too much to care."

Releasing her, he planted his hands behind him and leaned back on the bed. She frowned as he smiled at her.

"This is all you, beautiful," he said.

"I... I don't understand."

"Explore, learn, discover what pleases you. I'm merely here to make sure you come."

She wasn't entirely sure what he meant by that, but his words made her wetter as she slid along the length of him before shifting so the head of his shaft teased her entrance.

However, no matter how much she wanted him inside her, she enjoyed this far too much to end it now. She moved, shifted, teased, and played with him as she ran her hands over his chest and down his stomach.

She traced the dips and hollows of his chiseled abdomen before shifting to explore his cock. His breath quickened when she ran her fingers over it before stroking it.

She thrilled at her power over him as his breathing changed, his erection pulsed in her grip, and his body tensed. He didn't move as he continued to let her learn more about him, herself, and what they both liked.

When she finally took him inside her, Lexi was so aroused, she came almost instantly, but as she floated down from her high, he still didn't touch her.

"Keep going," he grated.

He said the words, but she saw the strain on his face as sweat beaded his forehead. Lexi leaned forward until her breasts rubbed against his chest.

She lifted her hips until he was nearly out of her again before sliding slowly back down. His head fell back as she ran her tongue across his chest.

She tasted sweat and man as his fingers entangled in her sheets and the corded muscles of his arms stood starkly out, but he still didn't touch her. She ran her tongue back up his chest, across his collarbone, and up to his neck before nipping at it.

"You better feed soon, love," he said. "I don't know how much longer I can take this."

He didn't need to encourage her anymore. With a hammering heart, she kissed his neck again before resting her mouth over the solid thump of his pulse. Her concern over harming him caused her to hesitate.

"Do it," he commanded.

And she found herself helpless to do anything but obey. Her lips skimmed back, and she sank her fangs into his throat. She cried out against his flesh as the hot wave of his blood pulsed into her mouth.

She'd never tasted anything so delicious as it slid down her throat and the power of it seeped into her veins. Out of her mind with desire, she tried to draw him closer. Sensing her frustration, his arms locked around her, and he pulled her flush against his chest.

Lexi wasn't convinced she would feel it when he fed, but then his power seeped out until it crackled the air around them. Beneath her hands, his muscles swelled and vibrated.

At first, she didn't understand what was happening, and then she realized he was growing stronger as he fed on the energy their joining emitted. The crackling in the air increased until it vibrated against her skin.

Oh yes, she could see why some believed it enhanced the pleasure as her skin came alive, the hair on her arms rose, and she craved more.

CHAPTER FIFTY-THREE

COLE DRANK in the power she emanated. In all of his many years, he'd never experienced a rush like the one she gave him, but he'd also never fed on his mate before—*his mate.*

He'd yet to claim her as a lycan would, but he was leaving his mark as only a dark fae could. She would remember him while he was gone, and she would be eagerly awaiting his return.

The dark fae didn't have fated lovers like the lycan, but the fact she was his mate caused her to satisfy him in a way no other had before. As her sexual pleasure heightened, he drank in more and more of it until the air swirled and pulsed around them.

When her back bowed beneath his hands, her fangs retracted, and her head fell back as she cried out. The tightness of her sheath clenching around his dick tore his release from him.

Even as he was coming, he almost sank his fangs into her shoulder, pushed her back on the bed, and fucked her until she begged him to stop. He almost staked his lycan claim on her, but to do so would be to use her in a way no woman who lost her virginity only two nights ago should be used.

He would scare her, and he would claim her before he ever got the chance to tell her what she was to him.

Trembling, clinging to her, and trying to control the rampaging lycan demanding to be satisfied as much as the dark fae, he buried his face in her breasts and shuddered as his softening erection hardened again.

He could often go for hours and days at a time when the dark fae part of him was in one of its more demanding feeding periods, but no one had so easily aroused him as this woman.

Despite that, he reluctantly withdrew from her. She was immortal, she healed fast, her body adapted and changed swiftly to new situations, but she was still so new to this, and if he didn't stop, he would claim her.

And since he wasn't about to tell her that she was his mate before returning to the Gloaming, he had to stop. He wasn't about to drop that news on her. It meant he'd have to claim her or deal with her rejection before leaving.

She collapsed against him and shivered as he ran his hands over her silken skin. He didn't want to part from her, but if he stayed much longer, he would start all over again, and he would never leave today.

Unfortunately, that couldn't happen.

He kissed her collarbone before tilting his head back to look up at her as she remained straddling his lap. "I'm coming back for you," he vowed.

Surprise flickered through her eyes before she smiled at him. "I'll understand if you don't. I know what the dark fae are."

"I've already told you that you don't know what *I* am," he growled. "I *am* coming back to you. I won't be gone more than a day or two."

She nodded, but he saw the doubt in her eyes. He hated that doubt, but his return would put an end to it. She would learn he had no intention of ever leaving her life.

"I'm going to leave a crow here; if anything happens, send a message to me. I'll return immediately," he said. "Let me know if Malakai returns."

He would prefer to send a dark fae to watch over her while he was in the Gloaming, but he couldn't have anyone else knowing about her yet. Eventually, word would get out that he'd mated—if she allowed him to do it—but until then, the best thing he could do to protect her was to keep her off the radar of his enemies.

Sending a guard to watch over would put an end to that. Word would rapidly spread amongst the immortals that he'd taken a special interest in someone.

"I mean it, Lexi," he said as he squeezed her ass. "If you need me for anything, or if Malakai steps foot on this property again, then send that crow."

"I will," she promised.

He wanted to do so much more for her, but it was the best he could do for now.

CHAPTER FIFTY-FOUR

LEXI BLINKED BACK the tears burning her eyes as she watched Cole and Brokk leave later that morning. In the tree above her head, the crow Cole left behind cawed loudly and ruffled its feathers but didn't take flight.

Cole assured her that even if this crow became surrounded by a murder of others, it would return to her the second she raised her arm. She was tempted to test this but decided against commanding the beautiful creature when it wasn't necessary.

When the brothers vanished from view, she turned away and trudged back to the manor. As she walked, she felt like the weight of the world was bearing down on her shoulders.

He'd said he would return, and she wanted to believe him, but as she walked, she prepared herself never to see him again.

He's a dark fae; she reminded herself for the umpteenth time.

But she had to keep doing it because she needed it to sink in, or she might end up with a shattered heart.

If he never returned, it might take her years to recover from the blow, but she would recover if she were expecting it. But if she had her hopes up and he never returned, it would make things so much worse.

He's also lycan. That niggling thought refused to die no matter how many times she tried to kill it. Such an idea was dangerous as it would only lead to her getting her hopes up.

The lycan could be the most loyal immortals when it came to their family and their mates, but she wasn't family, and he'd never mentioned mates to her.

Dark fae or not, his father loved his mother deeply.

But there was no mention of love between us!

She realized she was spiraling into a dark well of despair and hope that needed to end. She didn't know why he was so adamant about returning to her, but she wouldn't allow herself to believe it was for anything more than what they'd shared these past few days.

He liked her; she didn't doubt that. And she liked him, probably too much, but that didn't mean it was anything more.

He could quite possibly become completely distracted in the Gloaming and forget she existed.

She refused to get her hopes up too much about his return, but she wasn't going to turn into a moping, melancholy mess because he'd returned home... as she'd always known he would.

Even if he never returned, she had a life to live and things to do. One of those things might still be in her tunnels and most likely *seething* because she hadn't returned in days.

Lexi slipped back into the manor and headed for the kitchen. She'd fed well on Cole this morning, but she hadn't satisfied her human appetite yet.

Sahira was standing at the stove, stirring a pot as she worked to replenish the rest of her healing salves now that Brokk was gone. Sitting beside her, Shade was working to clean his paw, which he lowered to study Lexi when she entered the room.

"Have they left?" Sahira asked.

Lexi opened and closed a couple of cabinets, but most were empty. Thankfully, their garden would start yielding some produce soon, and the goats would provide milk and cheese while the chickens produced eggs.

They wouldn't have as much now that the market was gone, but they were better off than most, and they would get through this. If push came to shove, they could travel to another marketplace, but the closest one was now an hour away.

She didn't want to think about making that journey as she closed the cabinets and went to the fridge. She opened the refrigerator and removed a piece of cheese.

"Yes," she said as she took a knife from the drawer and sliced off a couple of pieces from the block.

"What happened to your neck?"

Lexi sighed. She'd dreaded this conversation and had hoped that Sahira wouldn't notice or question her on it, but now that she had…

"Cole," Lexi admitted, and Sahira's eyes darkened as her hand tightened on the knife. "It wasn't on purpose!"

Lexi told her what happened, and though she didn't think Cole would like her revealing his nightmares to her aunt, she couldn't hide them from Sahira. If her aunt didn't know the whole truth, she would hate Cole, and Lexi couldn't have that.

When she finished, Sahira's hand relaxed a little on the blade, but she still looked murderous.

"He's dangerous," Sahira said.

"Not to me."

"Your neck says differently."

"He's *not* dangerous to me. This was an accident. It won't happen again."

"If it does, I'll castrate him."

Lexi gulped. "He doesn't sleep when I'm there. He stays up the entire time instead because he wants me to stay with him."

Sahira's brow furrowed, and her mouth pursed. "That's… odd."

Lexi didn't respond.

"I still don't like it," Sahira said.

"I know."

Her aunt sighed and set down her knife. "Here." Sahira reached into her apron pocket and set a bottle of blue liquid on the counter near her.

"What's that?" Lexi asked around a mouthful of cheese.

"Birth control. Use it."

Lexi almost choked on her cheese but managed to swallow it. "Sahira—"

"Take a sip every night, and it will keep you from getting pregnant now and in the future."

Lexi cursed the blush creeping up her cheeks as she studied the liquid and her hand fell involuntarily to her belly. She knew it wasn't possible, but the idea of Cole's baby caused a small thrill of excitement to course through her.

"Cole is on birth control," she said.

"Hmm," Sahira grunted. "It won't hurt to have you both on it. Besides, he might have used it wrong or messed something up or forgotten to take it, so there is always that possibility. And...."

"And what?" Lexi prodded when Sahira's voice trailed off.

Sahira lifted her head, and their eyes met. Then she tossed some herbs into the pot. "And you'll be prepared for the next man."

Lexi felt like Sahira had slapped her, but she managed to keep herself from recoiling. She kept telling herself she was prepared for Cole not to return, but hearing Sahira say it slammed the reality of it home.

Her aunt didn't expect him to return, and she expected Lexi to prepare for the next man who entered her life. The idea of another man touching her the way Cole did made her stomach clench; she couldn't even consider that possibility right now.

"He said he would come back, but I'm not so sure," she admitted.

"Hmm," Sahira muttered.

When Lexi grasped the bottle, she didn't realize how close it was to the flames beneath Sahira's pot. She yelped and pulled her hand away when the fire burnt her finger.

"Are you okay?" Sahira asked.

Lexi sucked on her burnt finger as she slid the potion into her pocket. "I'm fine."

If Cole returned, she would use it when she was certain she wasn't pregnant, but not now. She couldn't bring herself to use it if there was a small chance she carried his child. It would be difficult to raise a human, vampire, lycan, dark fae baby on her own, but she would do it.

"Thank you," she said.

Sahira grunted again.

"I know he's a dark fae, but...." Lexi's gaze shifted to the window and the crow sitting in a tree across the way.

"But?" Sahira prompted.

"But I think he's a good man."

Sahira grunted again. Lexi kissed her cheek.

"I love you too, auntie," she teased.

Sahira rolled her eyes. "Ass kisser."

Lexi chuckled and folded the rest of the cheese into a napkin. "I'll be in the stables."

Sahira didn't reply as Lexi made her way out the door and toward the stables. She slipped inside and closed the door behind her. Taking a deep breath, she steadied herself before entering the feed room.

She lifted a couple of bags of feed and tossed them aside to expose the trapdoor beneath. The door blended so seamlessly into the floor that anyone who didn't know it was there would never see it even without the bags on top.

Removing the bottle from her pocket, Lexi hid it in one of the horse's feed tubs, so she didn't accidentally break it. Then she lifted the door and slipped into the shadows below.

She closed the door behind her. From experience, she knew the open space the moved bags created wouldn't attract any attention as there were other spaces like it within the feed room.

Lexi lifted the flashlight from the hook below the door and clicked it on before descending the steps. The beam played across the walls as she sped through the tunnels and in the direction of where she last saw Orin.

She didn't know if she expected him to be there or not; if he was, she imagined he was pretty *pissed* over her absence. Despite knowing that, she didn't feel any apprehension over encountering an irate dark fae down here. She'd had enough of bossy, overbearing men, and she wasn't about to let this one run all over her again.

She was almost to the place where she last saw Orin when low, gravelly words issued from the shadows. "Where the *fuck* have you been?"

CHAPTER FIFTY-FIVE

LEXI SIGHED and turned to face Orin. The beam found him standing in the corner of two adjoining tunnels. His black eyes glimmered with malice as he studied her with a look that made the hair on her nape rise, but she didn't back away from him.

"I was helping to save one of *your* brothers," she retorted.

Those words knocked some of the ire out of him, and he gaped at her before covering it up. Confronted with him again, that niggling guilt tugged at her again.

She'd kept his presence here a secret from Cole. But she was sure Cole had plenty of secrets of his own, and it wasn't like they were in a relationship and he'd told her everything.

She tried to reassure herself with this reasoning, but the guilt wouldn't let go.

"You could have left," she said. "Believe me, I would have preferred it if you did."

"I can't just pop out of here," he retorted. "I have no idea where any of these tunnels go or what I'd emerge into. Plus, you shut some of the gates, so I don't have many places to roam."

Lexi shrugged, but as much as she wanted him gone, she was

glad he hadn't decided to find his way out. It could have been disastrous, especially if one of those ways entered into the manor.

"What do you mean you helped save one of my brothers?" he asked.

She filled him in on what happened with Brokk but emitted all details about Cole and herself. She must have given something away though as his calculating eyes ran inquisitively over her.

"And you didn't tell them I was here?" he asked.

"You're still here, aren't you?"

Instead of answering her question, he asked another. "And how is Cole?"

She somehow, miraculously, managed not to blush as she responded. "Fine. They both returned to the Gloaming today, which means I can take you out of here."

She pulled the cheese from her pocket and tossed it to him. He caught it with ease.

"If you'll follow me," she said.

"And what if I decide not to go back out there?"

"Then that's your choice, but I'm not coming back here. You can let me lead you out somewhere safe, or you can wander around here until you're half-starved and desperate. Once that happens, you'll have to take the risk of leaving here and someone seeing you."

"And then they'll catch you too."

"I. Don't. Care," she enunciated.

It was a bald-faced lie; of course, she cared. They both knew that, but she was *not* going to be at his mercy anymore. She'd rather be crisp fried by a dragon than continue to live like this.

"I'm not going to keep putting myself at risk by continuing to come down here. Either leave now, or you're on your own."

He bit into the cheese and chewed before swallowing. "Lead the way, little human."

She glowered at him but refused to give him the satisfaction of telling him off. Turning on her heel, she didn't look back at him as she led the way to a door that opened into a shed on the edge of her property.

The shed housed all sorts of garden tools, fertilizer, and some seeds, but few knew its location as it was tucked within a copse of trees. She had no doubt it would be safe to emerge there.

Climbing the stairs to the door, she slid the bolts locking it free, grasped the handle, and pushed it up. The scent of dirt and earth enveloped her.

Though she was sure it was safe, she still poked her head cautiously out to look around before climbing into the shadowy interior of the shed. She stepped out of Orin's way before hurrying over to one of the three windows.

Even if someone had their face against the glass, they couldn't see into the shed. Her father had made sure of that with tinted windows.

Still, she approached the glass slowly before peaking outside. Nothing moved through the trees, so she went to one of the other windows.

She checked that one before going to the last window. The last window held her attention longer than the others. Through the trees encircling the shed, she could see smoke coiling insidiously into the air from the remains of the marketplace.

The smoke made her recall the thunderous booms that shook the earth and the way the dragon destroyed without remorse. Screams echoed in her head as that helpless feeling descended over her again.

She despised feeling so powerless in this new, uncertain world. There had to be something she could do to put an end to all the death and senseless violence, but she had no idea what.

Orin's reflection appeared in the glass as he came to stand behind her. "What happened there?" he inquired.

"The Lord decided there was a traitor in the marketplace."

"Was there?"

"I don't think so."

"That makes sense."

She turned to face him. "How does that make sense?"

He shrugged as he rubbed at the thick layer of stubble lining his chin. "Because the only thing the Lord does consistently is killing and destroying indiscriminately. Now that the war is over, he has to focus his bloodlust somewhere, and it doesn't matter to him if that focus deserves it or not. He enjoys killing too much to stop now."

Her blood ran cold; the beings in the marketplace were most likely innocent, but she wasn't. Harboring him made her a traitor, but that might not matter. The Lord could get bored and send his dragons here anyway.

She preferred to lessen her chances of that happening. Terror spurred her into action, and she pushed against Orin's solid chest as she nudged him toward the door. "You have to go."

She expected him to resist her or offer up some wiseass response, but he relented to her desperate hands. When he arrived at the door, he rested his hand on the knob and faced her.

"Don't ever tell anyone I was here," he said.

"Do I look like an idiot?" she retorted. "Don't ever come back. You'll find the shed locked as well as the entrance to the tunnel. I also plan on shutting some gates and blocking off this section of the tunnel."

His black eyes were as emotionless as a shark's as they roamed over her. She didn't shrink beneath his scrutiny. Instead, she scowled at him as a smile curved the edges of his mouth.

"Farewell then," he said.

He opened the door and stepped outside. She started to close the door behind him, but he held out his palm to stop her and nudged it back open.

"If I were you, I'd stay away from my brother. Cole's even more ruthless than me."

With those final words, he released the door and sauntered

away like he didn't have a care in the world. The bastard shoved his hands in his pockets and whistled while he walked.

It took everything Lexi had not to slam the door behind him. Instead, she quietly closed it and turned the locks. She would have to remember to bring the keys with her the next time she came to the shed; there was no way she was leaving this door unlocked again.

She refused to consider his words as she slipped into the tunnel and slid the bolts back into place before retreating into the tunnels. She closed a few gates behind her to ensure the tunnel was blocked off further.

When she finished, the only thing she had to do was think on Orin's parting words as she walked back toward the stables.

CHAPTER FIFTY-SIX

"You're home," his father said as he glided across the floor toward them.

He embraced Brokk first, and they hugged each other before breaking apart. His father grasped Brokk's shoulders and leaned back to study him. "How are you?"

"Much better now," Brokk replied. "Though I could use a shower and my clothes."

"Go do what you must and then meet me in my solar."

Brokk nodded before leaving.

"And how are you doing?" his father inquired as they embraced.

"I've been worse," Cole said. "But I have to agree about my clothes."

His father laughed and squeezed his shoulders. "Go on then; meet me in my solar as soon as you're finished."

Cole slipped away. He retreated to his room, where he showered and dressed in clothes that fit him. His clothes were far more comfortable, but he missed the ones he'd worn as they still smelled of Lexi.

The soap and water had washed her scent from him. However,

the memory of it teased his nostrils as he recalled the feel of her in his arms. And the sooner he returned to his father, the sooner he could see her again.

He left the room and practically jogged across the palace to his father's private solar. The candles floating in the air cast shadows across the dark floors and walls.

His steps reverberated off the stones as he passed countless closed doors to rooms he'd never entered. He had no idea what lay beyond most of them.

When he arrived at the solar, he knocked and waited for his father to bid him enter before stepping into the room. His father sat in his favorite chair with a glass of whiskey by his hand. The fire crackling in the hearth filled the room with the sweet aroma of fae wood.

Cole helped himself to a glass of the amber liquid and settled into the chair across from his dad. The warmth of the fire helped soothe some of his lingering anxiety, but he was impatient to get back to Lexi.

"What happened out there?" his father inquired.

Cole had only given him scant details in his letters, and now he filled him in on the rest of it.

"You were lucky to find the witch," his father said.

"Luck had nothing to do with it. I knew she was there."

"And how is that?"

"It was Del's mansion; his sister was the witch."

"I see. I recall her from the party. I also recall that his daughter is a beautiful woman."

"Yes, she is."

"You sound intrigued by the girl."

"It's more than that; she's my mate."

"Your *lycan* mate?"

"Yes."

Cole sipped his whiskey as he gazed over his father's shoulder.

One of the moons, Carpton, hung outside the window. The sight of it caused the lycan part of him to stir in a way it never had before.

He'd never transformed because of the moon's pull, but now that Lexi had awakened his more primitive urges, they were making themselves known more often than they had before. Lycans didn't transform with every full moon, but they felt connected to the moon's cycles that often drew the beast out of them as the moon became fuller.

His need to shift grew as he imagined feeling the earth beneath him and the wind in his hair while he raced back to her. The impulse was so strong his fangs lengthened, and the scent of the night air intensified as it filled his nose.

His fingers clenched on his glass. It would have shattered in his grasp if his father didn't lean across the distance separating them to remove it from his hand.

"Easy, son," he murmured as he set the glass on the table.

Cole took a steadying breath as he leashed the lycan part of him once more.

"Have you claimed her?" his father asked.

"No. I didn't have the chance to discuss it with her before your last letter asking us to return."

"It will be easier for you once you do. It was for your mother."

He fucking hoped so. He'd never liked feeling out of control; it was why he'd always identified more with his dark fae side, but the lycan was nowhere near as detached and calculating. It was making that clearly known.

"Do you care for her?" his father inquired.

"More than I ever believed possible."

Until he said the words, he hadn't realized how much he cared for Lexi. Not only was she his mate, but he liked her and admired her determination to keep her manor going and the ones she loved safe.

His father's grin lit his eyes. "I'm so happy for you!"

Cole didn't know how to reply, and before he could respond, the smile slid from his father's face.

"Protect her, Colburn," he said. "Don't lose her like I lost your mother. It's not something... it's not something you ever fully recover from."

His father's eyes flickered away as anguish briefly replaced his joy. When he looked at Cole again, his smile was back in place, but it no longer lit his eyes.

"I *will* keep her safe," Cole vowed.

"Good. Why didn't you bring her back with you?"

"She refused to come. She has responsibilities in the human realm, and she couldn't leave them. I plan to return to her as soon as I can."

"Ah, so she is stubborn."

"Very."

His father laughed as he sipped his whiskey. "I was with a stubborn woman once. She drove me crazy, but I wouldn't have had it any other way. I was fortunate I got the time I did with her and my firstborn son, but I've missed her every day since I lost her."

"So have I," Cole admitted.

It was these times, when it was just them, or them and his brothers, that Cole enjoyed the most. No one else would ever see this side of his father. It was reserved solely for his family.

His father was a ruthless ruler who didn't tolerate disobedience from his followers. He handed out punishments with no remorse and rarely smiled. But when he was alone with those he loved, he was an entirely different entity.

"I never thought I'd see the day when you would find a woman," his father murmured.

"Neither did I."

His father finished off his drink before pouring himself another. Then he dipped a hand into his shirt, pulled out the chain he wore around his neck, and unclasped it. Cole had seen the chain count-less times over the years, but he'd never seen his father remove it.

His dad slipped the two rings from the chain and hefted them in his hands. Sorrow radiated from him as he inspected them before rising and walking over to Cole. He tipped his head back as his dad stopped in front of him.

"Hold out your hand," his dad commanded.

Cole did as he said, and his father placed the rings on his palm.

"These were mine and your mother's," he said.

"I know," Cole murmured as he inspected the delicate bands.

The light reflecting off the silver bands emphasized the mark-ings etched onto them. His mother's ring was so delicate he was afraid he'd crush it in his fingers, but made of fae metal, it was far stronger than it looked.

He held them back out to his father, but his dad clasped his hand and closed his fingers over them. "Keep them. Give your mate your mother's ring."

"I can't do that."

"Yes, you can."

"They're yours. It's… it's Mom's."

"And now they're yours."

"You've worn them—"

"For six hundred and sixty-five years."

Had it been that long? He bowed his head as he stared at the rings and remembered the woman whose love he still felt after all these centuries.

As he gazed at her band, he recalled seeing it on her hand as she ran her fingers through his hair or worked in one of her many gardens.

"I don't need them to remember her," his father said as he rested his hand on Cole's shoulder. "She'll always be in my heart, and I have only to look at you to remember her."

Cole's head fell back, and he gazed up at his father. He hadn't expected the sheen of tears in his dad's eyes, but then his father blinked them away.

"Give your girl your mother's ring. It's what she would have wanted, and it would have made her so happy," his dad said.

"We're not anywhere near that stage."

"When you are, give it to her." His dad squeezed his shoulder before releasing him and returning to his chair. "If you're a fraction as happy with her as I was with your mother, you'll have a wonderful life together, and that is all I ever wanted for you and your brothers."

Before Cole could respond, Brokk breezed into the room with his wet hair hanging into his eyes and a smile on his face. "What did I miss?"

"Nothing," their father replied as he lifted his drink.

Cole slid the rings into his pocket. When he met his father's eyes again, they smiled at each other before his dad's face became more serious.

"We have a meeting with the others tomorrow," his father said. "They're arriving here at lunch."

Cole knew the others meant the coalition.

"What the Lord did to that marketplace never should have happened," Brokk said. "He's becoming more unstable and crueler."

"I know," their father murmured as he twisted his glass in his hands. "What we don't know is how to get at him and kill him."

And a solution to that would solve so many of their problems.

CHAPTER FIFTY-SEVEN

THEY SPENT the next few hours catching up and plotting, but none of them had any new ideas. In the end, they were no closer to a solution for the Lord, and if they didn't find one soon, he would destroy them all.

Every passing day was one more that the power of the throne ate into the increasingly rancid brain of the man sitting on it. But they still had no idea how to stop him.

This fact was becoming increasingly annoying. Cole felt as if they'd done nothing but talk about it for years, and, in truth, they had.

There had to be some weakness they were missing, but this Lord had learned from the mistakes of the other mad rulers who came before him. He wouldn't repeat the same mistakes that allowed others to be destroyed.

Cole was preparing to rise and send a crow to Lexi when a knock sounded on the door. They exchanged a look before his father set down his whiskey and rose. It was a clear rule that they were to be left alone when they were in the solar.

His father strode with elegant, fluid grace to the door and

opened it to reveal Sindri on the other side. The helot's black eyes glittered in the dim light.

A couple of hundred years ago, Sindri made the mistake of gathering an army to try to dethrone Tove. That army was ruthlessly slaughtered, but Tove kept Sindri alive. He had the dark fae's powers bound by a coven of witches and forced Sindri into servitude.

The coven was depleted for weeks afterward, but Tove gave them enough carisle to make it worth their while. He also allowed them to stay in the palace until they were strong enough to travel again.

No one in the palace trusted Sindri, but he was a neutered dog, and this punishment was far worse than death. Every day, Sindri repeatedly endured the humiliation of his defeat as he waited on the man he'd sought to depose.

"What is it, Sindri?" Tove demanded.

"There is a messenger here from the Lord, milord," Sindri murmured as he bowed his head.

The irritation vanished from Tove's face. "Then send him in."

"As you wish, mi—"

Sindri didn't get a chance to finish speaking before a warlock pushed past him and barged into the solar. The abrupt action and the audacity of the warlock caused Cole to set his glass down.

Rising, he braced his legs apart as he surveyed the haughty-looking warlock who practically sneered at his father.

This fucker deserves a beating.

Cole flexed his hands. *No one* entered his father's private room in such a way.

Beside him, Brokk also rose. The warlock seemed not to notice the increased hostility in the room as Tove kept his face expressionless, but Cole didn't miss the fury in his father's eyes.

"The Lord will speak with you," the messenger stated.

"Of course," Tove said. "Tell him that I will join him in the morning."

"He will see you *now*. You"—the warlock's eyes flicked to Cole— "and your eldest son."

Cole shoved aside the uneasy feeling the words created in his stomach. They'd never been summoned to the Lord in such a way, and Cole was *never* ordered to attend with his father.

He'd traveled to the Dragonian realm with his dad before, but he'd never been commanded there. After the events at the marketplace, this could not be good.

It took a few seconds for Tove to respond, and Cole heard the crackle of ire in his voice when he spoke. "Of course."

Beside Tove, Sindri smiled smugly, and his shoulders went back a little. Cole contemplated punching that smile off his face, but he couldn't reveal his anger to this warlock.

Once this was over, he would discuss destroying Sindri with his father. The man had served his punishment, and they were all better off without him in the palace.

His dad turned toward him and plastered on a smile that many wouldn't recognize as fake, but Cole saw through it. "Let us go, Colburn. Brokk, stay here and see over the realm."

"Of course, Father," Brokk murmured.

Cole glanced at the crow sitting on the windowsill. If he sent a message to Lexi now, the Lord's minion would report the crow's departure, and they might try to discover where the bird went.

The Lord could *not* know Lexi existed. He glanced at his brother, but he couldn't ask Brokk to look after her without the others overhearing him. And not in the mood to deal with Brokk's questions and teasing, he hadn't discussed what Lexi was to him with Brokk, so his brother wouldn't think to check on her.

She had to know he might be gone longer than he planned, but he didn't know how to tell her without revealing too much, and in the end, her safety was the most important thing to him. As he followed his father out the door, he could only hope they would return soon.

However, he had a bad feeling they wouldn't be returning soon… if they returned at all.

CHAPTER FIFTY-EIGHT

WHEN THE THIRD day passed without any word from Cole, Lexi's shoulders slumped a little and she felt like a weight was bearing down on them. By the time the fifth day passed, she was kicking herself for believing he would return.

She'd known better than to trust a dark fae; she'd repeatedly told herself *not* to trust him, but somehow, he slipped inside her defenses. And he'd forgotten her already.

Lexi had believed she'd prepared for him to forget her, but she hadn't. With every passing day, her sadness grew.

However, no matter how much it felt like someone was squeezing her heart in her chest, she didn't cry.

She *refused* to shed a tear over him even though some days she yearned to sit down and sob out her disappointment. But once she started, she wouldn't stop, and he wasn't worth her tears.

That fifth night, as she lay alone in bed, it took all she had not to roll over and cry into the pillows still smelling of him, but she didn't.

Instead, when the sun rose, she ripped her sheets, pillows, and comforter off the bed, carried them downstairs, and stuffed them in the washer. Thankfully, the electricity was working well as she washed them three times to ensure no hint of him remained on them.

The urge to cry was not so bad the following night.

On the seventh day, she learned she wasn't pregnant. Relief flowed through her, as did a little sadness. The last thing she needed was a baby in this crazy world, and one whose father would never know about its existence, but she couldn't shake her lingering disappointment.

She tucked Sahira's bottle of birth control into a cabinet where she wouldn't see it and closed the door. She wouldn't have any use for it again for a while. Asshole or not, it would be some time before she moved on from Cole.

Through it all, she realized that either Cole was not her consort, or she lacked another vampire trait. From what she'd heard, a vampire who lost their consort was inconsolable and often went to the grave soon after.

While she was grieving and lost, she didn't plan to die any time soon, and she wasn't inconsolable. Life went on, she would get over this, and one day, she would forget him just as he'd forgotten her.

Or at least she hoped she would.

At least she hadn't been foolish enough to love him. But as she told herself this, she recognized it as another lie.

On the morning of the eighth day, she went out to dispense as much food as they could spare to the dejected people rambling past the manor. Most were looking for work or food, but some seemed so broken that she wasn't sure they knew where they were anymore.

They couldn't spare much food, but their crops would soon be ready to harvest, and they were already gathering peas and tomatoes from the garden.

On the tenth day, she fed the people before heading into the woods. She had to gather some supplies from the shed before heading for the garden.

She emerged from the shed with a shovel and gloves when something zipped through the tree's shadows. It moved so fast she couldn't tell what it was, but it was something more than human, and that meant it was a threat.

Lexi dropped her gloves and shifted her hold on the shovel as she prepared to bash in the brains of whatever was moving through those trees. She caught another blur of movement to her right and turned to face it.

Whatever was out there was screwing with the wrong immortal. She'd never sought a fight before, but she'd gladly take her anger at Cole out on this asshole.

And then the blur vanished. She stared at the pine tree it stopped behind as she willed it to emerge. Was it Malakai?

Her heart raced at the possibility. She hadn't seen him since that day with Cole, but she didn't kid herself into thinking he wasn't coming back.

Lexi held her breath as she waited to see if Malakai had finally returned. After a few seconds, Orin stepped out.

At first, she was relieved to see him instead of Malakai, and then she recalled how much trouble he could cause her, and she scowled at him.

He grinned at her as he eyed the shovel and lifted his hands. "Easy there, killer."

She shifted her hold on the shovel. She'd told him *never* to come back here, and she'd meant it.

"What are you doing here?" she snapped.

His eyebrows rose, and even she was surprised by the vehemence of her tone. But she'd had enough of him and *all* dark fae. As far as she was concerned, they could all return to the Gloaming and rot there.

"What has your panties in a bunch?" he asked with wry humor.

"You're disgusting."

He grinned as he leaned against a tree. He crossed his legs and folded his arms over his lean chest. The striking similarities between him and Cole only made her want to hit him more.

"So I've been told," he murmured. "But I think I'm pretty amazing."

"You're the only one." She bent and lifted her gloves from the ground, hefted the shovel over her shoulder, and started through the woods. She'd prefer to smack him with the shovel, but she didn't want to be anywhere near him. "Get out of here."

"Would you like *all* of us to leave?"

His words froze her, and for a minute, she stared straight ahead as she watched the sun's rays playing through the trees and listened to the bird's song. It was such a peaceful, beautiful morning, and she'd been looking forward to losing herself in the garden. She wanted her hands in the dirt and the rich aroma of the earth filling her nostrils as it eased her heartache.

Instead, she was dealing with asshole number two of the dark fae realm. His older brother had taken over the title of asshole number one.

With a sigh, she turned back to him. She opened her mouth to ask what he was talking about, but before she could, more shadows moved through the trees and drew closer.

The first one to emerge was a young woman holding a small boy in her arms. The woman was human, but the tiny fangs on the boy indicated he was part vampire. Soot streaked their noses, cheeks, and torn clothes as they stared at her from haunted eyes. No child should have eyes that wise and sad, but suffering etched his face.

From behind them, more people and immortals emerged from the woods. In the end, three men, two women, a little girl, and the boy stood before her.

She stared at their battered countenances before shifting her attention to Orin. She'd prefer never to speak to him again, but she couldn't walk away from these people.

"What's going on?" she asked.

He stepped away from the tree and approached her. "They're being hunted."

"Why? And by who?"

"Because they survived the marketplace and by the Lord's followers. *No one* was supposed to survive the attack, but they did."

"I...." Her gaze flicked to them as Orin stopped before her. "I don't understand."

He clasped her elbow and led her a few feet away. She glowered at him as they walked, but she followed him. There was no point fighting when she wanted answers.

"Yes, you do," Orin said as he stopped and turned to face her. "They're on the run."

Lexi jerked her arm free of his grasp and gave him a seething look. "And *you're* helping to keep them alive?"

"Yes."

She studied him, but she didn't see anything smug in his gaze this time. No, all she saw was an earnestness that tempted her to punch him. He was an asshole, and she much preferred him that way.

She was sick of being used and manipulated by the dark fae, and even if Orin meant well, she'd told him never to return. He was using these people to manipulate her into doing what he wanted her to do.

And she was scared she knew what it was.

"I suppose you're helping them out of the kindness of your blackened heart?" she muttered sarcastically.

"You're a lot more bitter than the last time I saw you."

"I'm sick of your shit."

"Just mine or someone else's too?"

She swore the top of her head was going to blow off as her blood pressure skyrocketed. It took everything she had not to bash his brains in with the shovel. However, she was *not* in the mood to pick brains from her clothes.

"Leave, Orin, and don't come back," she said.

"They need a place to stay, or they're going to die. I'm running out of places to hide them, and the humans are slowing us down. Plus, I can't take the mortals into any of the Shadow Realms."

"I can't help you."

"There were more of them yesterday. We lost two; one was a child."

"Leave, Orin."

She hissed the words, but her gaze returned to where the others huddled together while they warily eyed the trees. The boy was gazing at her with his big blue eyes. When his mother wrapped her hand around his head and pressed it to her chest, he stuck his thumb in his mouth.

They were so broken and so helpless. Getting involved with this was a *very* bad idea, but how could she say no to the children? How could she turn any of them away?

Because it could lead to your death, the destruction of the manor, and possibly get Sahira killed.

Still, her heart ached for them, and her conviction to get rid of Orin wavered.

CHAPTER FIFTY-NINE

"Why are *you* trying to help them?" she asked distrustfully. "I know it's not from the goodness of your deadened heart."

"Ouch," Orin said and slapped his hands over his heart. "You wound me, milady."

Lexi shot him a look; he returned it with a smug grin.

"Don't screw with me," she warned.

"Seriously, who got your panties in such a bunch? Was it my big brother, or did he get them off?"

A muscle twitched in her jaw, and red filled her vision. She adjusted her hold on the shovel as she prepared to bash him with it, but he threw up his hands and edged back.

"Easy, killer," he murmured.

"I'm not in the mood, Orin."

"Obviously, but I'm not here to fight. I'm here to find help for these innocent souls."

"Why are *you* helping them?" she demanded.

"I'm not the hideous monster you think I am."

"Oh, no?"

"No," he said, and for the first time, there was no amusement in his gaze. "They need help, and I'm going to give it to them.

Plus, the more fighters we have to stand against the Lord, the better chance we have of defeating him."

"So, it's not entirely from the goodness of your heart?" she asked sarcastically.

He didn't respond.

"They're not fighters," she said.

She refrained from saying there was no way to beat the Lord as long as he had the dragons on his side, but she held her tongue. This day was depressing enough without adding more gloomy crap onto it.

"Not yet," Orin said.

The little girl let out a small sniffle and whispered, "Mommy."

The man holding her shushed her as he swayed her gently from side to side. At first, Lexi thought he was rocking to comfort her, but she realized he was doing it because he was about to fall over.

"We lost her mother yesterday," Orin said.

Lexi winced and lowered her shovel.

"Are you going to turn them away?" Orin asked.

She scowled at him, but when she glanced back at the refugees, some of her anger deflated. Then she looked toward what remained of the marketplace.

Smoke no longer rose from the ashes, but the stench of fire lingered in the air. For over a week now, she'd felt utterly helpless as she brought food to the broken masses passing her property.

The Lord must be stopped; it wouldn't be with this ragtag bunch of fugitives, but could she turn them away?

She glanced toward the manor, but she couldn't see it through the trees. However, she knew her home was there. The manor and Sahira were all she had left in this world.

No, they weren't all she had left. She also had herself, and how could she possibly live with herself if she turned these broken refugees away and the children died?

If she agreed to this, she was putting everyone and everything she loved at risk. What would her father think about her jeopardizing everything he worked to accomplish?

But she knew he wouldn't have turned any of them away. Her father had presented a gruff, tough exterior to the world, but he'd been a big old softie at heart. He'd fought for the Lord, but he *never* would have approved of what that monster did to the human realm.

The war over the mortal realm had been waged, but it wasn't over. Instead, a new war was beginning, and she had to choose a side.

But if she chose this side, it would pit her against Cole.

She immediately hated herself for thinking that. It didn't matter if they ended up on opposite sides of this new war. He wasn't coming back, and she had to accept that.

And even if he was coming back, this was *her* stance to take. No matter how much she cared for him, she wouldn't let any man dictate where she stood in this world.

She had to get on with her life, and no matter what side Cole and her father chose, she had to do what she believed was best. And there was only one decision that would allow her to have any respect for herself for the rest of her life.

What about Sahira?

Guilt tugged at her. Her aunt couldn't know about this; it would only put her in danger. If Lexi was caught, Sahira could truthfully plead that she hadn't known anything about this. It might be enough to save her.

I'll have to make sure I don't get caught. She didn't think it would be that simple, but she would do whatever it took to protect her aunt.

Knowing she was putting everything she loved at risk, she closed her eyes and took a deep breath before saying. "I don't have much food to spare."

She opened her eyes to find Orin grinning at her. Her teeth ground back and forth as she glowered at the arrogant prick.

"I'll help with feeding them," he said.

"I can't have you coming and going from the tunnels."

"I'll be careful and conceal myself in the shadows."

She swallowed the lump rising in her throat. If she made this choice, she couldn't turn back. She'd be putting her neck on the line for a bunch of strangers and a douchey fae as trustworthy as a crocodile with a toothache.

"Why are you *really* doing this?" she asked.

"The war against the Lord is taking on many forms. Undermining him every chance we get is only one of those forms."

She suspected it was more than that, but she couldn't bring herself to believe he might actually have a heart, even if it was a minuscule one.

"How many others are fighting on your side?" she asked.

"I can't reveal that."

"Will you reveal my tunnels to them?"

He hesitated before replying, "No. Your secret is safe with me."

She shifted her hold on the shovel and lowered her forehead to rub it with one hand. He was probably lying to her, but putting her decision off was pointless, and standing out here only put them at a greater risk of exposure.

They both knew she wasn't going to turn these poor fugitives away.

"Elexiandra." She lifted her head to look at him. "I won't tell anyone about these tunnels."

"You've already told these people."

He slipped a vial from inside his shirt pocket and held it before her. "It's a forgetting potion. Once they're safely ensconced inside, I'll give it to them."

She wished she'd had *that* to use on him.

"They'll never remember how to get here," he continued. "I will keep your secret safe because it benefits me to do so."

And that was a truth she could count on. While the tunnels

remained a secret, he would have a place to hide. Lowering her hands, she looked up at him.

"Were you planning on entering the tunnel no matter what?" she asked.

"You told me you were going to shut it off."

"Don't play your games with me; yes or no? Were you going to try to get into the tunnel without me?"

"Of course, but I don't have to do that now, do I?"

Her teeth were going to be nubs if she didn't stop grinding them. No matter what happened, when this was over, she was going to find a way to get back at this asshole for all the shit he'd put her through.

"I'll hide them," she bit out.

"I knew I could count on you," he said with a wink.

Without realizing she intended to do it, her hand fisted and she swung at him. Her punch was so hard and fast that he didn't have time to dodge it before it slammed into his nose. His head shot back, and his hands flew to his face.

"Fuck you!" she spat.

The fugitives all gasped and took a couple of steps away from her. She glared at Orin as he covered his nose and stared at her over the top of his fingers. She scented his blood on the air but couldn't see it.

Though she'd begged him to teach her how to fight, her dad would only show her how to punch. He said learning anything more was unladylike but did feel that she should know how to defend herself at least a little.

She'd never hit anyone out of anger before, and while she was still stunned by the action and her hand throbbed a little, she couldn't deny it felt *good*. The bastard deserved it.

This time, she was the one who smiled smugly.

"Okay," he muttered in a more nasally tone. "I'll give you that one. But *only* that one. Don't try it again."

She almost asked him what would happen if she *did* try it

again, but she decided not to test her luck by pushing him further. He may need her, but he was far more powerful, and he could hurt her.

"Do they know my name?" she asked in a low whisper that wouldn't carry to the others.

"No." Orin lowered his hands to reveal his swollen nose. He wiped away the trickle of blood seeping from one of his nostrils. "Your identity will remain hidden from them."

"They're *on* my land."

"They don't know that. We've been running so long that even the immortals have no idea where we are anymore. And the forgetting potion will erase any memories they might have of how they got here."

She despised him, but she believed him when he promised her this. He needed her help, and he would keep her protected while that remained true. What would happen afterward, she didn't know, but he could destroy her now, so it didn't matter.

Lexi plastered on a smile and turned to the fugitives. She did *not* feel like smiling as her stomach churned and her mind spun with all the ramifications of her actions, but she couldn't turn them away. She would never sleep again if she did.

"My name is Andi," she said with false cheeriness.

When she was a young girl, her father would sometimes call her Andi in a cute little rhyming game he made up. She recalled sitting on his lap and giggling while he tickled her and sang, "Andi Pandy smells like pickles and candy."

She pushed aside the grief that came with the memory as she continued speaking. "I'm going to help you."

It may be the worst decision she ever made, but the second the words left her mouth, the helplessness she'd experienced since the destruction of the marketplace vanished. She'd chosen a different side than her father, but he would have been so proud of her for doing it.

"Please, follow me. I'll take you somewhere safe," she promised as she led them into the shed.

CHAPTER SIXTY

CoLE TOOK his father's king as he declared, "Checkmate."

And it was about time. They'd played hundreds of matches over the past week and a half, and this was the first he'd won. He'd never been one for chess, but after days of being stuck in these small rooms, with windows as their only access to the outside world, he was becoming better at the game.

He'd also become better at rummy and keeping his building rage restrained.

It took everything he had not to launch to his feet and pace the small room containing only the gaming table and two chairs. No decorations hung on the walls, no fire crackled in the hearth, and the only door out was locked.

The place looked exactly like what it was… a prison.

Cole resisted pummeling the gray stone walls of the palace as he demanded to be released. However, he would not give the Lord the satisfaction of seeing him break, so he followed his father's lead of cool indifference while plotting the many ways he'd kill the Lord.

When the messenger showed them to this room, he told them they were the Lord's guests before he closed and locked the door behind them. Neither he nor his father ever said anything out loud to acknowledge it, but they were inmates.

So, they passed the time by discussing the realms' mundane politics and the games they played. His father never brought up Lexi, and Cole knew it was because he also sought to keep her secret from the Lord.

This was the Lord's palace, and even if they couldn't see any hearing device, Cole was certain they were somehow being listened to. They maintained an air of nonchalance as the days slipped past. He hoped they were boring their eavesdroppers to death.

Outside their tower prison, the dragons roamed the skies while inside it, their bellows reverberated around the stone rooms. Their incessant noise was grating on Cole's last nerve.

"Nice match," his father murmured.

"You weren't paying attention."

His father smiled. "You caught me."

Cole rose and stretched his back before walking over to the window. Cool air drifted through the opening in the stone wall as he stopped before it. The circular tower was at least a thousand feet in the air, which gave him a fantastic view of the Dragonian realm.

Despite the dragon's penchant for destroying everything they came across in the other realms, the fields surrounding the palace were lush and green. Stretching toward the mountains were numerous hills and valleys that rolled across the landscape.

The brilliant yellow sun sparkled off the glistening lake nestled outside the palace's colossal stone walls while dozens of other lakes dotted the land. This beautiful realm belonged to the dragons who soared through the air and swooped toward the earth and mountains.

There were hundreds of them, and they filled the sky with more abundance than the birds on Earth. And they were far, *far* more lethal.

The distant mountains were a different story than the lushness of the land. Their rocky surfaces stretched so high that many of their peaks obscured the pink clouds floating across the purple sky.

For the first few days, he'd believed those mountains were snow-topped. On the fourth day, he'd studied the scenery far more intently. It was then he realized it wasn't snow but thousands, if not *millions*, of bones littering those peaks.

The dragons were ravenous creatures.

One of them roared as it soared past the tower. It turned to the side, exposing its underbelly as it released a cry that some of its fellow destroyers echoed. The flap of its wings blew Cole's hair back and ruffled his wrinkled and dirty clothes.

The dragon was making it clear they were not to attempt an escape. They couldn't fly, but with the dark fae's ability to control air currents, they might be able to navigate their way down.

Although, their feet would never touch the ground before one of those dragons ate them. That knowledge was a bit of an escape deterrent.

If only there were some way we could harness the dragon's power and use it for our side. We could defeat the Lord then.

He tried to figure out a way to do this while watching the magnificent, vicious beasts, but he kept running up against a wall. The dragons were bound to this land and the power of the throne. Since the destruction of all the arachs, the dragons only followed whoever sat on that corrupting throne.

There were no arach left in this land, but immortals from other realms had moved here. The houses of those immortals dotted the landscape, and many of them wandered the roads. They approached or left the massive golden gates set into the towering, gray stone wall surrounding the palace.

Two dragons sat atop the golden gate. They eyed every immortal who entered and exited the courtyard. Most immortals ignored them, but a few cast them anxious glances before walking a little faster.

Cole rested his hand against the cool wall and glanced at the doorway to the small bedroom he'd taken after arriving here. His father had settled into the room across from his. Both rooms were sparsely furnished with only a bed and a small sink and toilet.

There was no shower, and though they were provided food, they weren't given clean clothes. They also weren't offered the sexual sustenance dark fae required, but Cole was glad for that.

He wouldn't partake even if partners arrived for them, and his celibacy would only pique the Lord's curiosity. And no matter what happened, the Lord could *not* know about Lexi. He would use her against Cole if he did.

Neither of them complained about their confines or showed their mounting frustration as each day passed, but it was only a matter of time before one of them lost their patience.

The Lord of the Shadow Realms ruled over all immortals, but his father was king of the dark fae, and *no* one had *ever* treated him with such blatant disrespect before and survived. However, there was little either of them could do about it while they remained locked away.

If they banged on the door and demanded to be released, they would only give the Lord the satisfaction of seeing them break. But they'd still be trapped here.

No, there was nothing either of them could do except play their games and act as if none of this bothered them. Their nonchalant attitude was probably infuriating the crazy bastard, which was the only bonus to this whole thing.

As he stared across the verdant land, Cole pondered how to get word to Lexi somehow, but he saw no way to reach her. By now, she probably assumed the worst and believed he wasn't returning. He couldn't blame her if she did, but she'd filled his thoughts over the passing days.

Was she safe? The possibility the Lord had unleashed another attack on Earth, and maybe her manor, caused him to toss and turn all night, as did the memory of her in his arms.

His hunger was increasing daily, and those memories only

enflamed it, but they also helped him get through the days. Once they were free, he would return to her, which was the only thing keeping him calm.

There was also Malakai. Had he returned for her?

Without him there to force Malakai away, she was far more vulnerable to that prick. A snarl curled his upper lip before he suppressed it. He couldn't think about Malakai or the possibility Lexi was in trouble; he'd lose his shit if he did.

Boredom, frustration, and barely contained fury had been his constant companions since arriving here, but he'd somehow managed to keep the lycan part of himself under restrained. He couldn't lose control of it now. That's *exactly* what the Lord wanted.

"How about some poker?" his father suggested.

Cole turned toward him as a click sounded in the door. Both their heads shot toward it as a key turned. A second later, the door swung open to reveal the same messenger who had escorted them from the Gloaming.

CHAPTER SIXTY-ONE

"The Lord will see you now," the man said.

Cole exchanged a look with his father, and then Tove smiled as he rose from his chair. He smoothed out his shirt and pants before striding toward the messenger. The warlock's eyes flickered nervously as Tove approached him, but he lifted his chin.

"Of course," his father said with an airy tone that belied the rage simmering beneath his surface.

Cole matched his dad's laid-back demeanor as he followed him from the room. They swept through the enclosed, gray stone hallway before arriving at a set of stairs. Those stairs spiraled down the middle of a circular opening that descended to the main entrance ten floors below.

Like the hallway, the walls here were all barren and lacked any color. He'd heard that when the arach who once ruled this land still lived here, the palace was alive with color, noise, parties, the arach, and other immortals, but none of that remained.

One of the mad Lords had stripped all the tapestries, rugs, and paintings from the palace and burned them in the courtyard. Now, not only was the place bleak, but it was also as hushed as a tomb.

There was no banister for the stairs, so they stayed close to the wall as they descended. Their footsteps echoing off the stone was the only sound until a dragon released a roar from somewhere within the palace. That roar reverberated off the walls and rebounded incessantly around them.

The hair on Cole's nape rose, but he kept his face impassive as they arrived on the first floor. The messenger led them down a hallway filled with statues of golden dragons situated in various positions.

Some of the statues had the ill-fated arach posed beside them. He suspected the only reason these statues survived the purge of all the other decorations was because they looked like they weighed a ton.

Cole examined the statues as they passed. It had been a thousand years since the last arach ruled the Shadow Realms and Dragonia. He'd never met an arach, but his father had known them and would sometimes tell stories of them.

Besides controlling the dragons, the powerful arach could withstand being burned by flames, throw fire from their hands, and cast spells like witches. Some of those spells remained on this palace as they blocked vampires from teleporting out.

No vampire could teleport into a residence, even if they were invited in at some point, but they could all teleport out unless something stopped them. And here, the lingering power of the arachs kept them trapped.

The arachs weaved a potent brand of magic, but despite their many powers, they were now the cautionary tale many children heard at bedtime and many rulers tried to avoid becoming.

The long-lost rulers of the dragons looked like most other immortal creatures. They didn't have wings like the pixies and didn't shapeshift like the lycan, but they had fangs like vampires, and if the statues were any indication, they had the arrogant stance of an immortal sure of their place in this world.

They shouldn't have been so confident as that place no longer existed.

His father once told him that in the beginning, the arach were a rather peaceful species. Still, disagreements on how to rule the Shadow Realms resulted in a civil war that dethroned the original ruling family and sent them into exile.

But the war didn't end there, and eventually, all the powerful creatures destroyed each other.

That war nearly destroyed the Shadow Realms when it spilled out of Dragonia. The dragons wreaked havoc throughout the realms as the arach battled to the death.

When the dust settled and nothing remained of the arach, their once-tamed dragons ran wild throughout the realms. His father once told him they'd believed they were all doomed. They'd managed to kill some of the dragons, but there were far too many, and the realms were falling apart.

However, when the first non-arach ruler sat on the throne, the dragons returned to Dragonia. That was when the immortals learned whoever held the throne controlled the beasts.

It didn't take them long to realize that whoever held the throne couldn't handle its power, and it eventually eroded their sanity until they became a corrupted, broken version of their old selves.

The first ruler had only taken the throne on a whim. The warlock entered Dragonia in the hopes of avoiding the dragons now living in the other realms. He'd been lured by the power of the throne and decided to sit on it. That decision was the turning point in the war against the dragons as his presence on the throne called them back to Dragonia.

That warlock went from a peace-loving man to one consumed by the paranoia that others were trying to kill him. He became determined to stop his imaginary assassins before they stopped him and set the dragons free again. That mistake cost him. He was dethroned by a lycan who moved in for the kill while the dragons were gone.

The lycan ascended to power only to suffer the same fate.

The messenger stopped outside a set of immense double doors.

Each door held the carving of a dragon in midflight. The dragons' tails curled before them, and their wings spread open as fire erupted from their mouths.

Almost everything within this place was drab, but these dragons were a splash of vivid, detailed color amid all the gray. The fire looked so real it seemed it would burn his fingers if he touched it. The rubies in their eyes gleamed in the rays of the sun streaming through the windows. The emeralds of their green scales cast green color across the floor.

The messenger pulled both doors open and stepped back. He gestured for them to enter the enormous, grand hall. It was at least the size of two football fields long and another football field wide. The room was so large that the throne on the other end, and the man sitting on it, were barely discernible.

Half a dozen dragons lounged inside the room. They were coiled up with their tails near their heads as they dozed contentedly in the sun streaming down on them.

When the doors opened, the dragon closest to them cracked its yellow eyes open and lifted its head. The spikes along its back rose before settling in a wave. Then it opened its colossal jaws and released a yawn that displayed its hundreds of razor-sharp teeth.

It settled its head on its front paws and closed its eyes, but Cole knew it remained focused on them. And though none of the other slumbering beasts stirred, he was certain they were aware of their presence.

His father plastered on a smile before descending the five steps to the great hall. Cole swiftly followed.

CHAPTER SIXTY-TWO

THEIR BOOTS THUDDED against the stone as they strode toward the throne at the end of the hall. Overhead, a domed ceiling arched a thousand feet above them. Black scorch marks surrounded the opening in the middle of it.

That opening revealed the clear blue sky beyond. Then the sun shining through vanished as a dragon soared overhead.

They were halfway to the throne when the dragon in front of them unfurled from its sleeping position and rose onto its hind legs. His father's footsteps didn't falter as the dragon bellowed, spread its wings, and launched off the ground.

Its wings made a loud, thumping sound, and the wind it created blew back their hair and plastered their clothes to them. It was nearly free of the hall when it released a blast of fire that charred the stones before it disappeared into the day.

Cole hid his apprehension, but he looked forward to getting out of this room and away from these nearly unstoppable killing machines.

"Tove!" the Lord exclaimed when they were twenty feet away. "How good to see you! I hope you didn't mind waiting, but I've been so busy that it took me far longer to get to you than I anticipated."

"Of course not, my Lord," his father replied.

They stopped only five feet away from the dais the throne sat on. The Lord sat fifteen feet above them.

"The wait allowed my son and I to work on his chess game. Besides, I needed a little vacation from the Gloaming," his father continued.

"That's why I like you, Tove. You're always so easygoing." The Lord steepled his fingers before him as he studied Tove. "The pressures of leadership are such a bore."

"They can be rather tedious."

The Lord's hazel eyes gleamed with malice as his mouth twisted in amusement. His brown hair hung to his broad shoulders in limp strands. The sharp angles of his face made the contours of his skull evident.

They were so close Cole could almost smell the Lord's blood on his hands. If he could get his hands on him, Cole could slaughter him. It was the getting his hands on him part that was tricky.

As he contemplated how he could kill the Lord before being eaten by a dragon, the gold-colored beast behind the throne lifted its head. Dragons couldn't read minds, but when the creature's green eyes locked on him, it slipped its tail around the throne like it was embracing the Lord.

The Lord leaned forward, and when he did, he provided a better view of the throne. The gold back of it was composed of two dragons with their wings spread wide. Behind the Lord's shoulders, those dragon heads nearly touched, and their tails created the seat holding a red cushion.

"I suppose you're curious as to why I wish to speak with you," the Lord said.

"I admit that I am," Tove replied.

Cole stiffened when a shuffling sound alerted him that a dragon was moving behind him. Though he wanted to know what was happening, he didn't look. He refused to let the Lord think these creatures unnerved him, even if they could swallow him like a frog with a fly.

"I'm hearing rumors about a growing rebellion," the Lord said.

"I'm sure they're just rumors, my Lord. The rebellion is broken, and the traitors are running," Tove replied. "As we speak, they are relentlessly hunted across the realms. I'm sure it's only a matter of time before they're all found and destroyed."

"Now you see, *that's* where I have a problem. I don't want it to be a matter of time. They should *all* be dead by now, including your sons."

The Lord's tone dripped venom, and his eyes shone with a malevolence the likes of which Cole had never seen. Cole glanced at his father as he sensed an unraveling in the monster sitting across from them.

"Varo and Orin are also being hunted as we speak," Tove replied. "I'm sure someone will find them soon."

"And if they're not?"

"Then I will personally help to hunt them down. I want all traitors persecuted as badly as you. I have two loyal sons who fought by my side and for you. That is enough for me."

The lie rolled so easily off his father's lips that Cole almost believed it. The Lord's gaze shifted to Cole.

"Yes, and here is one of those loyal sons," the Lord purred.

"Loyal to my father, to you, and the cause," Cole replied. "I had just returned from the human realm, where I was tracking Orin when you summoned us here."

"And did you have any luck in locating your brother?"

"No, but I did uncover a couple of leads. Unfortunately, my brother Brokk and I were ambushed by traitors before following through on those leads. Brokk was badly injured. However, I plan to return to hunting Orin and Varo as soon as I can."

And, he planned on making sure they stayed out of the Lord's hands once he found them.

"Wonderful," the Lord said and settled back on his throne. "Because some of those rumors claim that *Orin* is the one gathering more recruits for the rebellion."

Cole's blood ran cold. He wanted to look at his father, but he didn't dare take his eyes off this madman for one second.

"I'm sure they're rumors, my Lord," his father demurred. "But if not, then we will stop such a thing before it ever gets started."

The Lord didn't look at him as his gaze remained focused on Cole. "Oh, I'm sure I can count on you not to fail me."

"Of course, my Lord," Cole said.

"Because no matter how close they are, brothers always secretly hate each other. That hatred is ingrown into them. They compete for their parents' love and, in doing so, they grow to loathe one another."

Orin, Varo, Brokk, and all his brothers had pissed him off countless times over the years, but even when they were pummeling each other, he'd *never* hated them. Not even when his impetuous, stubborn brothers joined the rebellion did he hate them.

He'd grieved their deaths, and still did, but he wasn't going to correct the Lord. He'd let the crazy prick think he hated his brothers if it made the him happier.

"Unfortunately, no matter what a child does to its parent, that parent still retains some love for them. Isn't that true, Tove?" the Lord inquired.

An uneasy feeling twisted in Cole's stomach. He did not like the direction this conversation was taking.

His father hesitated before replying. "I love all my children, yes, but my loyalty is to *you*. Orin and Alvaro chose the wrong path and will face the consequences of their actions."

"That they will," the Lord agreed. "But I must question if you'll help them escape when the time comes."

"I would *never* help them escape, my Lord," Tove said.

Cole's uneasy feeling grew, and this time, he couldn't stop his gaze from traveling to the dragons. Two of the beasts had crept closer and were only ten feet away.

He contemplated grabbing his father and running from this place, but the dragons would never let them go.

"I want to believe you, Tove, I really do. However, though I have no children, I know the bond between a parent and their child is special. I do recall the love of my parents; my mother died to keep me alive," the Lord said.

Cole wished his mother hadn't been so selfless.

"I assure you, my Lord, that I would hand over any traitor, son or not," Tove replied.

The Lord tapped his fingers against his chin and stared down at them. "I truly want to believe you, but I can't. Kill him."

Cole had just processed the command when the dragon closest to them surged forward. With a snap of its powerful jaws, it consumed the top half of his father's body. Blood sprayed over Cole. His father had to be in serious pain, but he didn't make a sound when the dragon chomped down again.

Cole twisted his head away when the next snap of those jaws caused another wave of hot blood to spray him. And then the dragon swallowed.

CHAPTER SIXTY-THREE

It took a few seconds for the full impact of what happened to hit him. In that time, Cole became acutely aware of the blood sliding down his face and dripping off his chin. Each drop hitting the gray stone floor sounded like a gunshot fired inside a steel room.

His head slowly turned back to where he last saw the father he loved so much. In the place of the man who'd been his dad, mentor, and best friend was only a pool of red liquid.

The man who broke through his unbearable grief over the loss of Cole's mother and saved a lost boy who was drowning in his sorrow was gone. The man who, for a month after his mother's death, had come into Cole's room every night when he woke crying.

When Cole proved to be inconsolable, his father would carry him into his room and settle him in his bed. Nestled against his dad's side, Cole would finally fall asleep again.

Over the following five months, his dad didn't bother to put him in his room first but simply let him sleep beside him from the night's start. Cole had outgrown such things, but he still recalled those nights and the love sheltering him even after his mother's love was gone.

His father was as broken by her death, but his love for Cole triumphed over his sorrow. During those troubled days, he nursed his son back to life while a part of him remained dead forever.

Then Cole's shock and grief wore off, and a white-hot fury the likes of which he'd never known erupted through him. It was so intense that his claws lengthened and his fangs extended as the lycan broke free in a way it never had before.

He launched himself at the dragon. The creature reared back as Cole sank his claws into its throat. The dragon's eyes rolled as Cole sawed at the wall of muscle surrounding its throat. The beast's teeth snapped as it twisted its head to get at him, but Cole was wedged up beneath its head and out of the way of its powerful jaws.

"Stand down!" the Lord bellowed, but Cole barely heard the command, and he didn't obey it.

Animalistic snarls filled the room, and it took him a couple of seconds to realize those sounds were coming from *him*. However, they were not enough to deter him. He was lost to the mindlessness of the wolf and the thirst for vengeance.

The dragon swiveled enough that teeth raked his arm. He ignored the agony and blood those teeth created as he hacked through sinew as thick as steel. Warm breath plumed against his back as the dragon twisted its head to snap at him.

Smoke burst from its nostrils, and seconds before it released a plume of fire, Cole slid to the side to avoid it. He was too lost in the bloodlust of the lycan to be able to concerned about those flames. The dragon's fire blasted against its neck but didn't leave a mark on its flesh.

The blood soaking Cole dripped off and filled his mouth as he slashed through the monster's flesh. The metallic liquid caked his nostrils until he could barely breathe, but he continued to avoid the dragon's jaws while seeking to destroy the monster.

Around him, the slithering sounds of the others barely penetrated the beat of his heart rebounding in his ears.

"That is enough!" the Lord shouted. "Stay back!"

The command rebounded throughout the great hall, but Cole barely heard it as the dragon's movements grew sluggish and its head tilted at a funny angle. Then its powerful jaws sank onto his arm and clamped down.

The pain the bite created only fueled his desire to destroy as he sank the claws of his free hand into the gap he'd made in the beast's neck. His flesh gave way as the dragon's teeth scoured his bone.

As the creature sought to tear his arm from him, Cole lifted upward with his free hand. Sinew and skin gave way, and a hissing scream issued from the dragon as he tore the thing's neck upward.

Bone cracked and popped as a rending sound filled the air. The dragon bit down harder as its blood spilled over him.

Cole continued to pull upward until he severed its spinal cord and it couldn't hold onto him any longer. The dragon released its grip on his arm seconds before Cole succeeded in tearing its head the rest of the way off.

When the dragon's head fell to the ground with a wet thump, Cole released it and dropped down. His shoulders heaved as he spun on the Lord.

CHAPTER SIXTY-FOUR

WITH A SNARL, Cole stepped toward the Lord. He was about to rush up the steps of the dais, but the dragon behind the throne had slid its head in front of the Lord while Cole destroyed its friend.

Its face was only inches away from Cole's. Its hot breath blew Cole's hair back from his face when it bared its lethal, six-inch-long teeth at him.

Then he felt the hot breaths of the others and realized they'd all enclosed on him. He didn't turn to look at the monsters, but if the hate in the eyes of the one guarding the Lord was any indication, they were all pretty pissed.

None of them were as irate as him.

"Uh-ah." The Lord wagged his index finger at Cole like he was some kind of recalcitrant toddler throwing a tantrum.

It only enraged him more. His shoulders heaved, his muscles swelled, and his fangs filled his mouth as his breath came in ragged exhalations. His claws bit into his palms until his blood spilled free; it mixed with his father's and the dragon's while he glowered at the monster before him.

He might be able to kill this one too, but the others would be on him before he reached the Lord. A big part of him didn't give a fuck if he died trying to slaughter this prick. The other part told him he had to live to fight another day.

If he died here and the Lord survived, Lexi would be vulnerable. And he could not leave her unprotected in a world where this monster ruled.

If he could get to this monster and kill him, he would do it because it would keep her safer. However, he had no shot of succeeding. He'd managed to kill one dragon; he would not be able to battle his way through them all.

"Such a pity," the Lord said as his gaze fell on the slaughtered dragon. "She was one of my favorites." Then his attention returned to Cole, and a sly smile curved his mouth. "But *very* impressive. I don't think anyone has ever singlehandedly killed a dragon before."

Cole didn't speak as blood dripped off him to splatter on the ground.

"I should kill you for doing that to one of my babies. Her friends certainly want you dead, but you are of far more use to me alive."

The Lord stopped and stared expectantly at him, but Cole still didn't speak. If this lunatic gave the command to kill him, he planned to take out a few more of these monsters before he went.

"I bet you're thinking I've made a big enemy out of you and the dark fae," the Lord said.

Silence.

"Normally, I would say you're right, but you're wrong here. Your father's arrogance got him killed, as did his lies. He never planned to hand his sons over to me, but *you'll* have no qualms about doing so. You will not become my enemy, Cole, and do you know why?"

Cole kept his mouth shut as he eyed the dragons slithering around him. They were eager for his blood, but they didn't strike.

"Because if you become my enemy, countless dark fae will die. Do you understand me?"

He still didn't speak.

"Do not eat him, my friends," the Lord said and rubbed the back of the one protecting his throne. "If he decides not to play nice, you can have him, but that's not going to happen because he's going to be one of our best friends."

Cole's jaw clenched as images of tearing this bastard's head off and dancing around it filled his mind.

"Now," the Lord said as he steepled his hands before his face, "you're going to go back to the Gloaming, and as the eldest prince, you're going to take control of the dark fae. I know you're only a half-breed and you will have to endure the trials, but you *will* rule them.

"If you survive the trials, some will fight your rise to the throne, but that's not my problem. You *will* get the dark fae to fall in line, or I'll destroy the Gloaming. You will be my greatest ally, or I will label the dark fae as traitors and hunt them across the realms. Do you understand me?"

Cole scowled at him. Before this was over, he would make sure this *thing* was nothing more than pieces of meat strewn across the ground for his dragons. And then, he would slaughter all the dragons.

The Lord's eyes flicked past him, and a second later, a rush of hot air billowed against Cole's nape as a dragon exhaled behind him.

"Do you understand me?" the Lord repeated.

Cole didn't bother to look at the dragon, who was so close its nose brushed his skin, as he replied through gritted teeth, "Yes."

"Good, because it is time that all the leaders of the realms learn I am *not* fucking around, and they are *all* replaceable. They will do as I say. *You* will do as I say, or I'll kill them all."

He was crazier than Cole realized, and as the hot breath of the dragon continued to warm his neck, a chill ran through him.

"You just killed the king of the dark fae," Cole snarled. "The fae will not be excited to obey you."

"And I have crowned you the new king, and you should have no problem with making them fall in line."

There would be a huge problem. The dark fae had admired his father and followed him because he was powerful, fair, and quick to eradicate his enemies. They wouldn't have such faith in Cole, and they were going to be *pissed* the Lord had destroyed their king.

But even with all their powers, and even if they got help from the other immortals, they couldn't defeat the dragons. And there would be some who were glad Tove was dead; they would come for him and Brokk and try to destroy them.

The Lord had no idea the unrest he'd unleashed on the Gloaming by killing its king. If Cole couldn't keep the realm together, it would crumble into civil war, just like Dragonia once did.

"Do you understand?" the Lord demanded.

Cole started to tell him where he could shove his declarations, but when an image of Lexi entered his mind, he bit back the words. He had to return to make sure she was safe, and he had to let the other coalition members know what happened here. He couldn't do those things if he were dead.

"Yes," Cole growled.

The Lord grinned at him. "Good boy. Now, run along."

He waved his fingers at Cole as he shooed him away like an errant puppy. When Cole got the chance, he'd tear those fingers off and shove them up the Lord's ass.

Cole turned to look at the puddle of his father's blood again. It had mixed with the blood of the dragon, but it was still there beneath the dragon's head. Sorrow swelled to repress his rage, and then it burned hotly through him again.

"Don't worry, I'll make sure it's cleaned up," the Lord said. "Now, do as you were commanded and leave my hall, or I'll let my dragon eat one of your arms. I'm sure you couldn't survive the trials without it."

Though Cole only knew a little of what the trials entailed, it would be impossible to survive without it.

He bent and lifted the dragon's head from the ground. "I'm taking this with me."

"And if I say no?"

"You can say whatever you want, but if you want the dark fae to fall in line, then I'm taking the *fucking* head."

Cole didn't look back at him as he turned away. It took more willpower than he'd known he possessed to leave his father's remains. He wanted to gather what remained of the man he'd loved so much, but he had nothing to carry the blood in. However, not having a body to entomb beside his mother and brothers weighed heavily on his heart.

He met the eyes of the dragon behind him over the top of the thick scales lining its snout. Hatred glistened in those yellow eyes, but it was nothing compared to what Cole felt for these beasts.

"Let him pass," the Lord commanded, and after a few seconds, the dragon reluctantly slithered away.

CHAPTER SIXTY-FIVE

COLE'S FEET thudded against the floor as he strode down the hall and past the beasts. Hatred swelled in him as he sneered at the massive creatures, but none of them paid any attention to him as he stalked past.

With every step he took, his claws dug deeper into his palm while his other hand carried the dragon's head. If he didn't have this self-inflicted injury to keep him grounded in this form, Cole would transform completely, and if he did, he would go back for the Lord, and he would die.

Lexi! Thoughts of her helped to keep him grounded more than the pain, and for a second, the faint scent of strawberries pushed aside the coppery stench of the blood coating him.

The messenger still waited by the doors, and when Cole walked through them, the warlock closed them with a click. When Cole's head turned stiffly toward the man, he discovered the warlock staring at the wall with a blank expression on his face.

Do not kill him. But it was so tempting.

His claws scraped against the bones in his hand as he compelled himself to keep walking. He didn't look back as he strode to the front door. A servant opened it for him, and Cole walked outside.

The warm sun beat down on him, but he didn't see anything as he descended the steps and stalked out of the palace courtyard. As if he were a homing pigeon returning home, he found the Gloaming portal and entered it.

Once inside the protective, black walls of the portal, he slid his parents' rings from his pocket, put them in his mouth, and started running. He only made it three steps before the wolf took over.

His clothing ripped and fell away. His muscles and bones shifted and popped as he transformed into the beast he'd kept repressed for centuries. The dragon's bite ached and he limped, but he ignored both discomforts as he threw the head of the dragon into the air and caught it in his jaws.

Over the years, he'd transformed only a handful of times, and all those times were before he turned thirty. He tried to become comfortable in the wolf's skin during those times, but he hated the lack of control he experienced when the wolf was in charge.

The dark fae were known for their control and aloofness; nothing was controlled or reserved about the beast. It was wild, free, and ruled by the emotions the dark fae rarely displayed.

Now, he welcomed the loss of control as the wind whipped through his hair, and he was driven by an incessant compulsion to run faster. He couldn't escape what happened in the hall, but some of his fury and sorrow eased as he gave himself over to the freedom of the wolf's run.

Then he spotted a small glow at the end of the portal and emerged into the Gloaming. He didn't slow or return to his fae form as he ran up and down hills, past homesteads, and through fields full of crops.

As a fae, he was aware of his senses, but not like when he was a wolf. The scent of blood permeated the air, but beneath it, he detected the earth's rich aroma, the fae wheat crops, and the crisp, night air. His vision was more acute as a wolf, and he spotted thc tiny rodents darting back into the ground when he approached.

The sun had set, but the silvery radiance of the moons lit his way across an open field. His paws kicked up dirt that bounced off his back legs. The few fae who saw him cried out in surprise, but none knew it was him, and none dared to get in the way of a blood-drenched lycan.

He traversed miles, but he wasn't winded or tired when he arrived at the palace. Stopping outside the massive, metal gates, he closed his eyes as he willed himself to transform. It was more difficult than he'd anticipated; the wolf was reluctant to let go of its newfound freedom, but eventually the beast yielded.

Cole dropped the dragon head as his bones and joints popped back into place. He rose from all fours to stare at the closed gates. His hand heated as he wrapped it around the bars. Those bars recognized his touch, and when the lock sprang free, he opened one of the gates.

He lifted the dragon's head and drove it onto one of the fence spikes. That head would make a lot of the dark fae think twice before challenging him.

He would *not* let anyone or anything stand in the way of avenging his father's death. He glowered at the beast that slaughtered his father before turning away.

As he walked toward the towering palace half hidden in shadow, he removed the rings from under his tongue and slid his father's band onto his ring finger. It was a perfect fit.

His mother's ring barely made it to the knuckle of his pinky, but he fisted his hand to keep it securely in place there. The movement caused the dragon's bite to pull taut, but he barely noticed the discomfort.

He didn't care about his nudity as he strode through the empty courtyard, but he was glad no one was around to see the blood dripping from him. He wasn't in control enough to answer questions.

He ascended the steps to the large, silver front doors with the four moons etched onto them. Before he reached the doors, one of them swung open to reveal Sindri standing inside the threshold.

The helot's eyes ran over the blood, sliding down his flesh. Though Cole was barely in control of himself, he'd still managed to keep most of his ciphers hidden. Rage and sorrow could not erase centuries of discipline when it came to concealing the true depth of his power.

His father had drilled it into his head when he was only a young boy that *no* one could ever know the true number of ciphers on him, and no one did. Just as he didn't know how many ciphers the other dark fae possessed, including his brothers and father.

Sindri's eyes flickered behind him, and Cole saw understanding dawn in them a second before a cruel smile curved the man's lips.

"We have missed you, milord," he purred. "Where is your father?"

Sindri's smug smile widened as it ran over Cole once more.

"Or am I looking at him?" Sindri inquired.

Cole's claws extended, and with lightning speed, he sliced them across the helot's throat. Sindri's hands flew to his neck, and he staggered back as blood spilled from between his fingers. Cole didn't hesitate before slicing into him again.

His next blow caused Sindri's fingers to fall away; his throat opened enough to reveal his spine's white bone, and Cole seized it. Dawning horror and understanding bloomed in the helot's gaze a second before Cole snapped the spine in half.

Sindri's head hit the ground with a wet thud and rolled to settle at his feet. Cole stared at the unseeing eyes and parted mouth before bending to lift the head. He was rising when Sindri's body hit the ground.

Grasping the helot by his ankle, Cole dragged the body over to the fence and gazed up at the lethal spikes on top. He turned the head to look out on the Gloaming before slamming it onto one of the points. The metal rod burst out the top of Sindri's head.

He lifted the body next, turned it upside down, and plunged it onto another spike. The metal rod went all the way through Sindri's body and erupted out the other end. Along with his intestines, Sindri's testicles remained on top of the spike.

Stepping back, Cole examined the helot's body as he contemplated his next move. The dark fae would fight his ascension, but he wouldn't let it happen. He'd endure and survive the trials that killed many before his father, and he *would* become the king of the dark fae.

And once he was in charge, he didn't care what it took, he would destroy the Lord of the Shadow Realms.

∾

Turn the page for a sneak peek of book 2, *Shadows of Discovery*, or download now and continue reading: brendakdavies.com/SDwb

Stay in touch on updates, sales, and new releases by joining to the mailing list: brendakdavies.com/ESBKDNews

Visit the Erica Stevens/Brenda K. Davies Book Club on Facebook for exclusive giveaways and all things book related. Come join the fun: brendakdavies.com/ESBKDBookClub

SNEAK PEEK

SHADOWS OF DISCOVERY, THE SHADOW REALMS BOOK 2

Cole left bloody footprints behind him as he stalked up the palace steps toward the open doorway. A shadow fell across the stairs a second before Brokk skidded to a stop in the entrance. His aqua blue eyes widened, and his jaw dropped when he spotted Cole.

"Cole? Holy shit! What *happened* to you?"

Then his gaze went past Cole, and his eyes roamed over the pathway leading to the gate and fence surrounding the fae palace. Cole knew he was searching for their father, but he wouldn't find him.

When Brokk's eyes returned to him, dawning horror filled them as they ran over Cole's naked body and the blood covering him. It was the blood of their *father* mixed with that of a dragon.

"What happened?" Brokk croaked the words out. "Where's... where's father?"

Then his gaze went past Cole again, and his jaw dropped. He'd finally seen the body of their ex-helot, Sindri, and the dragon head Cole had staked to the fence.

"Is that a *dragon* head? And Sindri?" Brokk's eyes shot back to Cole. "What the *fuck* happened?"

"The Lord ordered a dragon to kill father."

Brokk blinked at him, but Cole's words didn't seem to register as he stared at the bloody remains sticking to the fence.

"Why?" Brokk whispered.

"Because he didn't think he would do enough to hunt Orin and Varo. He thinks *I* will do more. He intends for me to rule after I survive the trials."

Cole did not say *if* he survived the trials. He didn't care that many dark fae had failed to survive the trials. He. Would. Not. Fail. He would become the king of the dark fae and destroy the Lord of the Shadow Realms if it was the last thing he did.

Brokk didn't speak as he stared unblinkingly at the fence. Tears brimmed in his eyes, but he didn't shed them.

Cole knew Brokk's tears would come with time, and so would his, but right now, the horror of what happened to their father was hitting him. And though there was grief, there was also a fury so hot that it burned away the sorrow and left nothing but ashes in its wake.

"Where did the dragon head come from?" Brokk asked.

"I killed it, and I took it as a warning to all those who will think to stand in my way of claiming the throne."

If his brother's eyes got any bigger, they would pop out of his head. "You killed it by yourself?"

"Yes."

"How... *how* did you manage that?"

Cole still wasn't entirely sure how he'd managed to destroy the powerful creature and could only think of one answer. "Rage."

"And you killed Sindri because...?"

"He was happy to see me wearing father's blood."

"That would do it."

As Cole finished climbing the stairs, Brokk stepped back to let him enter the palace.

"Where are you going?" Brokk demanded.

"To see Lexi."

"Who?" And then Brokk's mind seemed to start working again, and he blurted. "*Del's* daughter?"

"Yes."

"You're going to see her *now?*"

"Yes."

"There are a thousand things that will have to be taken care of; why would you go see her now?"

"Because I have to."

The door slammed shut behind him, and then the padding sound of Brokk's soft boots sounded against the stone as he hurried after him. Cole didn't look back at his brother as he navigated the palace halls toward his room.

He'd spent his entire life within these walls, and during that time, he'd passed the numerous closed doors that would never open to him. Those rooms belonged to others, and they would not open to anyone but them, even if they were dead.

He wondered if the palace would seal off his father's room now, too; a pang broke through his rage to pierce his heart, but he swiftly buried it. This was not the time or place; he had to see Lexi then meet with the dark fae council and arrange to start the trials.

Once that was settled and the trials were over, he would use his power to help him find a way to sink his claws into the Lord and rip him to pieces. He would celebrate as that bastard's blood covered him.

"Cole." Brokk reached for his arm, but blood coated him so thickly that his brother hesitated before lowering his hand without touching him. "The fae council is going to descend on this palace as soon as they learn of father's death."

"I know."

"They won't want either of us ruling. We're only half breeds."

"They're not going to have a choice."

"Great. Fantastic. Glad to hear you say that because I'd really like to kill the Lord, and we're going to need the power of the fae throne behind us to help with that, but if you're not here when they arrive, then what? I don't want to throw myself in the ring as I want nothing to do with ruling the Gloaming."

"I know."

"You never wanted to rule it either."

"I still don't."

"Then—"

"I don't have a choice either. I *am* going to rule because if I don't, the Lord is going to destroy us all," Cole interrupted. "I will rule because I'm going to fucking kill that prick if it's the last thing I do. But I *have* to see Lexi first."

"Cole—"

Brokk stopped speaking and took a startled step back when Cole spun on him. "She's my mate, Brokk. She's *mine,* and I am going to see her. If the council shows up here before I return, then you will have to stall them. I don't care how you do it. Just *do* it."

Brokk gawked at him, and this time when Cole walked away from him, it was a few seconds before his brother scrambled to catch up again.

"Your mate as in your *lycan* mate?" Brokk demanded when he arrived at Cole's side again.

"Yes."

"Holy shit. Why didn't you say something? I could have checked on her."

"I wasn't expecting to be gone so long." Or to come back soaked in his father's blood. "I didn't expect any of this."

And he'd certainly never expected to watch his father die, to be forced to endure the trials, rule the Gloaming, or have the Lord breathing down his neck about his rebellious brothers. He hadn't expected to leave Lexi for nearly two weeks when he walked away from her manor.

Because of his dark fae nature, she probably thought he'd abandoned her, and she had every right to believe that, but he would make sure she learned the truth. And he had to make sure she was safe before starting the trials. He would never get through them if he were worried about her, and there was *no* way Cole could let her keep thinking that he'd used her and left her.

"Why didn't you tell me?" Brokk demanded.

"I wasn't ready."

Brokk didn't speak again as Cole continued to his room. He hated the silence that descended because with the silence came the memories, and every room and hallway he ever entered this place contained memories of his father.

His father had walked these halls. He'd ruled over and loved them, just as he'd loved his children. And his children loved him.

With every corner Cole turned, he expected to find his father gliding toward him. A smile would brighten his face when he saw Cole, and his arms would open for a quick embrace and pat on the back.

Tove, King of the dark fae, was a cold and ruthless ruler to the outside world. To his sons, he was a man who was loved, and they loved him in return.

Cole fingered the rings his father gave him before everything went to shit. The rings once belonged to his father and mother, and now they were his. And he hoped that one day Lexi would wear his mother's.

But that was an obstacle for a later time. Now, Cole just had to see her, to make sure she was safe, and return here to take control of the Gloaming.

He sneered at the reminder. He never thought anything would ever happen to his father. The man had ruled these lands for over seven hundred years; he was ruler before Cole was born. He'd been the longest-running dark fae king, and in a moment... just one, lightning-fast, hideous fucking moment, he was gone.

Cole shuddered as some of his rage ebbed, and the grief crept back in again. Except, he had no time for grief.

He had trials to survive, a throne to ascend, and hell to unleash.

∼

Download *Shadows of Discovery* and continue reading:
brendakdavies.com/SDwb

～

Stay in touch on updates, sales, and new releases by joining to the mailing list: brendakdavies.com/ESBKDNews

Visit the Erica Stevens/Brenda K. Davies Book Club on Facebook for exclusive giveaways and all things book related. Come join the fun: brendakdavies.com/ESBKDBookClub

FIND THE AUTHOR

Brenda K. Davies Mailing List:
brendakdavies.com/News

Facebook: brendakdavies.com/BKDfb

Brenda K. Davies Book Club:
brendakdavies.com/BKDBooks

Instagram: brendakdavies.com/BKDInsta
Twitter: brendakdavies.com/BKDTweet
Website: www.brendakdavies.com

ALSO FROM THE AUTHOR

Bound by Fate (Book 8)

Bound by Blood (Book 9)

Bound by Love (Book 10)

The Road to Hell Series

Good Intentions (Book 1)

Carved (Book 2)

The Road (Book 3)

Into Hell (Book 4)

Hell on Earth (Book 5)

Into the Abyss (Book 6)

Kiss of Death (Book 7)

Edge of the Darkness (Book 8)

The Shadow Realms

Shadows of Fire (Book 1)

Shadows of Discovery (Book 2)

Shadows of Betrayal (Book 3)

Shadows of Fury (Book 4)

Shadows of Destiny (Book 5)

Shadows of Light (Book 6)

Wicked Curses (Book 7)

Sinful Curses (Book 8)

Gilded Curses (Book 9)

Whispers of Ruin (Book 10)

Secrets of Ruin (Book 11)

Tempest of Shadows

A Tempest of Shadows (Book 1)

A Tempest of Thieves (Book 2)

A Tempest of Revelations (Book 3)

A Tempest of Intrigue (Book 4)

A Tempest of Chaos (Book 5)

Historical Romance

A Stolen Heart

Books written under the pen name

Erica Stevens

The Coven Series

Nightmares (Book 1)

The Maze (Book 2)

Dream Walker (Book 3)

The Captive Series

Captured (Book 1)

Renegade (Book 2)

Refugee (Book 3)

Salvation (Book 4)

Redemption (Book 5)

Vengeance (Book 6)

Unbound (Book 7)

Broken (Book 8 - Prequel)

The Kindred Series

Kindred (Book 1)

Ashes (Book 2)

Kindled (Book 3)

Inferno (Book 4)

Phoenix Rising (Book 5)

<u>The Fire & Ice Series</u>

Frost Burn (Book 1)

Arctic Fire (Book 2)

Scorched Ice (Book 3)

<u>The Ravening Series</u>

The Ravening (Book 1)

Taken Over (Book 2)

Reclamation (Book 3)

<u>The Survivor Chronicles</u>

The Upheaval (Book 1)

The Divide (Book 2)

The Forsaken (Book 3)

The Risen (Book 4)

ABOUT THE AUTHOR

Brenda K. Davies is the USA Today Bestselling author of the Vampire Awakening Series, Alliance Series, Road to Hell Series, Hell on Earth Series, The Shadow Realms Series, A Tempest of Shadows Series, and historical romantic fiction. She also writes under the pen name, Erica Stevens. When not out with friends and family, she can be found at home with her husband, son, and pets.

Printed in Dunstable, United Kingdom

68427565R00208